LAST WORDS

LAST WORDS

STEPHEN CRANE

WILDSIDE PRESS

LAST WORDS

Published by Wildside Press, LLC
www.wildsidebooks.com

CONTENTS

IRISH NOTES

SULLIVAN COUNTY SKETCHES

MISCELLANEOUS

THE RELUCTANT VOYAGERS

CHAPTER I

Two men sat by the sea waves.

"Well, I know I'm not handsome," said one gloomily. He was poking holes in the sand with a discontented cane.

The companion was watching the waves play. He seemed overcome with perspiring discomfort as a man who is resolved to set another man right.

Suddenly his mouth turned into a straight line. "To be sure you are not," he cried vehemently. "You look like thunder. I do not desire to be unpleasant, but I must assure you that your freckled skin continually reminds spectators of white wall paper with gilt roses on it. The top of your head looks like a little wooden plate. And your figure—heavens!"

For a time they were silent. They stared at the waves that purred near their feet like sleepy sea-kittens.

Finally the first man spoke.

"Well," said he, defiantly, "what of it?"

"What of it," exploded the other. "Why, it means that you'd look like blazes in a bathing-suit."

They were again silent. The freckled man seemed ashamed. His tall companion glowered at the scenery.

"I am decided," said the freckled man suddenly. He got boldly up from the sand and strode away. The tall man followed, walking sarcastically and glaring down at the round, resolute figure before him.

A bath-clerk was looking at the world with superior eyes through a hole in a board. To him the freckled man made application, waving his hands over his person in illustration of a snug fit. The bath-clerk thought profoundly. Eventually, he handed out a blue bundle with an air of having phenomenally solved the freckled man's dimensions.

The latter resumed his resolute stride.

"See here," said the tall man, following him, "I bet you've got a regular toga, you know. That fellow couldn't tell—"

"Yes, he could," interrupted the freckled man, "I saw correct mathematics in his eyes."

"Well, supposin' he has missed your size. Supposin'—"

"Tom," again interrupted the other, "produce your proud clothes and we'll go in."

The tall man swore bitterly. He went to one of a row of little wooden boxes and shut himself in it. His companion repaired to a similar box.

At first he felt like an opulent monk in a too-small cell, and he turned round two or three times to see if he could. He arrived finally into his bathing-dress. Immediately he dropped gasping upon a three-cornered bench. The suit fell in folds about his reclining form. There was silence, save for the caressing calls of the waves without.

Then he heard two shoes drop on the floor in one of the little coops. He began to clamour at the boards like a penitent at an unforgiving door.

"Tom," called he, "Tom—"

A voice of wrath, muffled by cloth, came through the walls. "You go t' blazes!"

The freckled man began to groan, taking the occupants of the entire row of coops into his confidence.

"Stop your noise," angrily cried the tall man from his hidden den. "You rented the bathing-suit, didn't you? Then—"

"It ain't a bathing-suit," shouted the freckled man at the boards. "It's an auditorium, a ballroom, or something. It ain't a bathing-suit."

The tall man came out of his box. His suit looked like blue skin. He walked with grandeur down the alley between the rows of coops. Stopping in front of his friend's door, he rapped on it with passionate knuckles.

"Come out of there, y' ol' fool," said he, in an enraged whisper. "It's only your accursed vanity. Wear it anyhow. What difference does it make? I never saw such a vain ol' idiot!"

As he was storming the door opened, and his friend confronted him. The tall man's legs gave way, and he fell against the opposite door.

The freckled man regarded him sternly.

"You're an ass," he said.

His back curved in scorn. He walked majestically down the alley. There was pride in the way his chubby feet patted the boards. The tall man followed, weakly, his eyes riveted upon the figure ahead.

As a disguise the freckled man had adopted the stomach of importance. He moved with an air of some sort of procession, across a board walk, down some steps, and out upon the sand.

There was a pug dog and three old women on a bench, a man and a maid with a book and a parasol, a seagull drifting high in the wind, and a distant, tremendous meeting of sea and sky. Down on the wet sand stood a girl being wooed by the breakers.

The freckled man moved with stately tread along the beach. The tall man, numb with amazement, came in the rear. They neared the girl.

Suddenly the tall man was seized with convulsions. He laughed, and the girl turned her head.

She perceived the freckled man in the bathing-suit. An expression of wonderment overspread her charming face. It changed in a moment to a pearly smile.

This smile seemed to smite the freckled man. He obviously tried to swell and fit his suit. Then he turned a shrivelling glance upon his companion, and fled up the beach. The tall man ran after him, pursuing with mocking cries that tingled his flesh like stings of insects. He seemed to be trying to lead the way out of the world. But at last he stopped and faced about.

"Tom Sharp," said he, between his clenched teeth, "you are an unutterable wretch! I could grind your bones under my heel."

The tall man was in a trance, with glazed eyes fixed on the bathing-dress. He seemed to be murmuring: "Oh, good Lord! Oh, good Lord! I never saw such a suit!"

The freckled man made the gesture of an assassin.

"Tom Sharp, you—"

The other was still murmuring: "Oh, good Lord! I never saw such a suit! I never—"

The freckled man ran down into the sea.

CHAPTER II

The cool, swirling waters took his temper from him, and it became a thing that is lost in the ocean. The tall man floundered in, and the two forgot and rollicked in the waves.

The freckled man, in endeavouring to escape from mankind, had left all save a solitary fisherman under a large hat, and three boys in bathing-dress, laughing and splashing upon a raft made of old spars.

The two men swam softly over the ground swells.

The three boys dived from their raft, and turned their jolly faces shorewards. It twisted slowly around and around, and began to move seaward on some unknown voyage. The freckled man laid his face to the water and swam toward the raft with a practised stroke. The tall man followed, his bended arm appearing and disappearing with the precision of machinery.

The craft crept away, slowly and wearily, as if luring. The little wooden plate on the freckled man's head looked at the shore like a round, brown eye, but his gaze was fixed on the raft that slyly appeared to be waiting. The tall man used the little wooden plate as a beacon.

At length the freckled man reached the raft and climbed aboard. He lay down on his back and puffed. His bathing-dress spread about him like a dead balloon. The tall man came, snorted, shook his tangled locks and lay down by the side of his companion.

They were overcome with a delicious drowsiness. The planks of the raft seemed to fit their tired limbs. They gazed dreamily up into the vast sky of summer.

"This is great," said the tall man. His companion grunted blissfully.

Gentle hands from the sea rocked their craft and lulled them to peace. Lapping waves sang little rippling sea-songs about them. The two men issued contented groans.

"Tom," said the freckled man.

"What?" said the other.

"This is great."

They lay and thought.

A fish-hawk, soaring, suddenly turned and darted at the waves. The tall man indolently twisted his head and watched the bird plunge its claws into the water. It heavily arose with a silver gleaming fish.

"That bird has got his feet wet again. It's a shame," murmured the tall man sleepily. "He must suffer from an endless cold in the head. He should wear rubber boots. They'd look great, too. If I was him, I'd—Great Scott!"

He has partly arisen, and was looking at the shore.

He began to scream. "Ted! Ted! Ted! Look!"

"What's matter?" dreamily spoke the freckled man. "You remind me of when I put the bird-shot in your leg." He giggled softly.

The agitated tall man made a gesture of supreme eloquence. His companion up-reared and turned a startled gaze shoreward.

"Lord," he roared, as if stabbed.

The land was a long, brown streak with a rim of green, in which sparkled the tin roofs of huge hotels. The hands from the sea had pushed them away. The two men sprang erect, and did a little dance of perturbation.

"What shall we do? What shall we do?" moaned the freckled man, wriggling fantastically in his dead balloon.

The changing shore seemed to fascinate the tall man, and for a time he did not speak.

Suddenly he concluded his minuet of horror. He wheeled about and faced the freckled man. He elaborately folded his arms.

"So," he said, in slow, formidable tones. "So! This all comes from your accursed vanity, your bathing-suit, your idiocy; you have murdered your best friend."

He turned away. His companion reeled as if stricken by an unexpected arm.

He stretched out his hands. "Tom, Tom," wailed he, beseechingly, "don't be such a fool."

The broad back of his friend was occupied by a contemptuous sneer.

Three ships fell off the horizon. Landward, the hues were blending. The whistle of a locomotive sounded from an infinite distance as if tooting in heaven.

"Tom! Tom! My dear boy," quavered the freckled man, "don't speak that way to me."

"Oh, no, of course not," said the other, still facing away and throwing the words over his shoulder. "You suppose I am going to accept all this calmly, don't you? Not make the slightest objection? Make no protest at all, hey?"

"Well, I—I—" began the freckled man.

The tall man's wrath suddenly exploded. "You've abducted me! That's the whole amount of it! You've abducted me!"

"I ain't," protested the freckled man. "You must think I'm a fool."

The tall man swore, and sitting down, dangled his legs angrily in the water. Natural law compelled his companion to occupy the other end of the raft.

Over the waters little shoals of fish spluttered, raising tiny tempests. Languid jelly-fish floated near, tremulously waving a thousand legs. A row of porpoises trundled along like a procession of cog-wheels. The sky became greyed save where over the land sunset colours were assembling.

The two voyagers, back to back and at either end of the raft, quarrelled at length.

"What did you want to follow me for?" demanded the freckled man in a voice of indignation.

"If your figure hadn't been so like a bottle, we wouldn't be here," replied the tall man.

CHAPTER III

The fires in the west blazed away, and solemnity spread over the sea. Electric lights began to blink like eyes. Night menaced the voyagers with a dangerous darkness, and fear came to bind their souls together. They huddled fraternally in the middle of the raft.

"I feel like a molecule," said the freckled man in subdued tones.

"I'd give two dollars for a cigar," muttered the tall man.

A V-shaped flock of ducks flew towards Barnegat, between the voyagers and a remnant of yellow sky. Shadows and winds came from the vanished eastern horizon.

"I think I hear voices," said the freckled man.

"That Dollie Ramsdell was an awfully nice girl," said the tall man.

When the coldness of the sea night came to them, the freckled man found he could by a peculiar movement of his legs and arms encase himself in his bathing-dress. The tall man was compelled to whistle and shiver. As night settled finally over the sea, red and green lights began to dot the blackness. There were mysterious shadows between the waves.

"I see things comin'," murmured the freckled man.

"I wish I hadn't ordered that new dress-suit for the hop to-morrow night," said the tall man reflectively.

The sea became uneasy and heaved painfully, like a lost bosom, when little forgotten heart-bells try to chime with a pure sound. The voyagers cringed at magnified foam on distant wave crests. A moon came and looked at them.

"Somebody's here," whispered the freckled man.

"I wish I had an almanac," remarked the tall man, regarding the moon.

Presently they fell to staring at the red and green lights that twinkled about them.

"Providence will not leave us," asserted the freckled man.

"Oh, we'll be picked up shortly. I owe money," said the tall man.

He began to thrum on an imaginary banjo.

"I have heard," said he, suddenly, "that captains with healthy ships beneath their feet will never turn back after having once started on a voyage. In that case we will be rescued by some ship bound for the golden seas of the south. Then, you'll be up to some of your confounded devilment, and we'll get put off. They'll maroon us! That's what they'll do! They'll maroon us! On an island with palm trees and sun-kissed maidens and all that. Sun-kissed maidens, eh? Great! They'd—"

He suddenly ceased and turned to stone. At a distance a great, green eye was contemplating the sea wanderers.

They stood up and did another dance. As they watched the eye grew larger.

Directly the form of a phantom-like ship came into view. About the great, green eye there bobbed small yellow dots. The wanderers could hear a far-away creaking of unseen tackle and flapping of shadowy sails. There came the melody of the waters as the ship's prow thrusted its way.

The tall man delivered an oration.

"Ha!" he exclaimed, "here comes our rescuers. The brave fellows! How I long to take the manly captain by the hand! You will soon see a white boat with a star on its bow drop from the side of yon ship. Kind sailors in blue and white will help us into the boat and conduct our wasted frames to the quarter-deck, where the handsome, bearded captain, with gold bands all around, will welcome us. Then in the hard-oak cabin, while the wine gurgles and the Havana's glow, we'll tell our tale of peril and privation."

The ship came on like a black hurrying animal with froth-filled maw. The two wanderers stood up and clasped hands. Then they howled out a wild duet that rang over the wastes of sea.

The cries seemed to strike the ship.

Men with boots on yelled and ran about the deck. They picked up heavy articles and threw them down. They yelled more. After hideous creakings and flappings, the vessel stood still.

In the meantime the wanderers had been chanting their song for help. Out in the blackness they beckoned to the ship and coaxed.

A voice came to them.

"Hello," it said.

They puffed out their cheeks and began to shout. "Hello! Hello! Hello!"

"Wot do yeh want?" said the voice.

The two wanderers gazed at each other, and sat suddenly down on the raft. Some pall came sweeping over the sky and quenched their stars.

But almost the tall man got up and brawled miscellaneous information. He stamped his foot, and frowning into the night, swore threateningly.

The vessel seemed fearful of these moaning voices that called from a hidden cavern of the water. And now one voice was filled with a menace. A number of men with enormous limbs that threw vast shadows over the sea as the lanterns flickered, held a debate and made gestures.

Off in the darkness, the tall man began to clamour like a mob. The freckled man sat in astounded silence, with his legs weak.

After a time one of the men of enormous limbs seized a rope that was tugging at the stern and drew a small boat from the shadows. Three giants clambered in and rowed cautiously toward the raft. Silver water flashed in the gloom as the oars dipped.

About fifty feet from the raft the boat stopped. "Who er you?" asked a voice.

The tall man braced himself and explained. He drew vivid pictures, his twirling fingers illustrating like live brushes.

"Oh," said the three giants.

The voyagers deserted the raft. They looked back, feeling in their hearts a mite of tenderness for the wet planks. Later, they wriggled up the side of the vessel and climbed over the railing.

On deck they met a man.

He held a lantern to their faces. "Got any chewin' tewbacca?" he inquired.

"No," said the tall man, "we ain't."

The man had a bronze face and solitary whiskers. Peculiar lines about his mouth were shaped into an eternal smile of derision. His feet were bare, and clung handily to crevices.

Fearful trousers were supported by a piece of suspender that went up the wrong side of his chest and came down the right side of his back, dividing him into triangles.

"Ezekiel P. Sanford, capt'in, schooner 'Mary Jones,' of N'yack, N.Y., genelmen," he said.

"Ah!" said the tall man, "delighted, I'm sure."

There were a few moments of silence. The giants were hovering in the gloom and staring.

Suddenly astonishment exploded the captain.

"Wot th' devil—" he shouted, "wot th' devil yeh got on?"

"Bathing-suits," said the tall man.

CHAPTER IV

The schooner went on. The two voyagers sat down and watched. After a time they began to shiver. The soft blackness of the summer night passed away, and grey mists writhed over the sea. Soon lights of early dawn went changing across the sky, and the twin beacons on the highlands grew dim and sparkling faintly, as if a monster were dying. The dawn penetrated the marrow of the two men in bathing-dress.

The captain used to pause opposite them, hitch one hand in his suspender, and laugh.

"Well, I be dog-hanged," he frequently said.

The tall man grew furious. He snarled in a mad undertone to his companion. "This rescue ain't right. If I had known—"

He suddenly paused, transfixed by the captain's suspender. "It's goin' to break," cried he, in an ecstatic whisper. His eyes grew large with excitement as he watched the captain laugh. "It'll break in a minute, sure."

But the commander of the schooner recovered, and invited them to drink and eat. They followed him along the deck, and fell down a square black hole into the cabin.

It was a little den, with walls of a vanished whiteness. A lamp shed an orange light. In a sort of recess two little beds were hiding. A wooden table, immovable, as if the craft had been builded around it, sat in the middle of the floor. Overhead the square hole was studded with a dozen stars. A foot-worn ladder led to the heavens.

The captain produced ponderous crackers and some cold broiled ham. Then he vanished in the firmament like a fantastic comet.

The freckled man sat quite contentedly like a stout squaw in a blanket. The tall man walked about the cabin and sniffed. He was angered at the crudeness of the rescue, and his shrinking clothes made him feel too large. He contemplated his unhappy state.

Suddenly, he broke out. "I won't stand this, I tell you! Heavens and earth, look at the—say, what in the blazes did you want to get me in this thing for, anyhow? You're a fine old duffer, you are! Look at that ham!"

The freckled man grunted. He seemed somewhat blissful. He was seated upon a bench, comfortably enwrapped in his bathing-dress.

The tall man stormed about the cabin.

"This is an outrage! I'll see the captain! I'll tell him what I think of—"

He was interrupted by a pair of legs that appeared among the stars. The captain came down the ladder. He brought a coffee pot from the sky.

The tall man bristled forward. He was going to denounce everything.

The captain was intent upon the coffee pot, balancing it carefully, and leaving his unguided feet to find the steps of the ladder.

But the wrath of the tall man faded. He twirled his fingers in excitement, and renewed his ecstatic whisperings to the freckled man.

"It's going to break! Look, quick, look! It'll break in a minute!"

He was transfixed with interest, forgetting his wrongs in staring at the perilous passage.

But the captain arrived on the floor with triumphant suspenders.

"Well," said he, "after yeh have eat, maybe ye'd like t'sleep some! If so, yeh can sleep on them beds."

The tall man made no reply, save in a strained undertone. "It'll break in about a minute! Look, Ted, look quick!"

The freckled man glanced in a little bed on which were heaped boots and oilskins. He made a courteous gesture.

"My dear sir, we could not think of depriving you of your beds. No, indeed. Just a couple of blankets if you have them, and we'll sleep very comfortable on these benches."

The captain protested, politely twisting his back and bobbing his head. The suspenders tugged and creaked. The tall man partially suppressed a cry, and took a step forward.

The freckled man was sleepily insistent, and shortly the captain gave over his deprecatory contortions. He fetched a pink quilt with yellow dots on it to the freckled man, and a black one with red roses on it to the tall man.

Again he vanished in the firmament. The tall man gazed until the last remnant of trousers disappeared from the sky. Then he wrapped himself up in his quilt and lay down. The freckled man was puffing contentedly, swathed like an infant. The yellow polka-dots rose and fell on the vast pink of his chest.

The wanderers slept. In the quiet could be heard the groanings of timbers as the sea seemed to crunch them together. The lapping of water along the vessel's side sounded like gaspings. An hundred spirits of the wind had got their wings entangled in the rigging, and, in soft voices, were pleading to be loosened.

The freckled man was awakened by a foreign noise. He opened his eyes and saw his companion standing by his couch.

His comrade's face was wane with suffering. His eyes glowed in the darkness. He raised his arms, spreading them out like a clergyman at a grave. He groaned deep in his chest.

"Good Lord!" yelled the freckled man, starting up. "Tom, Tom, what's th' matter?"

The tall man spoke in a fearful voice. "To New York," he said, "to New York in our bathing-suits."

The freckled man sank back. The shadows of the cabin threw mysteries about the figure of the tall man, arrayed like some ancient and potent astrologer in the black quilt with the red roses on it.

CHAPTER V

Directly the tall man went and lay down and began to groan.

The freckled man felt the miseries of the world upon him. He grew angry at the tall man awakening him. They quarrelled.

"Well," said the tall man, finally, "we're in a fix."

"I know that," said the other, sharply.

They regarded the ceiling in silence.

"What in the thunder are we going to do?" demanded the tall man, after a time. His companion was still silent. "Say," repeated he, angrily, "what in the thunder are we going to do?"

"I'm sure I don't know," said the freckled man in a dismal voice.

"Well, think of something," roared the other. "Think of something, you old fool. You don't want to make any more idiots of yourself, do you?"

"I ain't made an idiot of myself."

"Well, think. Know anybody in the city?"

"I know a fellow up in Harlem," said the freckled man.

"You know a fellow up in Harlem," howled the tall man. "Up in Harlem! How the dickens are we to—say, you're crazy!"

"We can take a cab," cried the other, waxing indignant.

The tall man grew suddenly calm. "Do you know any one else?" he asked, measuredly.

"I know another fellow somewhere on Park Place."

"Somewhere on Park Place," repeated the tall man in an unnatural manner. "Somewhere on Park Place." With an air of sublime resignation he turned his face to the wall.

The freckled man sat erect and frowned in the direction of his companion. "Well, now, I suppose you are going to sulk. You make me ill! It's the best we can do, ain't it? Hire a cab and go look that fellow up on Park—What's that? You can't afford it? What nonsense! You are getting—Oh! Well, maybe we can beg some clothes of the captain. Eh? Did I see 'im. Certainly, I saw 'im. Yes, it is improbable that a man who wears trousers like that can have clothes to lend. No, I won't wear oilskins and a sou'-wester. To Athens? Of course not! I don't know where it is. Do you? I thought not. With all your grumbling about other people, you never know anything important yourself. What? Broadway? I'll be hanged first. We can get off at Harlem, man alive. There are no cabs in Harlem. I don't think we can bribe a sailor to take us ashore and bring a cab to the dock, for the very simple reason that we have nothing to bribe him with. What? No, of course not. See here, Tom Sharp, don't you swear at me like that. I won't have it. What's that? I ain't, either. I ain't. What? I am not. It's no such thing. I ain't. I've got more than you have, anyway. Well, you ain't doing anything so very brilliant yourself—just lying there and cussin'." At length the tall man feigned to prodigiously snore. The freckled man thought with such vigour that he fell asleep.

After a time he dreamed that he was in a forest where bass drums grew on trees. There came a strong wind that banged the fruit about like empty pods. A frightful din was in his ears.

He awoke to find the captain of the schooner standing over him.

"We're at New York now," said the captain, raising his voice above the thumping and banging that was being done on deck, "an' I s'pose you fellers wanta go ashore." He chuckled in an exasperating manner. "Jes' sing out when yeh wanta go," he added, leering at the freckled man.

The tall man awoke, came over and grasped the captain by the throat.

"If you laugh again I'll kill you," he said.

The captain gurgled and waved his legs and arms.

"In the first place," the tall man continued, "you rescued us in a deucedly shabby manner. It makes me ill to think of it. I've a mind to mop you 'round just for that. In the second place, your vessel is bound for Athens, N.Y., and there's no sense in it. Now, will you or will you not turn this ship about and take us back where our clothes are, or to Philadelphia, where we belong?"

He furiously shook the captain. Then he eased his grip and awaited a reply.

"I can't," yelled the captain, "I can't. This vessel don't belong to me. I've got to—"

"Well, then," interrupted the tall man, "can you lend us some clothes?"

"Hain't got none," replied the captain, promptly. His face was red, and his eyes were glaring.

"Well, then," said the tall man, "can you lend us some money?"

"Hain't got none," replied the captain, promptly. Something overcame him and he laughed.

"Thunderation," roared the tall man. He seized the captain, who began to have wriggling contortions. The tall man kneaded him as if he were biscuits. "You infernal scoundrel," he bellowed, "this whole affair is some wretched plot, and you are in it. I am about to kill you."

The solitary whisker of the captain did acrobatic feats like a strange demon upon his chin. His eyes stood perilously from his head. The suspender wheezed and tugged like the tackle of a sail.

Suddenly the tall man released his hold. Great expectancy sat upon his features. "It's going to break," he cried, rubbing his hands.

But the captain howled and vanished in the sky.

The freckled man then came forward. He appeared filled with sarcasm.

"So!" said he. "So, you've settled the matter. The captain is the only man in the world who can help us, and I daresay he'll do anything he can now."

"That's all right," said the tall man. "If you don't like the way I run things you shouldn't have come on this trip at all."

They had another quarrel.

At the end of it they went on deck. The captain stood at the stern addressing the bow with opprobrious language. When he perceived the voyagers he began to fling his fists about in the air.

"I'm goin' to put yeh off," he yelled. The wanderers stared at each other.

"Hum," said the tall man.

The freckled man looked at his companion. "He's going to put us off, you see," he said, complacently.

The tall man began to walk about and move his shoulders. "I'd like to see you do it," he said, defiantly.

The captain tugged at a rope. A boat came at his bidding.

"I'd like to see you do it," the tall man repeated, continually. An imperturbable man in rubber boots climbed down in the boat and seized the oars. The captain motioned downward. His whisker had a triumphant appearance.

The two wanderers looked at the boat. "I guess we'll have to get in," murmured the freckled man.

The tall man was standing like a granite column. "I won't," said he. "I won't! I don't care what you do, but I won't!"

"Well, but—" expostulated the other. They held a furious debate.

In the meantime the captain was darting about making sinister gestures, but the back of the tall man held him at bay. The crew, much depleted by the departure of the imperturbable man into the boat, looked on from the bow.

"You're a fool," the freckled man concluded his argument.

"So?" inquired the tall man, highly exasperated.

"So? Well, if you think you're so bright, we'll go in the boat, and then you'll see."

He climbed down into the craft and seated himself in an ominous manner at the stern.

"You'll see," he said to his companion, as the latter floundered heavily down. "You'll see!"

The man in rubber boots calmly rowed the boat toward the shore. As they went, the captain leaned over the railing and laughed. The freckled man was seated very victoriously.

"Well, wasn't this the right thing after all?" he inquired in a pleasant voice. The tall man made no reply.

CHAPTER VI

As they neared the dock something seemed suddenly to occur to the freckled man.

"Great heavens," he murmured. He stared at the approaching shore.

"My, what a plight, Tommy," he quavered.

"Do you think so?" spoke up the tall man, "Why, I really thought you liked it." He laughed in a hard voice. "Lord, what a figure you'll cut."

This laugh jarred the freckled man's soul. He became mad.

"Thunderation, turn the boat around," he roared. "Turn 'er round, quick. Man alive, we can't—turn 'er round, d'ye hear."

The tall man in the stern gazed at his companion with glowing eyes.

"Certainly not," he said. "We're going on. You insisted upon it." He began to prod his companion with words.

The freckled man stood up and waved his arms.

"Sit down," said the tall man. "You'll tip the boat over."

The other man began to shout.

"Sit down," said the tall man again.

Words bubbled from the freckled man's mouth. There was a little torrent of sentences that almost choked him. And he protested passionately with his hands.

But the boat went on to the shadow of the docks. The tall man was intent upon balancing it as it rocked dangerously during his comrade's oration.

"Sit down," he continually repeated.

"I won't," raged the freckled man. "I won't do anything." The boat wobbled with these words.

"Say," he continued, addressing the oarsman, "just turn this boat round, will you. Where in the thunder are you taking us to, anyhow?"

The oarsman looked at the sky and thought. Finally he spoke. "I'm doin' what the cap'n sed."

"Well, what in th' blazes do I care what the cap'n sed?" demanded the freckled man. He took a violent step. "You just turn this round or—"

The small craft reeled. Over one side water came flashing in. The freckled man cried out in fear, and gave a jump to the other side. The tall man roared orders, and the oarsman made efforts. The boat acted for a moment like an animal on a slackened wire. Then it upset.

"Sit down," said the tall man, in a final roar as he was plunged into the water. The oarsman dropped his oars to grapple with the gunwale. He went down saying unknown words. The freckled man's explanation or apology was strangled by the water.

Two or three tugs let off whistles of astonishment, and continued on their paths. A man dosing on a dock aroused and began to caper. The passengers of a ferry-boat all ran to the near railing.

A miraculous person in a small boat was bobbing on the waves near the piers. He sculled hastily toward the scene. It was a swirl of waters in the midst of which the dark bottom of the boat appeared, whale-like.

Two heads suddenly came up. "839," said the freckled man, chokingly. "That's it! 839!"

"What is?" said the tall man.

"That's the number of that feller on Park Place. I just remembered."

"You're the bloomingest—" the tall man said.

"It wasn't my fault," interrupted his companion. "If you hadn't—" He tried to gesticulate, but one hand held to the keel of the boat, and the other was supporting the form of the oarsman. The latter had fought a battle with his immense rubber boots and had been conquered.

The rescuer in the other small boat came fiercely. As his craft glided up, he reached out and grasped the tall man by the collar and dragged him into the boat, interrupting what was, under the circumstances, a very brilliant flow of rhetoric directed at the freckled man. The oarsman of the wrecked craft was taken tenderly over the gunwale and laid in the bottom of the boat. Puffing and blowing, the freckled man climbed in.

"You'll upset this one before we can get ashore," the other voyager remarked.

As they turned toward the land they saw that the nearest dock was lined with people. The freckled man gave a little moan.

But the staring eyes of the crowd were fixed on the limp form of the man in rubber boots. A hundred hands reached down to help lift the body up. On the dock some men grabbed it and began to beat it and roll it. A policeman tossed the spectators about. Each individual in the heaving crowd sought to fasten his eyes on the blue-tinted face of the man in the rubber boots. They surged to and fro, while the policeman beat them indiscriminately.

The wanderers came modestly up the dock and gazed shrinkingly at the throng. They stood for a moment, holding their breath to see the first finger of amazement levelled at them.

But the crowd bended and surged in absorbing anxiety to view the man in rubber boots, whose face fascinated them. The sea-wanderers were as though they were not there.

They stood without the jam and whispered hurriedly.

"839," said the freckled man.

"All right," said the tall man.

Under the pommeling hands the oarsman showed signs of life. The voyagers watched him make a protesting kick at the leg of the crowd, the while uttering angry groans.

"He's better," said the tall man, softly; "let's make off."

Together they stole noiselessly up the dock. Directly in front of it they found a row of six cabs.

The drivers on top were filled with a mighty curiosity. They had driven hurriedly from the adjacent ferry-house when they had seen the first running sign of an accident. They were straining on their toes and gazing at the tossing backs of the men in the crowd.

The wanderers made a little detour, and then went rapidly towards a cab. They stopped in front of it and looked up.

"Driver," called the tall man, softly.

The man was intent.

"Driver," breathed the freckled man. They stood for a moment and gazed imploringly.

The cabman suddenly moved his feet. "By Jimmy, I bet he's a

gonner," he said, in an ecstacy, and he again relapsed into a statue.

The freckled man groaned and wrung his hands. The tall man climbed into the cab.

"Come in here," he said to his companion. The freckled man climbed in, and the tall man reached over and pulled the door shut. Then he put his head out the window.

"Driver," he roared, sternly, "839 Park Place—and quick."

The driver looked down and met the eye of the tall man. "Eh?— Oh—839? Park Place? Yessir." He reluctantly gave his horse a clump on the back. As the conveyance rattled off the wanderers huddled back among the dingy cushions and heaved great breaths of relief.

"Well, it's all over," said the freckled man, finally. "We're about out of it. And quicker than I expected. Much quicker. It looked to me sometimes that we were doomed. I am thankful to find it not so. I am rejoiced. And I hope and trust that you—well, I don't wish, to— perhaps it is not the proper time to—that is, I don't wish to intrude a moral at an inopportune moment, but, my dear, dear fellow, I think the time is ripe to point out to you that your obstinacy, your selfishness, your villainous temper, and your various other faults can make it just as unpleasant for your ownself, my dear boy, as they frequently do for other people. You can see what you brought us to, and I most sincerely hope, my dear, dear fellow, that I shall soon see those signs in you which shall lead me to believe that you have become a wiser man."

SPITZBERGEN TALES

THE KICKING TWELFTH

The Spitzbergen army was backed by tradition of centuries of victory. In its chronicles, occasional defeats were not printed in italics, but were likely to appear as glorious stands against overwhelming odds. A favourite way to dispose of them was frankly to attribute them to the blunders of the civilian heads of government. This was very good for the army, and probably no army had more self-confidence. When it was announced that an expeditionary force was to be sent to Rostina to chastise an impudent people, a hundred barrack squares filled with excited men, and a hundred sergeant-majors hurried silently through the groups, and succeeded in looking as if they were the repositories of the secrets of empire. Officers on leave sped joyfully back to their harness, and recruits were abused with unflagging devotion by every man, from colonels to privates of experience.

The Twelfth Regiment of the Line—the Kicking Twelfth—was consumed with a dread that it was not to be included in the expedition, and the regiment formed itself into an informal indignation meeting. Just as they had proved that a great outrage was about to be perpetrated, warning orders arrived to hold themselves in readiness for active service abroad—in Rostina. The barrack yard was in a flash transferred into a blue-and-buff pandemonium, and the official bugle itself hardly had power to quell the glad disturbance.

Thus it was that early in the spring the Kicking Twelfth—sixteen hundred men in service equipment—found itself crawling along a road in Rostina. They did not form part of the main force, but belonged to a column of four regiments of foot, two batteries of field guns, a battery of mountain howitzers, a regiment of horse, and a company of engineers. Nothing had happened. The long column had crawled without amusement of any kind through a broad green valley. Big white farm-houses dotted the slopes; but there was no sign of man or beast, and no smoke from the chimneys. The column was operating from its own base, and its general was expected to form a junction with the main body at a given point.

A squadron of the cavalry was fanned out ahead, scouting, and day by day the trudging infantry watched the blue uniforms of the horsemen as they came and went. Sometimes there would sound the faint thuds of a few shots, but the cavalry was unable to find anything to engage.

The Twelfth had no record of foreign service, and it could hardly be said that it had served as a unit in the great civil war, when His Majesty the King had whipped the Pretender. At that time the regiment had suffered from two opinions, so that it was impossible for either side to depend upon it. Many men had deserted to the standard of the Pretender, and a number of officers had drawn their swords for him. When the King, a thorough soldier, looked at the remnant, he saw that they lacked the spirit to be of great help to him in the tremendous battles which he was waging for his throne. And so this emaciated Twelfth was sent off to a corner of the kingdom to guard a dockyard, where some of the officers so plainly expressed their disapproval of this policy that the regiment received its steadfast name, the Kicking Twelfth.

At the time of which I am writing the Twelfth had a few veteran officers and well-bitten sergeants; but the body of the regiment was composed of men who had never heard a shot fired excepting on the rifle-range. But it was an experience for which they longed, and when the moment came for the corps' cry—"Kim up, the Kickers"—there was not likely to be a man who would not go tumbling after his leaders.

Young Timothy Lean was a second lieutenant in the first company of the third battalion, and just at this time he was pattering along at the flank of the men, keeping a fatherly lookout for boots that hurt and packs that sagged. He was extremely bored. The mere far-away sound of desultory shooting was not war as he had been led to believe it.

It did not appear that behind that freckled face and under that red hair there was a mind which dreamed of blood. He was not extremely anxious to kill somebody, but he was very fond of soldiering—it had been the career of his father and of his grandfather—and he understood that the profession of arms lost much of its point unless a man shot at people and had people shoot at him. Strolling in the sun through a practically deserted country might be a proper occupation for a divinity student on a vacation, but the soul of Timothy Lean was in revolt at it. Some times at night he would go morosely to the camp of the cavalry and hear the infant subalterns laughingly exaggerate the comedy side of the adventures which they had had out with small patrols far ahead. Lean would sit and listen in glum silence to these tales, and dislike the young officers—many of them old military school friends—for having had experience in modern warfare.

"Anyhow," he said savagely, "presently you'll be getting into a lot of trouble, and then the Foot will have to come along and pull you out. We always do. That's history."

"Oh, we can take care of ourselves," said the Cavalry, with good-natured understanding of his mood.

But the next day even Lean blessed the cavalry, for excited troopers came whirling back from the front, bending over their speeding horses, and shouting wildly and hoarsely for the infantry to clear the way. Men yelled at them from the roadside as courier followed courier, and from the distance ahead sounded in quick succession six booms from field guns. The information possessed by the couriers was no longer precious. Everybody knew what a battery meant when it spoke. The bugles cried out, and the long column jolted into a halt. Old Colonel Sponge went bouncing in his saddle back to see the general, and the regiment sat down in the grass by the roadside, and waited in silence. Presently the second squadron of the cavalry trotted off along the road in a cloud of dust, and in due time old Colonel Sponge came bouncing back, and palavered his three majors and his adjutant. Then there was more talk by the majors, and gradually through the correct channels spread information which in due time reached Timothy Lean.

The enemy, 5000 strong, occupied a pass at the head of the valley some four miles beyond. They had three batteries well posted. Their infantry was entrenched. The ground in their front was crossed and lined with many ditches and hedges; but the enemy's batteries were so posted that it was doubtful if a ditch would ever prove convenient as shelter for the Spitzbergen infantry.

There was a fair position for the Spitzbergen artillery 2300 yards from the enemy. The cavalry had succeeded in driving the enemy's skirmishers back upon the main body; but, of course, had only tried to worry them a little. The position was almost inaccessible on the enemy's right, owing to steep hills, which had been crowned by small parties of infantry. The enemy's left, although guarded by a much larger force, was approachable, and might be flanked. This was what the cavalry had to say, and it added briefly a report of two troopers killed and five wounded.

Whereupon Major-General Richie, commanding a force of 7500

men of His Majesty of Spitzbergen, set in motion, with a few simple words, the machinery which would launch his army at the enemy. The Twelfth understood the orders when they saw the smart young aide approaching old Colonel Sponge, and they rose as one man, apparently afraid that they would be late. There was a clank of accoutrements. Men shrugged their shoulders tighter against their packs, and thrusting their thumbs between their belts and their tunics, they wriggled into a closer fit with regard to the heavy ammunition equipment. It is curious to note that almost every man took off his cap, and looked contemplatively into it as if to read a maker's name. Then they replaced their caps with great care. There was little talking, and it was not observable that a single soldier handed a token or left a comrade with a message to be delivered in case he should be killed. They did not seem to think of being killed; they seemed absorbed in a desire to know what would happen, and how it would look when it was happening. Men glanced continually at their officers in a plain desire to be quick to understand the very first order that would be given; and officers looked gravely at their men, measuring them, feeling their temper, worrying about them.

A bugle called; there were sharp cries, and the Kicking Twelfth was off to battle.

The regiment had the right of line in the infantry brigade, and the men tramped noisily along the white road, every eye was strained ahead; but, after all, there was nothing to be seen but a dozen farms—in short, a country-side. It resembled the scenery in Spitzbergen; every man in the Kicking Twelfth had often confronted a dozen such farms with a composure which amounted to indifference. But still down the road came galloping troopers, who delivered information to Colonel Sponge and then galloped on. In time the Twelfth came to the top of a rise, and below them on the plain was the heavy black streak of a Spitzbergen squadron, and behind the squadron loomed the grey bare hill of the Rostina position.

There was a little of skirmish firing. The Twelfth reached a knoll, which the officers easily recognised as the place described by the cavalry as suitable for the Spitzbergen guns. The men swarmed up it in a peculiar formation. They resembled a crowd coming off a race track; but, nevertheless, there was no stray sheep. It was simply that the ground on which actual battles are fought is not like a chess board. And after them came swinging a six-gun battery, the guns wagging from side to side as the long line turned out of the road, and the drivers using their whips as the leading horses scrambled at the hill. The halted Twelfth lifted its voice and spoke amiably, but with point, to the battery.

"Go on, Guns! We'll take care of you. Don't be afraid. Give it to them!" The teams—lead, swing and wheel—struggled and slipped over the steep and uneven ground; and the gunners, as they clung to their springless positions, wore their usual and natural airs of unhappiness. They made no reply to the infantry. Once upon the top of the hill, however, these guns were unlimbered in a flash, and directly the infantry could hear the loud voice of an officer drawling out the time for fuses. A moment later the first 3·2 bellowed out, and there could be heard the swish and the snarl of a fleeting shell.

Colonel Sponge and a number of officers climbed to the battery's position; but the men of the regiment sat in the shelter of the hill, like so many blindfolded people, and wondered what they would have been able to see if they had been officers. Sometimes the shells of the enemy came sweeping over the top of the hill, and burst in great brown explosions in the fields to the rear. The men looked after them and laughed. To the rear could be seen also the mountain battery coming at a comic trot, with every man obviously in a deep rage with every mule. If a man can put in long service with a mule battery and come out of it with an amiable disposition, he should be presented with a medal weighing many ounces. After the mule battery came a long black winding thing, which was three regiments of Spitzbergen infantry; and at the backs of them and to the right was an inky square, which was the remaining Spitzbergen guns. General Richie and his staff clattered up the hill. The blindfolded Twelfth sat still. The inky square suddenly became a long racing line. The howitzers joined their little bark to the thunder of the guns on the hill, and the three regiments of infantry came on. The Twelfth sat still.

Of a sudden a bugle rang its warning, and the officers shouted. Some used the old cry, "Attention! Kim up, the Kickers!"—and the Twelfth knew that it had been told to go on. The majority of the men expected to see great things as soon as they rounded the shoulder of the hill; but there was nothing to be seen save a complicated plain and the grey knolls occupied by the enemy. Many company commanders in low voices worked at their men, and said things which do not appear in the written reports. They talked soothingly; they talked indignantly; and they talked always like fathers. And the men heard no sentences completely; they heard no specific direction, these wide-eyed men. They understood that there was being delivered some kind of exhortation to do as they had been taught, and they also understood that a superior intelligence was anxious over their behaviour and welfare.

There was a great deal of floundering through hedges, climbing of walls and jumping of ditches. Curiously original privates tried to find new and easier ways for themselves, instead of following the men in front of them. Officers had short fits of fury over these people. The more originality they possessed, the more likely they were to become separated from their companies. Colonel Sponge was making an exciting progress on a big charger. When the first song of the bullets came from above, the men wondered why he sat so high; the charger seemed as tall as the Eiffel Tower. But if he was high in the air, he had a fine view, and that supposedly is why people ascend the Eiffel Tower. Very often he had been a joke to them, but when they saw this fat, old gentleman so coolly treating the strange new missiles which hummed in the air, it struck them suddenly that they had wronged him seriously; and a man who could attain the command of a Spitzbergen regiment was entitled to general respect. And they gave him a sudden, quick affection—an affection that would make them follow him heartily, trustfully, grandly—this fat, old gentleman, seated on a too-big horse. In a flash his tousled grey head, his short, thick legs, even his paunch, had become specially and humorously endeared to them. And this is the way of soldiers.

But still the Twelfth had not yet come to the place where tumbling bodies begin their test of the very heart of a regiment. They backed through more hedges, jumped more ditches, slid over more walls. The Rostina artillery had seemed to be asleep; but suddenly the guns aroused like dogs from their kennels, and around the Twelfth there began a wild, swift screeching. There arose cries to hurry, to come on; and, as the rifle bullets began to plunge into them, the men saw the high, formidable hills of the enemy's right, and perfectly understood that they were doomed to storm them. The cheering thing was the sudden beginning of a tremendous uproar on the enemy's left.

Every man ran, hard, tense, breathless. When they reached the foot of the hills, they thought they had won the charge already, but they were electrified to see officers above them waving their swords and yelling with anger, surprise, and shame. With a long murmurous outcry the Twelfth began to climb the hill; and as they went and fell, they could hear frenzied shouts—"Kim up, the Kickers!" The pace was slow. It was like the rising of a tide; it was determined, almost relentless in its appearance, but it was slow. If a man fell there was a chance that he would land twenty yards below the point where he was hit. The Kickers crawled, their rifles in their left hands as they pulled and tugged themselves up with their right hands. Ever arose the shout, "Kim up, the Kickers!" Timothy Lean, his face flaming, his eyes wild, yelled it back as if he were delivering the gospel.

The Kickers came up. The enemy—they had been in small force, thinking the hills safe enough from attack—retreated quickly from this preposterous advance, and not a bayonet in the Twelfth saw blood; bayonets very seldom do.

The homing of this successful charge wore an unromantic aspect. About twenty windless men suddenly arrived, and threw themselves upon the crest of the hill, and breathed. And these twenty were joined by others, and still others, until almost 1100 men of the Twelfth lay upon the hilltop, while the regiment's track was marked by body after body, in groups and singly. The first officer—perchance the first man, one never can be certain—the first officer to gain the top of the hill was Timothy Lean, and such was the situation that he had the honour to receive his colonel with a bashful salute.

The regiment knew exactly what it had done; it did not have to wait to be told by the Spitzbergen newspapers. It had taken a formidable position with the loss of about five hundred men, and it knew it. It knew, too, that it was great glory for the Kicking Twelfth; and as the men lay rolling on their bellies, they expressed their joy in a wild cry—"Kim up, the Kickers!" For a moment there was nothing but joy, and then suddenly company commanders were besieged by men who wished to go down the path of the charge and look for their mates. The answers were without the quality of mercy; they were short, snapped, quick words, "No; you can't."

The attack on the enemy's left was sounding in great rolling crashes. The shells in their flight through the air made a noise as of red-hot iron plunged into water, and stray bullets nipped near the ears of the Kickers.

The Kickers looked and saw. The battle was below them. The enemy were indicated by a long, noisy line of gossamer smoke, although there could be seen a toy battery with tiny men employed at the guns. All over the field the shrapnel was bursting, making quick bulbs of white smoke. Far away, two regiments of Spitzbergen infantry were charging, and at the distance this charge looked like a casual stroll. It appeared that small black groups of men were walking meditatively toward the Rostina entrenchments.

There would have been orders given sooner to the Twelfth, but unfortunately Colonel Sponge arrived on top of the hill without a breath of wind in his body. He could not have given an order to save the regiment from being wiped off the earth. Finally he was able to gasp out something and point at the enemy. Timothy Lean ran along the line yelling to the men to sight at 800 yards; and like a slow and ponderous machine the regiment again went to work. The fire flanked a great part of the enemy's trenches.

It could be said that there were only two prominent points of view expressed by the men after their victorious arrival on the crest. One was defined in the exulting use of the corps' cry. The other was a grief-stricken murmur which is invariably heard after a fight—"My God, we're all cut to pieces!"

Colonel Sponge sat on the ground and impatiently waited for his wind to return. As soon as it did, he arose and cried out, "Form up, and we'll charge again! We will win this battle as soon as we can hit them!" The shouts of the officers sounded wild, like men yelling on ship-board in a gale. And the obedient Kickers arose for their task. It was running down hill this time. The mob of panting men poured over the stones.

But the enemy had not been blind to the great advantage gained by the Twelfth, and they now turned upon them a desperate fire of small arms. Men fell in every imaginable way, and their accoutrements rattled on the rocky ground. Some landed with a crash, floored by some tremendous blows; others dropped gently down like sacks of meal; with others, it would positively appear that some spirit had suddenly seized them by their ankles and jerked their legs from under them. Many officers were down, but Colonel Sponge, stuttering and blowing, was still upright. He was almost the last man in the charge, but not to his shame, rather to his stumpy legs. At one time it seemed that the assault would be lost. The effect of the fire was somewhat as if a terrible cyclone were blowing in the men's faces. They wavered, lowering their heads and shouldering weakly, as if it were impossible to make headway against the wind of battle. It was the moment of despair, the moment of the heroism which comes to the chosen of the war-god.

The colonel's cry broke and screeched absolute hatred; other officers simply howled; and the men, silent, debased, seemed to tighten their muscles for one last effort. Again they pushed against this mysterious power of the air, and once more the regiment was charging. Timothy Lean, agile and strong, was well in advance; and afterwards he reflected that the men who had been nearest to him were an old grizzled sergeant who would have gone to hell for the honour of the regiment, and a pie-faced lad who had been obliged to lie about his age in order to get into the army.

There was no shock of meeting. The Twelfth came down on a corner of the trenches, and as soon as the enemy had ascertained that the Twelfth was certain to arrive, they scuttled out, running close to the earth and spending no time in glances backward. In these days it is not discreet to wait for a charge to come home. You observe the charge, you attempt to stop it, and if you find that you can't, it is better to retire immediately to some other place. The Rostina soldiers were not heroes, perhaps, but they were men of sense. A maddened and badly-frightened mob of Kickers came tumbling into the trench, and shot at the backs of fleeing men. And at that very moment the action was won, and won by the Kickers. The enemy's flank was entirely crippled, and, knowing this, he did not await further and more disastrous information. The Twelfth looked at themselves and knew that they had a record. They sat down and grinned patronisingly as they saw the batteries galloping to advance position to shell the retreat, and they really laughed as the cavalry swept tumultuously forward.

The Twelfth had no more concern with the battle. They had won it, and the subsequent proceedings were only amusing.

There was a call from the flank, and the men wearily adjusted themselves as General Richie, stern and grim as a Roman, looked with his straight glance at a hammered and thin and dirty line of figures, which was His Majesty's Twelfth Regiment of the Line. When opposite old Colonel Sponge, a podgy figure standing at attention, the general's face set in still more grim and stern lines. He took off his helmet. "Kim up, the Kickers!" said he. He replaced his helmet and rode off. Down the cheeks of the little fat colonel rolled tears. He stood like a stone for a long moment, and wheeled in supreme wrath upon his surprised adjutant. "Delahaye, you d—d fool, don't stand there staring like a monkey! Go, tell young Lean I want to see him." The adjutant jumped as if he were on springs, and went after Lean. That young officer presented himself directly, his face covered with disgraceful smudges, and he had also torn his breeches. He had never seen the colonel in such a rage. "Lean, you young whelp! you—you're a good boy." And even as the general had turned away from the colonel, the colonel turned away from the lieutenant.

THE UPTURNED FACE

"What will we do now?" said the adjutant, troubled and excited.

"Bury him," said Timothy Lean.

The two officers looked down close to their toes where lay the body of their comrade. The face was chalk-blue; gleaming eyes stared at the sky. Over the two upright figures was a windy sound of bullets, and on the top of the hill Lean's prostrate company of Spitzbergen infantry was firing measured volleys.

"Don't you think it would be better—" began the adjutant, "we might leave him until to-morrow."

"No," said Lean. "I can't hold that post an hour longer. I've got to fall back, and we've got to bury old Bill."

"Of course," said the adjutant, at once. "Your men got intrenching tools?"

Lean shouted back to his little line, and two men came slowly, one with a pick, one with a shovel. They started in the direction of the Rostina sharpshooters. Bullets cracked near their ears. "Dig here," said Lean gruffly. The men, thus caused to lower their glances to the turf, became hurried and frightened merely because they could not look to see whence the bullets came. The dull beat of the pick striking the earth sounded amid the swift snap of close bullets. Presently the other private began to shovel.

"I suppose," said the adjutant, slowly, "we'd better search his clothes for—things."

Lean nodded. Together in curious abstraction they looked at the body. Then Lean stirred his shoulders suddenly, arousing himself.

"Yes," he said, "we'd better see what he's got." He dropped to his knees, and his hands approached the body of the dead officer. But his hands wavered over the buttons of the tunic. The first button was brick-red with drying blood, and he did not seem to dare touch it.

"Go on," said the adjutant, hoarsely.

Lean stretched his wooden hand, and his fingers fumbled the blood-stained buttons. At last he rose with ghastly face. He had gathered a watch, a whistle, a pipe, a tobacco pouch, a handkerchief, a little case of cards and papers. He looked at the adjutant. There was a silence. The adjutant was feeling that he had been a coward to make Lean do all the grizzly business.

"Well," said Lean, "that's all, I think. You have his sword and revolver?"

"Yes," said the adjutant, his face working, and then he burst out in a sudden strange fury at the two privates. "Why don't you hurry up with that grave? What are you doing, anyhow? Hurry, do you hear? I never saw such stupid—"

Even as he cried out in his passion the two men were labouring for their lives. Ever overhead the bullets were spitting.

The grave was finished. It was not a masterpiece—a poor little shallow thing. Lean and the adjutant again looked at each other in a curious silent communication.

Suddenly the adjutant croaked out a weird laugh. It was a terrible laugh, which had its origin in that part of the mind which is first moved by the singing of the nerves. "Well," he said, humorously to Lean, "I suppose we had best tumble him in."

"Yes," said Lean. The two privates stood waiting, bent over their implements. "I suppose," said Lean, "it would be better if we laid him in ourselves."

"Yes," said the adjutant. Then apparently remembering that he had made Lean search the body, he stooped with great fortitude and took hold of the dead officer's clothing. Lean joined him. Both were particular that their fingers should not feel the corpse. They tugged away; the corpse lifted, heaved, toppled, flopped into the grave, and the two officers, straightening, looked again at each other—they were always looking at each other. They sighed with relief.

The adjutant said, "I suppose we should—we should say something. Do you know the service, Tim?"

"They don't read the service until the grave is filled in," said Lean, pressing his lips to an academic expression.

"Don't they?" said the adjutant, shocked that he had made the mistake.

"Oh, well," he cried, suddenly, "let us—let us say something—while he can hear us."

"All right," said Lean. "Do you know the service?"

"I can't remember a line of it," said the adjutant.

Lean was extremely dubious. "I can repeat two lines, but—"

"Well, do it," said the adjutant. "Go as far as you can. That's better than nothing. And the beasts have got our range exactly."

Lean looked at his two men. "Attention," he barked. The privates came to attention with a click, looking much aggrieved. The adjutant lowered his helmet to his knee. Lean, bareheaded, stood over the grave. The Rostina sharpshooters fired briskly.

"Oh Father, our friend has sunk in the deep waters of death, but his spirit has leaped toward Thee as the bubble arises from the lips of the drowning. Perceive, we beseech, Oh Father, the little flying bubble, and—"

Lean, although husky and ashamed, had suffered no hesitation up to this point, but he stopped with a hopeless feeling and looked at the corpse.

The adjutant moved uneasily. "And from Thy superb heights—" he began, and then he too came to an end.

"And from Thy superb heights," said Lean.

The adjutant suddenly remembered a phrase in the back part of the Spitzbergen burial service, and he exploited it with the triumphant manner of a man who has recalled everything, and can go on.

"Oh God, have mercy—"

"Oh God, have mercy—" said Lean.

"Mercy," repeated the adjutant, in quick failure.

"Mercy," said Lean. And then he was moved by some violence of feeling, for he turned suddenly upon his two men and tigerishly said, "Throw the dirt in."

The fire of the Rostina sharpshooters was accurate and continuous.

* * * * * * *

One of the aggrieved privates came forward with his shovel. He lifted his first shovel-load of earth, and for a moment of inexplicable hesitation it was held poised above this corpse, which from its chalk-blue face looked keenly out from the grave. Then the soldier emptied his shovel on—on the feet.

Timothy Lean felt as if tons had been swiftly lifted from off his forehead. He had felt that perhaps the private might empty the shovel on—on the face. It had been emptied on the feet. There was a great point gained there—ha, ha!—the first shovelful had been emptied on the feet. How satisfactory!

The adjutant began to babble. "Well, of course—a man we've messed with all these years—impossible—you can't, you know, leave your intimate friends rotting on the field. Go on, for God's sake, and shovel, you."

The man with the shovel suddenly ducked, grabbed his left arm with his right hand, and looked at his officer for orders. Lean picked the shovel from the ground. "Go to the rear," he said to the wounded man. He also addressed the other private. "You get under cover, too; I'll finish this business."

The wounded man scrambled hard still for the top of the ridge without devoting any glances to the direction from whence the bullets came, and the other man followed at an equal pace; but he was different, in that he looked back anxiously three times.

This is merely the way—often—of the hit and unhit.

Timothy Lean filled the shovel, hesitated, and then in a movement which was like a gesture of abhorrence he flung the dirt into the grave, and as it landed it made a sound—plop. Lean suddenly stopped and mopped his brow—a tired labourer.

"Perhaps we have been wrong," said the adjutant. His glance wavered stupidly. "It might have been better if we hadn't buried him just at this time. Of course, if we advance to-morrow the body would have been—"

"Damn you," said Lean, "shut your mouth." He was not the senior officer.

He again filled the shovel and flung the earth. Always the earth made that sound—plop. For a space Lean worked frantically, like a man digging himself out of danger.

Soon there was nothing to be seen but the chalk-blue face. Lean filled the shovel. "Good God," he cried to the adjutant. "Why didn't you turn him somehow when you put him in? This—" Then Lean began to stutter.

The adjutant understood. He was pale to the lips. "Go on, man," he cried, beseechingly, almost in a shout. Lean swung back the shovel. It went forward in a pendulum curve. When the earth landed it made a sound—plop.

THE SHRAPNEL OF THEIR FRIENDS

From over the knolls came the tiny sound of a cavalry bugle singing out the recall, and later, detached parties of His Majesty's 2nd Hussars came trotting back to where the Spitzbergen infantry sat complacently on the captured Rostina position. The horsemen were well pleased, and they told how they had ridden thrice through the helterskelter of the fleeing enemy. They had ultimately been checked by the great truth, and when a good enemy runs away in daylight he sooner or later finds a place where he fetches up with a jolt, and turns face the pursuit—notably if it is a cavalry pursuit. The Hussars had discreetly withdrawn, displaying no foolish pride of corps at that time.

There was a general admission that the Kicking Twelfth had taken the chief honours of the day, but the artillery added that if the guns had not shelled so accurately the Twelfth's charge could not have been made so successfully, and the three other regiments of infantry, of course, did not conceal their feelings, that their attack on the enemy's left had withdrawn many rifles that would have been pelting at the Twelfth. The cavalry simply said that but for them the victory would not have been complete.

Corps' prides met each other face to face at every step, but the Kickers smiled easily and indulgently. A few recruits bragged, but they bragged because they were recruits. The older men did not wish it to appear that they were surprised and rejoicing at the performance of the regiment. If they were congratulated they simply smirked, suggesting that the ability of the Twelfth had been long known to them, and that the charge had been a little thing, you know, just turned off in the way of an afternoon's work.

Major-General Richie encamped his troops on the position which they had from the enemy. Old Colonel Sponge of the Twelfth redistributed his officers, and the losses had been so great that Timothy Lean got command of a company. It was not much of a company. Fifty-three smudged and sweating men faced their new commander. The company had gone into action with a strength of eighty-six. The heart of Timothy Lean beat high with pride. He intended to be some day a general, and if he ever became a general, that moment of promotion was not equal in joy to the moment when he looked at his new possession of fifty-three vagabonds. He scanned the faces, and recognised with satisfaction one old sergeant and two bright young corporals. "Now," said he to himself, "I have here a snug little body of men with which I can do something." In him burned the usual fierce fire to make them the best company in the regiment. He had adopted them; they were his men. "I will do what I can for you," he said. "Do you the same for me."

The Twelfth bivouacked on the ridge. Little fires were built, and there appeared among the men innumerable blackened tin cups, which were so treasured that a faint suspicion in connection with the loss of one could bring on the grimmest of fights. Meantime certain of the privates silently readjusted their kits as their names were called out by the sergeants. These were the men condemned to picket duty after a hard day of marching and fighting. The dusk came slowly, and the colour of the countless fires, spotting the ridge and the plain, grew in the falling darkness. Far-away pickets fired at something.

One by one the men's heads were lowered to the earth until the ridge was marked by two long shadowy rows of men. Here and there an officer sat musing in his dark cloak with a ray of a weakening fire gleaming on his sword-hilt. From the plain there came at times the sound of battery horses moving restlessly at their tethers, and one could imagine he heard the throaty, grumbling curse of the drivers. The moon died swiftly through flying light clouds. Far-away pickets fired at something.

In the morning the infantry and guns breakfasted to the music of a racket between the cavalry and the enemy, which was taking place some miles up the valley.

The ambitious Hussars had apparently stirred some kind of a hornet's nest, and they were having a good fight with no officious friends near enough to interfere. The remainder of the army looked toward the fight musingly over the tops of tin cups. In time the column crawled lazily forward to see.

The Twelfth, as it crawled, saw a regiment deploy to the right, and saw a battery dash to take position. The cavalry jingled back grinning with pride and expecting to be greatly admired. Presently the Twelfth was bidden to take seat by the roadside and await its turn. Instantly the wise men—and there were more than three— came out of the east and announced that they had divined the whole plan. The Kicking Twelfth was to be held in reserve until the critical moment of the fight, and then they were to be sent forward to win a victory. In corroboration, they pointed to the fact that the general in command was sticking close to them, in order, they said, to give the word quickly at the proper moment. And in truth, on a small hill to the right, Major-General Richie sat on his horse and used his glasses, while back of him his staff and the orderlies bestrode their champing, dancing mounts.

It is always good to look hard at a general, and the Kickers were transfixed with interest. The wise men again came out of the east and told what was inside the Richie head, but even the wise men wondered what was inside the Richie head.

Suddenly an exciting thing happened. To the left and ahead was a pounding Spitzbergen battery, and a toy suddenly appeared on the slope behind the guns. The toy was a man with a flag—the flag was white save for a square of red in the centre. And this toy began to wig-wag wag-wig, and it spoke to General Richie under the authority of the captain of the battery. It said: "The 88th are being driven on my centre and right."

Now, when the Kicking Twelfth had left Spitzbergen there was an average of six signalmen in each company. A proportion of these signallers had been destroyed in the first engagement, but enough remained so that the Kicking Twelfth read, as a unit, the news of the 88th. The word ran quickly. "The 88th are being driven on my centre and right."

Richie rode to where Colonel Sponge sat aloft on his big horse, and a moment later a cry ran along the column: "Kim up, the Kickers." A large number of the men were already in the road, hitching and twisting at their belts and packs. The Kickers moved forward.

They deployed and passed in a straggling line through the battery, and to the left and right of it. The gunners called out to them carefully, telling them not to be afraid.

The scene before them was startling. They were facing a country cut up by many steep-sided ravines, and over the resultant hills were retreating little squads of the 88th. The Twelfth laughed in its exultation. The men could now tell by the volume of fire that the 88th were retreating for reasons which were not sufficiently expressed in the noise of the Rostina shooting. Held together by the bugle, the Kickers swarmed up the first hill and laid on the crest. Parties of the

88th went through their lines, and the Twelfth told them coarsely its several opinions. The sights were clicked up to 600 yards, and, with a crashing volley, the regiment entered its second battle.

A thousand yards away on the right the cavalry and a regiment of infantry were creeping onward. Sponge decided not to be backward, and the bugle told the Twelfth to go ahead once more. The Twelfth charged, followed by a rabble of rallied men of the 88th, who were crying aloud that it had been all a mistake.

A charge in these days is not a running match. Those splendid pictures of levelled bayonets, dashing at headlong pace towards the closed ranks of the enemy are absurd as soon as they are mistaken for the actuality of the present. In these days charges are likely to cover at least the half of a mile, and to go at the pace exhibited in the pictures a man would be obliged to have a little steam engine inside of him.

The charge of the Kicking Twelfth somewhat resembled the advance of a great crowd of beaters who, for some reason, passionately desired to start the game. Men stumbled; men fell; men swore; there were cries: "This way!" "Come this way!" "Don't go that way!" "You can't get up that way!" Over the rocks the Twelfth scrambled, red in the face, sweating and angry. Soldiers fell because they were struck by bullets, and because they had not an ounce of strength left in them. Colonel Sponge, with a face like a red cushion, was being dragged windless up the steeps by devoted and athletic men. Three of the older captains lay afar back, and swearing with their eyes because their tongues were temporarily out of service.

And yet-and-yet, the speed of the charge was slow. From the position of the battery, it looked as if the Kickers were taking a walk over some extremely difficult country.

The regiment ascended a superior height, and found trenches and dead men. They took seat with the dead, satisfied with this company until they could get their wind. For thirty minutes purple-faced stragglers rejoined from the rear. Colonel Sponge looked behind him, and saw that Richie, with his staff, had approached by another route, and had evidently been near enough to see the full extent of the Kickers' exertions. Presently Richie began to pick a way for his horse towards the captured position. He disappeared in a gully between two hills.

Now it came to pass that a Spitzbergen battery on the far right took occasion to mistake the identity of the Kicking Twelfth, and the captain of these guns, not having anything to occupy him in front, directed his six 3·2's upon the ridge where the tired Kickers lay side by side with the Rostina dead. A shrapnel came swinging over the Kickers, seething and fuming. It burst directly over the trenches, and the shrapnel, of course, scattered forward, hurting nobody. But a man screamed out to his officer: "By God, sir, that is one of our own batteries!" The whole line quivered with fright. Five more shells streaked overhead, and one flung its hail into the middle of the 3rd battalion's line, and the Kicking Twelfth shuddered to the very centre of its heart, and arose, like one man, and fled.

Colonel Sponge, fighting, frothing at the month, dealing blows with his fist right and left, found himself confronting a fury on horse-back. Richie was as pale as death, and his eyes sent out sparks. "What does this conduct mean?" he flashed out between his fastened teeth.

Sponge could only gurgle: "The battery—the battery—the battery!"

"The battery?" cried Richie, in a voice which sounded like pistol shots. "Are you afraid of the guns you almost took yesterday? Go back there, you white-livered cowards! You swine! You dogs! Curs! Curs! Curs! Go back there!"

Most of the men halted and crouched under the lashing tongue of their maddened general. But one man found desperate speech, and yelled: "General, it is our own battery that is firing on us!"

Many say that the General's face tightened until it looked like a mask. The Kicking Twelfth retired to a comfortable place, where they were only under the fire of the Rostina artillery. The men saw a staff officer riding over the obstructions in a manner calculated to break his neck directly.

The Kickers were aggrieved, but the heart of the colonel was cut in twain. He even babbled to his major, talking like a man who is about to die of simple rage. "Did you hear what he said to me? Did you hear what he called us? *Did you hear what he called us?*"

The majors searched their minds for words to heal a deep wound.

The Twelfth received orders to go into camp upon the hill where they had been insulted. Old Sponge looked as if he were about to knock the aide out of the saddle, but he saluted, and took the regiment back to the temporary companionship of the Rostina dead.

Major-General Richie never apologised to Colonel Sponge. When you are a commanding officer you do not adopt the custom of apologising for the wrong done to your subordinates. You ride away; and they understand, and are confident of the restitution to honour. Richie never opened his stern, young lips to Sponge in reference to the scene near the hill of the Rostina dead, but in time there was a general order No. 20, which spoke definitely of the gallantry of His Majesty's 12th regiment of the line and its colonel. In the end Sponge was given a high decoration, because he had been badly used by Richie on that day. Richie knew that it is hard for men to withstand the shrapnel of their friends.

A few days later the Kickers, marching in column on the road, came upon their friend the battery, halted in a field; and they addressed the battery, and the captain of the battery blanched to the tips of his ears. But the men of the battery told the Kickers to go to the devil—frankly, freely, placidly, told the Kickers to go to the devil.

And this story proves that it is sometimes better to be a private.

"AND IF HE WILLS,
WE MUST DIE"

A sergeant, a corporal, and fourteen men of the Twelfth Regiment of the Line had been sent out to occupy a house on the main highway. They would be at least a half of a mile in advance of any other picket of their own people. Sergeant Morton was deeply angry at being sent on this duty. He said that he was over-worked. There were at least two sergeants, he claimed furiously, whose turn it should have been to go on this arduous mission. He was treated unfairly; he was abused by his superiors; why did any damned fool ever join the army? As for him he would get out of it as soon as possible; he was sick of it; the life of a dog. All this he said to the corporal, who listened attentively, giving grunts of respectful assent. On the way to this post two privates took occasion to drop to the rear and pilfer in the orchard of a deserted plantation. When the sergeant discovered this absence, he grew black with a rage which was an accumulation of all his irritations. "Run, you!" he howled. "Bring them here! I'll show them—" A private ran swiftly to the rear. The remainder of the squad began to shout nervously at the two delinquents, whose figures they could see in the deep shade of the orchard, hurriedly picking fruit from the ground and cramming it within their shirts, next to their skins. The beseeching cries of their comrades stirred the criminals more than did the barking of the sergeant. They ran to rejoin the squad, while holding their loaded bosoms and with their mouths open with aggrieved explanations.

Jones faced the sergeant with a horrible cancer marked in bumps on his left side. The disease of Patterson showed quite around the front of his waist in many protuberances. "A nice pair!" said the sergeant, with sudden frigidity. "You're the kind of soldiers a man wants to choose for a dangerous outpost duty, ain't you?"

The two privates stood at attention, still looking much aggrieved. "We only—" began Jones huskily.

"Oh, you 'only!'" cried the sergeant. "Yes, you 'only.' I know all about that. But if you think you are going to trifle with me—"

A moment later the squad moved on towards its station. Behind the sergeant's back Jones and Patterson were slyly passing apples and pears to their friends while the sergeant expounded eloquently to the corporal "You see what kind of men are in the army now. Why, when I joined the regiment it was a very different thing, I can tell you. Then a sergeant had some authority, and if a man disobeyed orders, he had a very small chance of escaping something extremely serious. But now! Good God! If I report these men, the captain will look over a lot of beastly orderly sheets and say—'Haw, eh, well, Sergeant Morton, these men seem to have very good records; very good records, indeed. I can't be too hard on them; no, not too hard.'" Continued the sergeant: "I tell you, Flagler, the army is no place for a decent man."

Flagler, the corporal, answered with a sincerity of appreciation which with him had become a science. "I think you are right, sergeant," he answered.

Behind them the privates mumbled discreetly. "Damn this sergeant of ours. He thinks we are made of wood. I don't see any reason for all this strictness when we are on active service. It isn't like being at home in barracks! There is no great harm in a couple of men dropping out to raid an orchard of the enemy when all the world knows that we haven't had a decent meal in twenty days."

The reddened face of Sergeant Morton suddenly showed to the rear. "A little more marching and less talking," he said.

When he came to the house he had been ordered to occupy the sergeant sniffed with disdain. "These people must have lived like cattle," he said angrily. To be sure, the place was not alluring. The ground floor had been used for the housing of cattle, and it was dark and terrible. A flight of steps led to the lofty first floor, which was denuded but respectable. The sergeant's visage lightened when he saw the strong walls of stone and cement. "Unless they turn guns on us, they will never get us out of here," he said cheerfully to the squad. The men, anxious to keep him in an amiable mood, all hurriedly grinned and seemed very appreciative and pleased. "I'll make this into a fortress," he announced. He sent Jones and Patterson, the two orchard thiefs, out on sentry-duty. He worked the others, then, until he could think of no more things to tell them to do. Afterwards he went forth, with a major-general's serious scowl, and examined the ground in front of his position. In returning he came upon a sentry, Jones, munching an apple. He sternly commanded him to throw it away.

The men spread their blankets on the floors of the bare rooms, and putting their packs under their heads and lighting their pipes, they lived in easy peace. Bees hummed in the garden, and a scent of flowers came through the open window. A great fan-shaped bit of sunshine smote the face of one man, and he indolently cursed as he moved his primitive bed to a shadier place.

Another private explained to a comrade: "This is all nonsense anyhow. No sense in occupying this post. They—"

"But, of course," said the corporal, "when she told me herself that she cared more for me than she did for him, I wasn't going to stand any of his talk—" The corporal's listener was so sleepy that he could only grunt his sympathy.

There was a sudden little spatter of shooting. A cry from Jones rang out. With no intermediate scrambling, the sergeant leaped straight to his feet. "Now," he cried, "let us see what you are made of! If," he added bitterly, "you are made of anything!"

A man yelled: "Good God, can't you see you're all tangled up in my cartridge belt?"

Another man yelled: "Keep off my legs! Can't you walk on the floor?"

To the windows there was a blind rush of slumberous men, who brushed hair from their eyes even as they made ready their rifles. Jones and Patterson came stumbling up the steps, crying dreadful information. Already the enemy's bullets were spitting and singing over the house.

The sergeant suddenly was stiff and cold with a sense of the importance of the thing. "Wait until you see one," he drawled loudly and calmly, "then shoot."

For some moments the enemy's bullets swung swifter than lightning over the house without anybody being able to discover a target. In this interval a man was shot in the throat. He gurgled, and then lay down on the floor. The blood slowly waved down the brown skin of his neck while he looked meekly at his comrades.

There was a howl. "There they are! There they come!" The rifles crackled. A light smoke drifted idly through the rooms. There was a strong odour as if from burnt paper and the powder of fire-crackers. The men were silent. Through the windows and about the house the bullets of an entirely invisible enemy moaned, hummed, spat, burst, and sang.

The men began to curse. "Why can't we see them?" they muttered through their teeth. The sergeant was still frigid. He answered sooth- ingly as if he were directly reprehensible for this behaviour of the enemy. "Wait a moment. You will soon be able to see them. There! Give it to them." A little skirt of black figures had appeared in a field. It was really like shooting at an upright needle from the full length of a ball-room. But the men's spirits improved as soon as the enemy— this mysterious enemy—became a tangible thing, and far off. They had believed the foe to be shooting at them from the adjacent garden.

"Now," said the sergeant ambitiously, "we can beat them off easily if you men are good enough."

A man called out in a tone of quick, great interest. "See that fellow on horseback, Bill? Isn't he on horseback? I thought he was on horse- back."

There was a fusilade against another side of the house. The sergeant dashed into the room which commanded that situation. He found a dead soldier on the floor. He rushed out howling: "When was Knowles killed? When was Knowles killed? Damn it, when was Knowles killed?" It was absolutely essential to find out the exact moment this man died. A blackened private turned upon his sergeant and demanded: "How in hell do I know?" Sergeant Morton had a sense of anger so brief that in the next second he cried: "Patterson!" He had even forgotten his vital interest in the time of Knowles' death.

"Yes?" said Patterson, his face set with some deep-rooted quality of determination. Still, he was a mere farm boy.

"Go in to Knowles' window and shoot at those people," said the sergeant hoarsely. Afterwards he coughed. Some of the fumes of the fight had made way to his lungs.

Patterson looked at the door into this other room. He looked at it as if he suspected it was to be his death-chamber. Then he entered and stood across the body of Knowles and fired vigorously into a group of plum trees.

"They can't take this house," declared the sergeant in a contemp- tuous and argumentative tone. He was apparently replying to some- body. The man who had been shot in the throat looked up at him. Eight men were firing from the windows. The sergeant detected in a corner three wounded men talking together feebly. "Don't you think there is anything to do?" he bawled. "Go and get Knowles' cartridges and give them to somebody who can use them! Take Simpson's too." The man who had been shot in the throat looked at him. Of the three wounded men who had been talking, one said: "My leg is all doubled up under me, sergeant." He spoke apologetically.

Meantime the sergeant was re-loading his rifle. His foot slipped in the blood of the man who had been shot in the throat, and the military boot made a greasy red streak on the floor.

"Why, we can hold this place," shouted the sergeant jubilantly. "Who says we can't?"

Corporal Flagler suddenly spun away from his window and fell in a heap.

"Sergeant," murmured a man as he dropped to a seat on the floor out of danger, "I can't stand this. I swear I can't. I think we should run away."

Morton, with the kindly eyes of a good shepherd, looked at the man. "You are afraid, Johnston, you are afraid," he said softly. The man struggled to his feet, cast upon the sergeant a gaze full of admiration, reproach, and despair, and returned to his post. A moment later he pitched forward, and thereafter his body hung out of the window, his arms straight and the fists clenched. Incidentally this corpse was pierced afterwards by chance three times by bullets of the enemy.

The sergeant laid his rifle against the stone-work of the window-frame and shot with care until his magazine was empty. Behind him a man, simply grazed on the elbow, was wildly sobbing like a girl. "Damn it, shut up," said Morton, without turning his head. Before him was a vista of a garden, fields, clumps of trees, woods, populated at the time with little fleeting figures.

He grew furious. "Why didn't he send me orders?" he cried aloud. The emphasis on the word "he" was impressive. A mile back on the road a galloper of the Hussars lay dead beside his dead horse.

The man who had been grazed on the elbow still set up his bleat. Morton's fury veered to this soldier. "Can't you shut up? Can't you shut up? Can't you shut up? Fight! That's the thing to do. Fight!"

A bullet struck Morton, and he fell upon the man who had been shot in the throat. There was a sickening moment. Then the sergeant rolled off to a position upon the blood floor. He turned himself with a last effort until he could look at the wounded who were able to look at him.

"Kim up, the Kickers," he said thickly. His arms weakened and he dropped on his face.

After an interval a young subaltern of the enemy's infantry, followed by his eager men, burst into this reeking interior. But just over the threshold he halted before the scene of blood and death. He turned with a shrug to his sergeant. "God, I should have estimated them at least one hundred strong."

WYOMING VALLEY TALES

I. — THE SURRENDER
OF FORTY FORT

Immediately after the battle of 3rd July, my mother said, "We had best take the children and go into the Fort."

But my father replied, "I will not go. I will not leave my property. All that I have in the world is here, and if the savages destroy it they may as well destroy me also."

My mother said no other word. Our household was ever given to stern silence, and such was my training that it did not occur to me to reflect that if my father cared for his property it was not my property, and I was entitled to care somewhat for my life.

Colonel Denison was true to the word which he had passed to me at the Fort before the battle. He sent a messenger to my father, and this messenger stood in the middle of our living-room and spake with a clear, indifferent voice. "Colonel Denison bids me come here and say that John Bennet is a wicked man, and the blood of his own children will be upon his head." As usual, my father said nothing. After the messenger had gone, he remained silent for hours in his chair by the fire, and this stillness was so impressive to his family that even my mother walked on tip-toe as she went about her work. After this long time my father said, "Mary!"

Mother halted and looked at him. Father spoke slowly, and as if every word was wrested from him with violent pangs. "Mary, you take the girls and go to the Fort. I and Solomon and Andrew will go over the mountain to Stroudsberg."

Immediately my mother called us all to set about packing such things as could be taken to the Fort. And by nightfall we had seen them within its pallisade, and my father, myself, and my little brother Andrew, who was only eleven years old, were off over the hills on a long march to the Delaware settlements. Father and I had our rifles, but we seldom dared to fire them, because of the roving bands of Indians. We lived as well as we could on blackberries and raspberries. For the most part, poor little Andrew rode first on the back of my father and then on my back. He was a good little man, and only cried when he would wake in the dead of night very cold and very hungry. Then my father would wrap him in an old grey coat that was so famous in the Wyoming country that there was not even an Indian who did not know of it. But this act he did without any direct display of tenderness, for the fear, I suppose, that he would weaken little Andrew's growing manhood. Now, in these days of safety, and even luxury, I often marvel at the iron spirit of the people of my young days. My father, without his coat and no doubt very cold, would then sometimes begin to pray to his God in the wilderness, but in low voice, because of the Indians. It was July, but even July nights are cold in the pine mountains, breathing a chill which goes straight to the bones.

But it is not my intention to give in this section the ordinary adventures of the masculine part of my family. As a matter of fact, my mother and the girls were undergoing in Forty Fort trials which made as nothing the happenings on our journey, which ended in safety.

My mother and her small flock were no sooner established in the crude quarters within the pallisade than negotiations were opened between Colonel Denison and Colonel Zebulon Butler on the American side, and "Indian Butler" on the British side, for the capitulation of the Fort with such arms and military stores as it contained, the lives of the settlers to be strictly preserved. But "Indian Butler" did not seem to feel free to promise safety for the lives of the Continental Butler and the pathetic little fragment of the regular troops. These men always fought so well against the Indians that whenever the Indians could get them at their mercy there was small chances of anything but a massacre. So every regular left before the surrender; and I fancy that Colonel Zebulon Butler considered himself a much-abused man, for if we had left ourselves entirely under his direction there is no doubt but what we could have saved the valley. He had taken us out on 3rd July because our militia officers had almost threatened him. In the end he had said, "Very well, I can go as far as any of you." I was always on Butler's side of the argument, but owing to the singular arrangement of circumstances, my opinion at the age of sixteen counted upon neither the one side nor the other.

The Fort was left in charge of Colonel Denison. He had stipulated before the surrender that no Indians should be allowed to enter the stockade and molest these poor families of women whose fathers and brothers were either dead or fled over the mountains, unless their physical debility had been such that they were able neither to get killed in the battle nor to take the long trail to the Delaware. Of course, this excepts those men who were with Washington.

For several days the Indians, obedient to the British officers, kept out of the Fort, but soon they began to enter in small bands and went sniffing and poking in every corner to find plunder. Our people had hidden everything as well as they were able, and for a period little was stolen. My mother told me that the first thing of importance to go was Colonel Denison's hunting shirt, made of "fine forty" linen. It had a double cape, and was fringed about the cape and about the wristbands. Colonel Denison at the time was in my mother's cabin. An Indian entered, and, rolling a thieving eye about the place, sighted first of all the remarkable shirt which Colonel Denison was wearing. He seized the shirt and began to tug, while the Colonel backed away, tugging and protesting at the same time. The women folk saw at once that the Colonel would be tomahawked if he did not give up his shirt, and they begged him to do it. He finally elected not to be tomahawked, and came out of his shirt. While my mother unbuttoned the wristbands, the Colonel cleverly dropped into the lap of a certain Polly Thornton a large packet of Continental bills, and his money was thus saved for the settlers.

Colonel Denison had several stormy interviews with "Indian Butler," and the British commander finally ended in frankly declaring that he could do nothing with the Indians at all. They were beyond control, and the defenceless people in the Fort would have to take the consequence. I do not mean that Colonel Denison was trying to recover his shirt; I mean that he was objecting to a situation which was now almost unendurable. I wish to record also that the Colonel lost a large beaver hat. In both cases he willed to be tomahawked and killed rather than suffer the indignity, but mother prevailed over him. I must confess to this discreet age that my mother engaged in fisticuffs with a squaw. This squaw came into the cabin, and, without preliminary discussion, attempted to drag from my mother the petticoat she was wearing. My mother forgot the fine advice she had given to Colonel Denison. She proceeded to beat the squaw out of the cabin, and although the squaw appealed to some warriors who were standing without the warriors only laughed, and my mother kept her petticoat.

The Indians took the feather beds of the people, and, ripping them open, flung the feathers broadcast. Then they stuffed these sacks full of plunder, and flung them across the backs of such of the settlers' horses as they had been able to find. In the old days my mother had

had a side saddle, of which she was very proud when she rode to meeting on it. She had also a brilliant scarlet cloak, which every lady had in those days, and which I can remember as one of the admirations of my childhood. One day my mother had the satisfaction of seeing a squaw ride off from the Fort with this prize saddle reversed on a small nag, and with the proud squaw thus mounted wearing the scarlet cloak, also reversed. My sister Martha told me afterwards that they laughed, even in their misfortunes. A little later they had the satisfaction of seeing the smoke from our house and barn arising over the tops of the trees.

When the Indians first began their pillaging, an old Mr. Sutton, who occupied a cabin near my mother's cabin, anticipated them by donning all his best clothes. He had had a theory that the Americans would be free to retain the clothes that they wore. And his best happened to be a suit of Quaker grey, from beaver to boots, in which he had been married. Not long afterwards my mother and my sisters saw passing the door an Indian arrayed in Quaker grey, from beaver to boots. The only odd thing which impressed them was that the Indian had appended to the dress a long string of Yankee scalps. Sutton was a good Quaker, and if he had been wearing the suit there would have been no string of scalps.

They were, in fact, badgered, insulted, robbed by the Indians so openly that the British officers would not come into the Fort at all. They stayed in their camp, affecting to be ignorant of what was happening. It was about all they could do. The Indians had only one idea of war, and it was impossible to reason with them when they were flushed with victory and stolen rum.

The hand of fate fell heavily upon one rogue whose ambition it was to drink everything that the Fort contained. One day he inadvertently came upon a bottle of spirits of camphor, and in a few hours he was dead.

But it was known that General Washington contemplated sending a strong expedition into the valley, to clear it of the invaders and thrash them. Soon there were no enemies in the country save small roving parties of Indians, who prevented work in the fields and burned whatever cabins that earlier torches had missed.

The first large party to come into the valley was composed mainly of Captain Spaulding's company of regulars, and at its head rode Colonel Zebulon Butler. My father, myself, and little Andrew returned with this party to set to work immediately to build out of nothing a prosperity similar to that which had vanished in the smoke.

II. — "OL' BENNET"
AND THE INDIANS

My father was so well known of the Indians that, as I was saying, his old grey coat was a sign through the northern country. I know of no reason for this save that he was honest and obstreperously minded his own affairs, and could fling a tomahawk better than the best Indian. I will not declare upon how hard it is for a man to be honest and to mind his own affairs, but I fully know that it is hard to throw a tomahawk as my father threw it, straighter than a bullet from a duelling pistol. He had always dealt fairly with the Indians, and I cannot tell why they paled him so bitterly, unless it was that when an Indian went foolishly drunk my father would deplore it with his foot, if it so happened that the drunkenness was done in our cabin. It is true to say that when the war came, a singular large number of kicked Indians journeyed from the Canadas to re-visit with torch and knife the scenes of the kicking.

If people had thoroughly known my father he would have had no enemies. He was the best of men. He had a code of behaviour for himself, and for the whole world as well. If people wished his good opinion they only had to do exactly as he did, and to have his views. I remember that once my sister Martha made me a waistcoat of rabbits' skins, and generally it was considered a great ornament. But one day my father espied me in it, and commanded me to remove it for ever. Its appearance was indecent, he said, and such a garment tainted the soul of him who wore it. In the ensuing fortnight a poor pedlar arrived from the Delaware, who had suffered great misfortunes in the snows. My father fed him and warmed him, and when he gratefully departed, gave him the rabbits' skin waistcoat, and the poor man went off clothed indecently in a garment that would taint his soul. Afterwards, in a daring mood, I asked my father why he had so cursed this pedlar, and he recommended that I should study my Bible more closely, and there read that my own devious ways should be mended before I sought to judge the enlightened acts of my elders. He set me to ploughing the upper twelve acres, and I was hardly allowed to loose my grip of the plough handles until every furrow was drawn.

The Indians called my father "Ol' Bennet," and he was known broadcast as a man whose doom was sealed when the redskins caught him. As I have said, the feeling is inexplicable to me. But Indians who had been ill-used and maltreated by downright ruffians, against whom revenge could with a kind of propriety be directed—many of these Indians avowedly gave up a genuine wrong in order to direct a fuller attention to the getting of my father's scalp. This most unfair disposition of the Indians was a great, deep anxiety to all of us up to the time when General Sullivan and his avenging army marched through the valley and swept our tormentors afar.

And yet great calamities could happen in our valley even after the coming and passing of General Sullivan. We were partly mistaken in our gladness. The British force of Loyalists and Indians met Sullivan in one battle, and finding themselves over-matched and beaten, they scattered in all directions. The Loyalists, for the most part, went home, but the Indians cleverly broke up into small bands, and General Sullivan's army had no sooner marched beyond the Wyoming Valley than some of these small bands were back into the valley plundering outlying cabins and shooting people from the thickets and woods that bordered the fields.

General Sullivan had left a garrison at Wilkesbarre, and at this time we lived in its strong shadow. It was too formidable for the Indians to attack, and it could protect all who valued protection enough to remain under its wings, but it could do little against the flying small bands. My father chafed in the shelter of the garrison. His best lands lay beyond Forty Fort, and he wanted to be at his ploughing. He made several brief references to his ploughing that led us to believe that his ploughing was the fundamental principle of life. None of us saw any means of contending him. My sister Martha began to weep, but it no more mattered than if she had began to laugh. My mother said nothing. Aye, my wonderful mother said nothing. My father said he would go plough some of the land above Forty Fort. Immediately this was with us some sort of a law. It was like a rain, or a wind, or a drought.

He went, of course. My young brother Andrew went with him, and he took the new span of oxen and a horse. They began to plough a meadow which lay in a bend of the river above Forty Fort. Andrew rode the horse hitched ahead of the oxen. At a certain thicket the horse shied so that little Andrew was almost thrown down. My father seemed to have begun a period of apprehension at this time, but it was of no service. Four Indians suddenly appeared out of the thicket. Swiftly, and in silence, they pounced with tomahawk, rifle, and knife upon my father and my brother, and in a moment they were captives of the redskins—that fate whose very phrasing was a thrill to the heart of every colonist. It spelled death, or that horrible simple absence, vacancy, mystery, which is harder than death.

As for us, he had told my mother that if he and Andrew were not returned at sundown she might construe a calamity. So at sundown we gave the news to the Fort, and directly we heard the alarm gun booming out across the dusk like a salute to the death of my father, a solemn, final declaration. At the sound of this gun my sisters all began newly to weep. It simply defined our misfortune. In the morning a party was sent out, which came upon the deserted plough, the oxen calmly munching, and the horse still excited and affrighted. The soldiers found the trail of four Indians. They followed the trail some distance over the mountains, but the redskins with their captives had a long start, and pursuit was but useless. The result of this expedition was that we knew at least that father and Andrew had not been massacred immediately. But in those days this was a most meagre consolation. It was better to wish them well dead.

My father and Andrew were hurried over the hills at a terrible pace by the four Indians. Andrew told me afterwards that he could think sometimes that he was dreaming of being carried off by goblins. The redskins said no word, and their mocassined feet made no sound. They were like evil spirits. But it was as he caught glimpses of father's pale face, every wrinkle in it deepened and hardened, that Andrew saw everything in its light. And Andrew was but thirteen years old. It is a tender age at which to be burned at the stake.

In time the party came upon two more Indians, who had as a prisoner a man named Lebbeus Hammond. He had left Wilkesbarre in search of a strayed horse. He was riding the animal back to the Fort when the Indians caught him. He and my father knew each other well, and their greeting was like them.

"What! Hammond! You here?"

"Yes, I'm here."

As the march was resumed, the principal Indian bestrode Hammond's horse, but the horse was very high-nerved and scared, and the bridle was only a temporary one made from hickory withes. There was no saddle. And so finally the principal Indian came off with a crash, alighting with exceeding severity upon his head. When he got upon his feet he was in such a rage that the three captives thought to see him dash his tomahawk into the skull of the trembling horse, and, indeed, his arm was raised for the blow, but suddenly he thought better of it. He had been touched by a real point of Indian inspiration. The party was passing a swamp at the time, so he mired the horse almost up to its eyes, and left it to the long death.

I had said that my father was well known of the Indians, and yet I have to announce that none of his six captors knew him. To them he was a complete stranger, for upon camping the first night they left my father unbound. If they had had any idea that he was "Ol' Bennet" they would never have left him unbound. He suggested to Hammond that they try to escape that night, but Hammond seemed not to care to try it yet.

In time they met a party of over forty Indians, commanded by a Loyalist. In that band there were many who knew my father. They cried out with rejoicing when they perceived him. "Ha!" they shouted, "Ol' Bennet!" They danced about him, making gestures expressive of the torture. Later in the day my father accidentally pulled a button from his coat, and an Indian took it from him.

My father asked to be allowed to have it again, for he was a very careful man, and in those days all good husbands were trained to bring home the loose buttons. The Indians laughed, and explained that a man who was to die at Wyallusing—one day's march—need not be particular about a button.

The three prisoners were now sent off in care of seven Indians, while the Loyalist took the remainder of his men down the valley to further harass the settlers. The seven Indians were now very careful of my father, allowing him scarce a wink. Their tomahawks came up at the slightest sign. At the camp that night they bade the prisoners lie down, and then placed poles across them. An Indian lay upon either end of these poles. My father managed, however, to let Hammond know that he was determined to make an attempt to escape. There was only one night between him and the stake, and he was resolved to make what use he could of it. Hammond seems to have been dubious from the start, but the men of that time were not daunted by broad risks. In his opinion the rising would be a failure, but this did not prevent him from agreeing to rise with his friend. My brother Andrew was not considered at all. No one asked him if he wanted to rise against the Indians. He was only a boy, and supposed to obey his elders. So, as none asked his views, he kept them to himself; but I wager you he listened, all ears, to the furtive consultations, consultations which were mere casual phrases at times, and at other times swift, brief sentences shot out in a whisper.

The band of seven Indians relaxed in vigilance as they approached their own country, and on the last night from Wyallusing the Indian part of the camp seemed much inclined to take deep slumber after the long and rapid journey. The prisoners were held to the ground by poles as on the previous night, and then the Indians pulled their blankets over their heads and passed into heavy sleep. One old warrior sat by the fire as guard, but he seems to have been a singularly inefficient man, for he was continuously drowsing, and if the captives could have got rid of the poles across their chests and legs they would have made their flight sooner.

The camp was on a mountain side amid a forest of lofty pines. The night was very cold, and the blasts of wind swept down upon the crackling, resinous fire. A few stars peeped through the feathery pine branches. Deep in some gulch could be heard the roar of a mountain stream. At one o'clock in the morning three of the Indians arose, and, releasing the prisoners, commanded them to mend the fire. The prisoners brought dead pine branches; the ancient warrior on watch sleepily picked away with his knife at the deer's head which he had roasted; the other Indians retired again to their blankets, perhaps each depending upon the other for the exercise of precautions. It was a tremendously slack business; the Indians were feeling security because they knew that the prisoners were too wise to try to run away.

The warrior on watch mumbled placidly to himself as he picked at the deer's head. Then he drowsed again, just the short nap of a man who had been up too long. My father stepped quickly to a spear, and backed away from the Indian; then he drove it straight through his chest. The Indian raised himself spasmodically, and then collapsed into that camp fire which the captives had made burn so brilliantly, and as he fell he screamed. Instantly his blanket, his hair, he himself began to burn, and over him was my father tugging frantically to get the spear out again.

My father did not recover the spear. It had so gone through the old warrior that it could not readily be withdrawn, and my father left it.

The scream of the watchman instantly aroused the other warriors, who, as they scrambled in their blankets, found over them a terrible white-lipped creature with an axe—an axe, the most appallingly brutal of weapons. Hammond buried his weapon in the head of the leader of the Indians even as the man gave out his first great cry. The second blow missed an agile warrior's head, but caught him in the nape of the neck, and he swung, to bury his face in the red-hot ashes at the edge of the fire.

Meanwhile my brother Andrew had been gallantly snapping empty guns. In fact he snapped three empty guns at the Indians, who were in the purest panic. He did not snap the fourth gun, but took it by the barrel, and, seeing a warrior rush past him, he cracked his skull with the clubbed weapon. He told me, however, that his snapping of the empty guns was very effective, because it made the Indians jump and dodge.

Well, this slaughter continued in the red glare of the fire on the lonely mountain side until two shrieking creatures ran off through the trees, but even then my father hurled a tomahawk with all his strength. It struck one of the fleeing Indians on the shoulder. His blanket dropped from him, and he ran on practically naked.

The three whites looked at each other, breathing deeply. Their work was plain to them in the five dead and dying Indians underfoot. They hastily gathered weapons and mocassins, and in six minutes from the time when my father had hurled the spear through the Indian sentinel they had started to make their way back to the settlements, leaving the camp fire to burn out its short career alone amid the dead.

III. — THE BATTLE OF FORTY FORT

The Congress, sitting at Philadelphia, had voted our Wyoming country two companies of infantry for its protection against the Indians, with the single provision that we raise the men and arm them ourselves. This was not too brave a gift, but no one could blame the poor Congress, and indeed one could wonder that they found occasion to think of us at all, since at the time every gentleman of them had his coat-tails gathered high in his hands in readiness for flight to Baltimore. But our two companies of foot were no sooner drilled, equipped, and in readiness to defend the colony when they were ordered off down to the Jerseys to join General Washington. So it can be seen what service Congress did us in the way of protection. Thus the Wyoming Valley, sixty miles deep in the wilderness, held its log-houses full of little besides mothers, maids, and children. To the clamour against this situation the badgered Congress could only reply by the issue of another generous order, directing that one full company of foot be raised in the town of Westmoreland for the defence of said town, and that the said company find their own arms, ammunition, and blankets. Even people with our sense of humour could not laugh at this joke.

When the first two companies were forming, I had thought to join one, but my father forbade me, saying that I was too young, although I was full sixteen, tall, and very strong. So it turned out that I was not off fighting with Washington's army when Butler with his rangers and Indians raided Wyoming. Perhaps I was in the better place to do my duty, if I could.

When wandering Indians visited the settlements, their drunkenness and insolence were extreme, but the few white men remained calm, and often enough pretended oblivion to insults which, because of their wives and families, they dared not attempt to avenge. In my own family, my father's imperturbability was scarce superior to my mother's coolness, and such was our faith in them that we twelve children also seemed to be fearless. Neighbour after neighbour came to my father in despair of the defenceless condition of the valley, declaring that they were about to leave everything and flee over the mountains to Stroudsberg. My father always wished them God-speed and said no more. If they urged him to fly also, he usually walked away from them.

Finally there came a time when all the Indians vanished. We rather would have had them tipsy and impudent in the settlements; we knew what their disappearance portended. It was the serious sign. Too soon the news came that "Indian Butler" was on his way.

The valley was vastly excited. People with their smaller possessions flocked into the block-houses, and militia officers rode everywhere to rally every man. A small force of Continentals—regulars of the line—had joined our people, and the little army was now under the command of a Continental officer, Major Zebulon Butler.

I had thought that with all this hubbub of an impending life and death struggle in the valley that my father would allow the work of our farm to slacken. But in this I was notably mistaken. The milking and the feeding and the work in the fields went on as if there never had been an Indian south of the Canadas. My mother and my sisters continued to cook, to wash, to churn, to spin, to dye, to mend, to make soap, to make maple sugar. Just before the break of each day, my younger brother Andrew and myself tumbled out for some eighteen hours' work, and woe to us if we departed the length of a dog's tail from the laws which our father had laid down. It was a life with which I was familiar, but it did seem to me that with the Indians almost upon us he might have allowed me, at least, to go to the Fort and see our men drilling.

But one morning we aroused as usual at his call at the foot of the ladder, and, dressing more quickly than Andrew, I climbed down from the loft to find my father seated by a blazing fire reading by its light in his Bible.

"Son," said he.

"Yes, father?"

"Go and fight."

Without a word more I made hasty preparation. It was the first time in my life that I had a feeling that my father would change his mind. So strong was this fear that I did not even risk a good-bye to my mother and sisters. At the end of the clearing I looked back. The door of the house was open, and in the blazing light of the fire I saw my father seated as I had left him.

At Forty Fort I found between three and four hundred under arms, while the stockade itself was crowded with old men, and women and children. Many of my acquaintances welcomed me; indeed, I seemed to know everybody save a number of the Continental officers. Colonel Zebulon Butler was in chief command, while directly under him was Colonel Denison, a man of the valley, and much respected. Colonel Denison asked news of my father, whose temper he well knew. He said to me—"If God spares Nathan Denison I shall tell that obstinate old fool my true opinion of him. He will get himself and all his family butchered and scalped."

I joined Captain Bidlack's company for the reason that a number of my friends were in it. Every morning we were paraded and drilled in the open ground before the Fort, and I learned to present arms and to keep my heels together, although to this day I have never been able to see any point to these accomplishments, and there was very little of the presenting of arms or of the keeping together of heels in the battle which followed these drills. I may say truly that I would now be much more grateful to Captain Bidlack if he had taught us to run like a wild horse.

There was considerable friction between the officers of our militia and the Continental officers. I believe the Continental officers had stated themselves as being in favour of a cautious policy, whereas the men of the valley were almost unanimous in their desire to meet "Indian Butler" more than half way. They knew the country, they said, and they knew the Indians, and they deduced that the proper plan was to march forth and attack the British force near the head of the valley. Some of the more hot-headed ones rather openly taunted the Continentals, but these veterans of Washington's army remained silent and composed amid more or less wildness of talk. My own concealed opinions were that, although our people were brave and determined, they had much better allow the Continental officers to manage the valley's affairs.

At the end of June, we heard the news that Colonel John Butler, with some four hundred British and Colonial troops, which he called the Rangers, and with about five hundred Indians, had entered the valley at its head and taken Fort Wintermoot after an opposition of a perfunctory character. I could present arms very well, but I do not think that I could yet keep my heels together. But "Indian Butler" was marching upon us, and even Captain Bidlack refrained from being annoyed at my refractory heels.

The officers held councils of war, but in truth both fort and camp rang with a discussion in which everybody joined with great vigour and endurance. I may except the Continental officers, who told us what they thought we should do, and then, declaring that there was no more to be said, remained in a silence which I thought was rather grim. The result was that on the 3rd of July our force of about 300 men marched away, amid the roll of drums and the proud career of flags, to meet "Indian Butler" and his two kinds of savages. There yet remains with me a vivid recollection of a close row of faces above the stockade of Forty Fort which viewed our departure with that profound anxiety which only an imminent danger of murder and scalping can produce. I myself was never particularly afraid of the Indians, for to my mind the great and almost the only military virtue of the Indians was that they were silent men in the woods. If they were met squarely on terms approaching equality, they could always be whipped. But it was another matter to a fort filled with women and children and cripples, to whom the coming of the Indians spelled pillage, arson, and massacre. The British sent against us in those days some curious upholders of the honour of the King, and although Indian Butler, who usually led them, afterwards contended that everything was performed with decency and care for the rules, we always found that such of our dead whose bodies we recovered invariably lacked hair on the tops of their heads, and if worse wasn't done to them we wouldn't even use the word mutilate.

Colonel Zebulon Butler rode along the column when we halted once for water. I looked at him eagerly, hoping to read in his face some sign of his opinions. But on the soldierly mask I could read nothing, although I am certain now that he felt that the fools among us were going to get us well beaten. But there was no vacillation in the direction of our march. We went straight until we could hear through the woods the infrequent shots of our leading party at retreating Indian scouts.

Our Colonel Butler then sent forward four of his best officers, who reconnoitered the ground in the enemy's front like so many engineers marking the place for a bastion. Then each of the six companies were told their place in the line. We of Captain Bidlack's company were on the extreme right. Then we formed in line and marched into battle, with me burning with the high resolve to kill Indian Butler and bear his sword into Forty Fort, while at the same time I was much shaken that one of Indian Butler's Indians might interfere with the noble plan.

We moved stealthily among the pine trees, and I could not forbear looking constantly to right and left to make certain that everybody was of the same mind about this advance. With our Captain Bidlack was Captain Durkee of the regulars. He was also a valley man, and it seemed that every time I looked behind me I met the calm eye of this officer, and I came to refrain from looking behind me.

Still, I was very anxious to shoot Indians, and if I had doubted my ability in this direction I would have done myself a great injustice, for I could drive a nail to the head with a rifle ball at respectable range. I contend that I was not at all afraid of the enemy, but I much feared that certain of my comrades would change their minds about the expediency of battle on the 3rd July, 1778.

But our company was as steady and straight as a fence. I do not know who first saw dodging figures in the shadows of the trees in our front. The first fire we received, however, was from our flank, where some hidden Indians were yelling and firing, firing and yelling. We did not mind the war-whoops. We had heard too many drunken Indians in the settlements before the war. They wounded the lieutenant of the company next to ours, and a moment later they killed Captain Durkee. But we were steadily advancing and firing regular volleys into the shifting frieze of figures before us. The Indians gave their cries as if the imps of Hades had given tongue to their emotions. They fell back before us so rapidly and so cleverly that one had to watch his chance as the Indians sped from tree to tree. I had a sudden burst of rapture that they were beaten, and this was accentuated when I stepped over the body of an Indian whose forehead had a hole in it as squarely in the middle as if the location had been previously surveyed. In short, we were doing extremely well.

Soon we began to see the slower figures of white men through the trees, and it is only honest to say that they were easier to shoot. I myself caught sight of a fine officer in a uniform that seemed of green and buff. His sword-belt was fastened by a great shining brass plate, and, no longer feeling the elegancies of marksmanship, I fired at the brass plate. Such was the conformation of the ground between us that he disappeared as if he had sunk in the sea. We, all of us, were loading behind the trees and then charging ahead with fullest confidence.

But suddenly from our own left came wild cries from our men, while at the same time the yells of Indians redoubled in that direction.

Our rush checked itself instinctively. The cries rolled toward us. Once I heard a word that sounded like "Quarte." Then, to be truthful, our line wavered. I heard Captain Bidlack give an angry and despairing shout, and I think he was killed before he finished it.

In a word, our left wing had gone to pieces. It was in complete rout. I know not the truth of the matter; but it seems that Colonel Denison had given an order which was misinterpreted for the order to retreat. At any rate, there can be no doubt of how fast the left wing ran away.

We ran away too. The company on our immediate left was the company of regulars, and I remember some red-faced and powder-stained men bellowing at me contemptuously. That company stayed, and, for the most part, died. I don't know what they mustered when we left the Fort, but from the battle eleven worn and ragged men emerged. In my running was wisdom. The country was suddenly full of fleet Indians, upon us with the tomahawk. Behind me as I ran I could hear the screams of men cleaved to the earth. I think the first things that most of us discarded were our rifles. Afterward, upon serious reflection, I could not recall where I gave my rifle to the grass.

I ran for the river. I saw some of our own men running ahead of me and I envied them. My point of contact with the river was the top of a high bank. But I did not hesitate to leap for the water with all my ounces of muscle. I struck out strongly for the other shore. I expected to be shot in the water. Up stream, and down stream, I could hear the crack of rifles, but none of the enemy seemed to be paying direct heed to me. I swam so well that I was soon able to put my feet on the slippery round stones and wade. When I reached a certain sandy beach, I lay down and puffed and blew my exhaustion. I watched the scene on the river. Indians appeared in groups on the opposite bank, firing at various heads of my comrades, who, like me, had chosen the Susquehanna as their refuge. I saw more than one hand fling up and the head turn sideways and sink.

I set out for home. I set out for home in that perfect spirit of dependence which I had always felt toward my father and my mother. When I arrived I found nobody in the living room but my father seated in his great chair and reading his Bible, even as I had left him.

The whole shame of the business came upon me suddenly. "Father," I choked out, "we have been beaten."

"Aye," said he, "I expected it."

LONDON IMPRESSIONS

CHAPTER I

London at first consisted of a porter with the most charming manners in the world, and a cabman with a supreme intelligence, both observing my profound ignorance without contempt or humour of any kind observable in their manners. It was in a great resounding vault of a place where there were many people who had come home, and I was displeased because they knew the detail of the business, whereas I was confronting the inscrutable. This made them appear very stony-hearted to the sufferings of one of whose existence, to be sure, they were entirely unaware, and I remember taking great pleasure in disliking them heartily for it. I was in an agony of mind over my baggage, or my luggage, or my—perhaps it is well to shy around this terrible international question; but I remember that when I was a lad I was told that there was a whole nation that said luggage instead of baggage, and my boyish mind was filled at the time with incredulity and scorn. In the present case it was a thing that I understood to involve the most hideous confessions of imbecility on my part, because I had evidently to go out to some obscure point and espy it and claim it, and take trouble for it; and I would rather have had my pockets filled with bread and cheese, and had no baggage at all.

Mind you, this was not at all a homage that I was paying to London. I was paying homage to a new game. A man properly lazy does not like new experiences until they become old ones. Moreover, I have been taught that a man, any man, who has a thousand times more points of information on a certain thing than I have will bully me because of it, and pour his advantages upon my bowed head until I am drenched with his superiority. It was in my education to concede some licence of the kind in this case, but the holy father of a porter and the saintly cabman occupied the middle distance imperturbably, and did not come down from their hills to clout me with knowledge. From this fact I experienced a criminal elation. I lost view of the idea that if I had been brow-beaten by porters and cabmen from one end of the United States to the other end I should warmly like it, because in numbers they are superior to me, and collectively they can have a great deal of fun out of a matter that would merely afford me the glee of the latent butcher.

This London, composed of a porter and a cabman, stood to me subtly as a benefactor. I had scanned the drama, and found that I did not believe that the mood of the men emanated unduly from the feature that there was probably more shillings to the square inch of me than there were shillings to the square inch of them. Nor yet was it any manner of palpable warm-heartedness or other natural virtue. But it was a perfect artificial virtue; it was drill, plain, simple drill. And now was I glad of their drilling, and vividly approved of it, because I saw that it was good for me. Whether it was good or bad for the porter and the cabman I could not know; but that point, mark you, came within the pale, of my respectable rumination.

I am sure that it would have been more correct for me to have alighted upon St. Paul's and described no emotion until I was overcome by the Thames Embankment and the Houses of Parliament. But as a matter of fact I did not see them for some days, and at this time they did not concern me at all. I was born in London at a railroad station, and my new vision encompassed a porter and a cabman. They deeply absorbed me in new phenomena, and I did not then care to see the Thames Embankment nor the Houses of Parliament. I considered the porter and the cabman to be more important.

CHAPTER II.

The cab finally rolled out of the gas-lit vault into a vast expanse of gloom. This changed to the shadowy lines of a street that was like a passage in a monstrous cave. The lamps winking here and there resembled the little gleams at the caps of the miners. They were not very competent illuminations at best, merely being little pale flares of gas that at their most heroic periods could only display one fact concerning this tunnel—the fact of general direction. But at any rate I should have liked to have observed the dejection of a search-light if it had been called upon to attempt to bore through this atmosphere. In it each man sat in his own little cylinder of vision, so to speak. It was not so small as a sentry-box nor so large as a circus tent, but the walls were opaque, and what was passing beyond the dimensions of his cylinder no man knew.

It was evident that the paving was very greasy, but all the cabs that passed through my cylinder were going at a round trot, while the wheels, shod in rubber, whirred merely like bicycles. The hoofs of the animals themselves did not make that wild clatter which I knew so well. New York, in fact, roars always like ten thousand devils. We have ingenuous and simple ways of making a din in New York that cause the stranger to conclude that each citizen is obliged by statute to provide himself with a pair of cymbals and a drum. If anything by chance can be turned into a noise it is promptly turned. We are engaged in the development of a human creature with very large, sturdy, and doubly-fortified ears.

It was not too late at night, but this London moved with the decorum and caution of an undertaker. There was a silence, and yet there was no silence. There was a low drone, perhaps a humming contributed inevitably by closely-gathered thousands, and yet on second thoughts it was to me silence. I had perched my ears for the note of London, the sound made simply by the existence of five million people in one place. I had imagined something deep, vastly deep, a bass from a mythical organ, but found, as far as I was concerned, only a silence.

New York in numbers is a mighty city, and all day and all night it cries its loud, fierce, aspiring cry, a noise of men beating upon barrels, a noise of men beating upon tin, a terrific racket that assails the abject skies. No one of us seemed to question this row as a certain consequence of three or four million people living together and scuffling for coin, with more agility, perhaps, but otherwise in the usual way. However, after this easy silence of London, which in numbers is a mightier city, I began to feel that there was a seduction in this idea of necessity. Our noise in New York was not a consequence of our rapidity at all. It was a consequence of our bad pavements.

Any brigade of artillery in Europe that would love to assemble its batteries, and then go on a gallop over the land, thundering and thundering, would give up the idea of thunder at once if it could hear Tim Mulligan drive a beer waggon along one of the side streets of cobbled New York.

CHAPTER III.

Finally, a great thing came to pass. The cab horse, proceeding at a sharp trot, found himself suddenly at the top of an incline, where through the rain the pavement shone like an expanse of ice. It looked to me as if there was going to be a tumble. In an accident of such a kind a hansom becomes really a cannon in which a man finds that he has paid shillings for the privilege of serving as a projectile. I was making a rapid calculation of the arc that I would describe in my flight, when the horse met his crisis with a masterly device that I could not have imagined. He tranquilly braced his four feet like a bundle of stakes, and then, with a gentle gaiety of demeanour, he slid swiftly and gracefully to the bottom of the hill as if he had been a toboggan. When the incline ended he caught his gait again with great dexterity, and went pattering off through another tunnel.

I at once looked upon myself as being singularly blessed by this sight. This horse had evidently originated this system of skating as a diversion, or, more probably, as a precaution against the slippery pavement; and he was, of course, the inventor and sole proprietor—two terms that are not always in conjunction. It surely was not to be supposed that there could be two skaters like him in the world. He deserved to be known and publicly praised for this accomplishment. It was worthy of many records and exhibitions. But when the cab arrived at a place where some dipping streets met, and the flaming front of a music-hall temporarily widened my cylinder, behold there were many cabs, and as the moment of necessity came the horses were all skaters. They were gliding in all directions. It might have been a rink. A great omnibus was hailed by a hand under an umbrella on the side walk, and the dignified horses bidden to halt from their trot did not waste time in wild and unseemly spasms. They, too, braced their legs and slid gravely to the end of their momentum.

It was not the feat, but it was the word which had at this time the power to conjure memories of skating parties on moonlit lakes, with laughter ringing over the ice, and a great red bonfire on the shore among the hemlocks.

CHAPTER IV.

A terrible thing in nature is the fall of a horse in his harness. It is a tragedy. Despite their skill in skating there was that about the pavement on the rainy evening which filled me with expectations of horses going headlong. Finally it happened just in front. There was a shout and a tangle in the darkness, and presently a prostrate cab horse came within my cylinder. The accident having been a complete success and altogether concluded, a voice from the side walk said, "*Look* out, now! *Be* more careful, can't you?"

I remember a constituent of a Congressman at Washington who had tried in vain to bore this Congressman with a wild project of some kind. The Congressman eluded him with skill, and his rage and despair ultimately culminated in the supreme grievance that he could not even get near enough to the Congressman to tell him to go to Hades.

This cabman should have felt the same desire to strangle this man who spoke from the side walk. He was plainly impotent; he was deprived of the power of looking out. There was nothing now for which to look out. The man on the side walk had dragged a corpse from a pond and said to it, "*Be* more careful, can't you, or you'll drown?" My cabman pulled up and addressed a few words of reproach to the other. Three or four figures loomed into my cylinder, and as they appeared spoke to the author or the victim of the calamity in varied terms of displeasure. Each of these reproaches was couched in terms that defined the situation as impending. No blind man could have conceived that the precipitate phrase of the incident was absolutely closed. "*Look* out now, cawnt you?" And there was nothing in his mind which approached these sentiments near enough to tell them to go to Hades.

However, it needed only an ear to know presently that these expressions were formulæ. It was merely the obligatory dance which the Indians had to perform before they went to war. These men had come to help, but as a regular and traditional preliminary they had first to display to this cabman their idea of his ignominy.

The different thing in the affair was the silence of the victim. He retorted never a word. This, too, to me seemed to be an obedience to a recognised form. He was the visible criminal, if there was a criminal, and there was born of it a privilege for them.

They unfastened the proper straps and hauled back the cab. They fetched a mat from some obscure place of succour, and pushed it carefully under the prostrate thing. From this panting, quivering mass they suddenly and emphatically reconstructed a horse. As each man turned to go his way he delivered some superior caution to the cabman while the latter buckled his harness.

CHAPTER V.

There was to be noticed in this band of rescuers a young man in evening clothes and top-hat. Now, in America a young man in evening clothes and a top-hat may be a terrible object. He is not likely to do violence, but he is likely to do impassivity and indifference to the point where they become worse than violence. There are certain of the more idle phases of civilisation to which America has not yet awakened—and it is a matter of no moment if she remains unaware. This matter of hats is one of them. I recall a legend recited to me by an esteemed friend, ex-Sheriff of Tin Can, Nevada. Jim Cortright, one of the best gun-fighters in town, went on a journey to Chicago, and while there he procured a top-hat. He was quite sure how Tin Can would accept this innovation, but he relied on the celerity with which he could get a six-shooter in action. One Sunday Jim examined his guns with his usual care, placed the top-hat on the back of his head, and sauntered coolly out into the streets of Tin Can.

Now, while Jim was in Chicago some progressive citizen had decided that Tin Can needed a bowling alley. The carpenters went to work the next morning, and an order for the balls and pins was telegraphed to Denver. In three days the whole population was concentrated at the new alley betting their outfits and their lives.

It has since been accounted very unfortunate that Jim Cortright had not learned of bowling alleys at his mother's knee nor even later in the mines. This portion of his mind was singularly belated. He might have been an Apache for all he knew of bowling alleys.

In his careless stroll through the town, his hands not far from his belt and his eyes going sideways in order to see who would shoot first at the hat, he came upon this long, low shanty where Tin Can was betting itself hoarse over a game between a team from the ranks of Excelsior Hose Company No. 1 and a team composed from the *habi-*

tues of the "Red Light" saloon.

Jim, in blank ignorance of bowling phenomena, wandered casually through a little door into what must always be termed the wrong end of a bowling alley. Of course, he saw that the supreme moment had come. They were not only shooting at the hat and at him, but the low-down cusses were using the most extraordinary and hellish ammunition. Still, perfectly undaunted, however, Jim retorted with his two Colts, and killed three of the best bowlers in Tin Can.

The ex-Sheriff vouched for this story. He himself had gone head-long through the door at the firing of the first shot with that simple courtesy which leads Western men to donate the fighters plenty of room. He said that afterwards the hat was the cause of a number of other fights, and that finally a delegation of prominent citizens were obliged to wait upon Cortright and ask him if he wouldn't take that thing away somewhere and bury it. Jim pointed out to them that it was his hat, and that he would regard it as a cowardly concession if he submitted to their dictation in the matter of his headgear. He added that he purposed to continue to wear his top-hat on every occasion when he happened to feel that the wearing of a top-hat was a joy and a solace to him.

The delegation sadly retired, and announced to the town that Jim Cortright had openly defied them, and had declared his purpose of forcing his top-hat on the pained attention of Tin Can whenever he chose. Jim Cortright's plug hat became a phrase with considerable meaning to it.

However, the whole affair ended in a great passionate outburst of popular revolution. Spike Foster was a friend of Cortright, and one day, when the latter was indisposed, Spike came to him and borrowed the hat. He had been drinking heavily at the "Red Light," and was in a supremely reckless mood. With the terrible gear hanging jauntily over his eye and his two guns drawn, he walked straight out into the middle of the square in front of the Palace Hotel, and drew the attention of all Tin Can by a blood-curdling imitation of the yowl of a mountain lion.

This was when the long-suffering populace arose as one man. The top-hat had been flaunted once too often. When Spike Foster's friends came to carry him away they found nearly a hundred and fifty men shooting busily at a mark—and the mark was the hat.

My informant told me that he believed he owed his popularity in

Tin Can, and subsequently his election to the distinguished office of Sheriff, to the active and prominent part he had taken in the proceedings.

The enmity to the top-hat expressed by the convincing anecdote exists in the American West at present, I think, in the perfection of its strength; but disapproval is not now displayed by volleys from the citizens, save in the most aggravating cases. It is at present usually a matter of mere jibe and general contempt. The East, however, despite a great deal of kicking and gouging, is having the top-hat stuffed slowly and carefully down its throat, and there now exist many young men who consider that they could not successfully conduct their lives without this furniture.

To speak generally, I should say that the headgear then supplies them with a kind of ferocity of indifference. There is fire, sword, and pestilence in the way they heed only themselves. Philosophy should always know that indifference is a militant thing. It batters down the walls of cities, and murders the women and children amid flames and the purloining of altar vessels. When it goes away it leaves smoking ruins, where lie citizens bayoneted through the throat. It is not a children's pastime like mere highway robbery.

Consequently in America we may be much afraid of these young men. We dive down valleys so that we may not kow-tow. It is a fearsome thing.

Taught thus a deep fear of the top-hat in its effect upon youth, I was not prepared for the move of this particular young man when the cab-horse fell. In fact, I grovelled in my corner that I might not see the cruel stateliness of his passing. But in the meantime he had crossed the street, and contributed the strength of his back and some advice, as well as the formal address, to the cabman on the importance of looking out immediately.

I felt that I was making a notable collection. I had a new kind of porter, a cylinder of vision, horses that could skate, and now I added a young man in a top-hat who would tacitly admit that the beings around him were alive. He was not walking a churchyard filled with inferior headstones. He was walking the world, where there were people, many people.

But later I took him out of the collection. I thought he had rebelled against the manner of a class, but I soon discovered that the top-hat was not the property of a class. It was the property of rogues, clerks, theatrical agents, damned seducers, poor men, nobles, and others. In fact, it was the universal rigging. It was the only hat; all other forms might as well be named ham, or chops, or oysters. I retracted my admiration of the young man because he may have been merely a rogue.

CHAPTER VI.

There was a window whereat an enterprising man by dodging two placards and a calendar was entitled to view a young woman. She was dejectedly writing in a large book. She was ultimately induced to open the window a trifle. "What nyme, please?" she said wearily. I was surprised to hear this language from her. I had expected to be addressed on a submarine topic. I have seen shell fishes sadly writing in large books at the bottom of a gloomy aquarium who could not ask me what was my "nyme."

At the end of the hall there was a grim portal marked "Lift." I pressed an electric button and heard an answering tinkle in the heavens. There was an upholstered settle near at hand, and I discovered the reason. A deer-stalking peace drooped upon everything, and in it a man could invoke the passing of a lazy pageant of twenty years of his life.

The dignity of a coffin being lowered into a grave surrounded the ultimate appearance of the lift. The expert we in America call the elevator-boy stepped from the car, took three paces forward, faced to attention, and saluted. This elevator-boy could not have been less than sixty years of age; a great white beard streamed towards his belt. I saw that the lift had been longer on its voyage than I had suspected.

Later in our upward progress a natural event would have been an establishment of social relations. Two enemies imprisoned together during the still hours of a balloon journey would, I believe, suffer a mental amalgamation. The overhang of a common fate, a great principal fact, can make an equality and a truce between any pair. Yet, when I disembarked, a final survey of the grey beard made me recall that I had failed even to ask the boy whether he had not taken probably three trips on this lift.

My windows overlooked simply a great sea of night, in which were swimming little gas fishes.

CHAPTER VII.

I have of late been led to wistfully reflect that many of the illustrators are very clever. In an impatience, which was denoted by a certain economy of apparel, I went to a window to look upon day-lit London. There were the 'buses parading the streets with the miens of elephants. There were the police looking precisely as I had been informed by the prints. There were the sandwich-men. There was almost everything.

But the artists had not told me the sound of London. Now, in New York the artists are able to pourtray sound, because in New York a dray is not a dray at all; it is a great potent noise hauled by two or more horses. When a magazine containing an illustration of a New York street is sent to me, I always know it beforehand. I can hear it coming through the mails. As I have said previously, this which I must call sound of London was to me only a silence.

Later, in front of the hotel a cabman that I hailed said to me—"Are you gowing far, sir? I've got a byby here, and want to giv'er a bit of a blough." This impressed me as being probably a quotation from an early Egyptian poet, but I learned soon enough that the word "byby" was the name of some kind or condition of horse. The cabman's next remark was addressed to a boy who took a perilous dive between the byby's nose and a cab in front. "That's roight. Put your head in there and get it jammed—a whackin good place for it, I should think." Although the tone was low and circumspect, I have never heard a better off-handed declamation. Every word was cut clear of disreputable alliances with its neighbours. The whole thing was as clean as a row of pewter mugs. The influence of indignation upon the voice caused me to reflect that we might devise a mechanical means of inflaming some in that constellation of mummers which is the heritage of the Anglo-Saxon race.

Then I saw the drilling of vehicles by two policemen. There were four torrents converging at a point, and when four torrents converge at one point engineering experts buy tickets for another place.

But here, again, it was drill, plain, simple drill. I must not falter in saying that I think the management of the traffic—as the phrase goes—to be distinctly illuminating and wonderful. The police were not ruffled and exasperated. They were as peaceful as two cows in a pasture.

I remember once remarking that mankind, with all its boasted modern progress, had not yet been able to invent a turnstile that will commute in fractions. I have now learned that 756 rights-of-way cannot operate simultaneously at one point. Right-of-way, like fighting women, requires space. Even two rights-of-way can make a scene which is only suited to the tastes of an ancient public.

This truth was very evidently recognised. There was only one right-of-way at a time. The police did not look behind them to see if their orders were to be obeyed; they knew they were to be obeyed. These four torrents were drilling like four battalions. The two blue-cloth men manœuvred them in solemn, abiding peace, the silence of London.

I thought at first that it was the intellect of the individual, but I looked at one constable closely and his face was as afire with intelligence as a flannel pin-cushion. It was not the police, and it was not the crowd. It was the police and the crowd. Again, it was drill.

CHAPTER VIII.

I have never been in the habit of reading signs. I don't like to read signs. I have never met a man that liked to read signs. I once invented a creature who could play the piano with a hammer, and I mentioned him to a professor in Harvard University whose peculiarity was Sanscrit. He had the same interest in my invention that I have in a certain kind of mustard. And yet this mustard has become a part of me. Or, I have become a part of this mustard. Further, I know more of an ink, a brand of hams, a kind of cigarette, and a novelist than any man living. I went by train to see a friend in the country, and after passing through a patent mucilage, some more hams, a South African Investment Company, a Parisian millinery firm, and a comic journal, I alighted at a new and original kind of corset. On my return journey the road almost continuously ran through soap.

I have accumulated superior information concerning these things, because I am at their mercy. If I want to know where I am I must find the definitive sign. This accounts for my glib use of the word mucilage, as well as the titles of other staples.

I suppose even the Briton in mixing his life must sometimes consult the labels on 'buses and streets and stations, even as the chemist consults the labels on his bottles and boxes. A brave man would possibly affirm that this was suggested by the existence of the labels.

The reason that I did not learn more about hams and mucilage in New York seems to me to be partly due to the fact that the British advertiser is allowed to exercise an unbridled strategy in his attack with his new corset or whatever upon the defensive public. He knows that the vulnerable point is the informatory sign which the citizen must, of course, use for his guidance, and then, with horse, foot, guns, corsets, hams, mucilage, investment companies, and all, he hurls himself at the point.

Meanwhile I have discovered a way to make the Sanscrit scholar heed my creature who plays the piano with a hammer.

NEW YORK SKETCHES

STORIES TOLD BY AN ARTIST IN NEW YORK

A Tale about How "Great Grief" got His Holiday Dinner.

Wrinkles had been peering into the little dry-goods box that acted as a cupboard.

"There are only two eggs and a half of a loaf of bread left," he announced brutally.

"Heavens!" said Warwickson, from where he lay smoking on the bed. He spoke in his usual dismal voice. By it he had earned his popular name of Great Grief.

Wrinkles was a thrifty soul. A sight of an almost bare cupboard maddened him. Even when he was not hungry, the ghosts of his careful ancestors caused him to rebel against it. He sat down with a virtuous air. "Well, what are we going to do?" he demanded of the others. It is good to be the thrifty man in a crowd of unsuccessful artists, for then you can keep the others from starving peacefully. "What are we going to do?"

"Oh, shut up, Wrinkles," said Grief from the bed. "You make me think."

Little Pennoyer, with head bended afar down, had been busily scratching away at a pen and ink drawing. He looked up from his board to utter his plaintive optimism.

"The *Monthly Amazement* may pay me to-morrow. They ought to. I've waited over three months now. I'm going down there to-morrow, and perhaps I'll get it."

His friends listened to him tolerantly, but at last Wrinkles could not omit a scornful giggle. He was such an old man, almost twenty-eight, and he had seen so many little boys be brave. "Oh, no doubt, Penny, old man." Over on the bed Grief croaked deep down in his throat. Nothing was said for a long time thereafter.

The crash of the New York streets came faintly. Occasionally one could hear the tramp of feet in the intricate corridors of this begrimed building that squatted, slumbering and aged, between two exalted commercial structures that would have had to bend afar down to perceive it. The light snow beat pattering into the window corners, and made vague and grey the vista of chimneys and roofs. Often the wind scurried swiftly and raised a long cry.

Great Grief leaned upon his elbow. "See to the fire, will you, Wrinkles?"

Wrinkles pulled the coal-box out from under the bed and threw open the stove door preparatory to shovelling some fuel. A red glare plunged in the first faint shadow of dusk. Little Pennoyer threw down his pen and tossed his drawing over on the wonderful heap of stuff that hid the table. "It's too dark to work." He lit his pipe and walked about, stretching his shoulders like a man whose labour was valuable.

When dusk came it saddened these youths. The solemnity of darkness always caused them to ponder. "Light the gas, Wrinkles," said Grief.

The flood of orange light showed clearly the dull walls lined with scratches, the tousled bed in one corner, the mass of boxes and trunks in another, the little fierce stove, and the wonderful table. Moreover, there were some wine-coloured draperies flung in some places, and on a shelf, high up, there was a plaster cast dark with dust in the creases. A long stove-pipe wandered off in the wrong direction, and then twined impulsively toward a hole in the wall. There were some extensive cobwebs on the ceilings.

"Well, let's eat," said Grief.

Later, there came a sad knock at the door. Wrinkles, arranging a tin pail on the stove, little Pennoyer busy at slicing the bread, and Great Grief affixing the rubber tube to the gas stove, yelled: "Come in!"

The door opened and Corinson entered dejectedly. His overcoat was very new. Wrinkles flashed an envious glance at it, but almost immediately he cried: "Hello, Corrie, old boy!"

Corinson sat down and felt around among the pipes until he found a good one. Great Grief had fixed the coffee to boil on the gas stove, but he had to watch it closely, for the rubber tube was short, and a chair was balanced on a trunk, and then the gas stove was balanced on the chair. Coffee making was a feat.

"Well," said Grief, with his back turned, "how goes it, Corrie? How's Art, hey?" He fastened a terrible emphasis upon the word.

"Crayon portraits," said Corinson.

"What?" They turned towards him with one movement, as if from a lever connection. Little Pennoyer dropped his knife.

"Crayon portraits," repeated Corinson. He smoked away in

profound cynicism. "Fifteen dollars a week or more this time of year, you know." He smiled at them like a man of courage.

Little Pennoyer picked up his knife again. "Well, I'll be blowed," said Wrinkles. Feeling it incumbent upon him to think, he dropped into a chair and began to play serenades on his guitar and watch to see when the water for the eggs would boil. It was a habitual pose.

Great Grief, however, seemed to observe something bitter in the affair. "When did you discover that you couldn't draw?" he said stiffly.

"I haven't discovered it yet," replied Corinson, with a serene air. "I merely discovered that I would rather eat."

"Oh!" said Grief.

"Hand me the eggs, Grief," said Wrinkles. "The water's boiling."

Little Pennoyer burst into the conversation. "We'd ask you to dinner, Corrie, but there's only three of us and there's two eggs. I dropped a piece of bread on the floor, too. I'd shy one."

"That's all right, Penny," said the other; "don't trouble yourself. You artists should never be hospitable. I'm going anyway. I've got to make a call. Well, good night, boys. I've got to make a call. Drop in and see me."

When the door closed upon him, Grief said: "The coffee's done; I hate that fellow. That overcoat cost thirty dollars, if it cost a red. His egotism is so tranquil. It isn't like yours, Wrinkles. He—"

The door opened again and Corinson thrust in his head. "Say, you fellows, you know it's Thanksgiving to-morrow?"

"Well, what of it?" demanded Grief.

Little Pennoyer said: "Yes, I know it is, Corrie, I thought of it this morning."

"Well, come out and have a table d'hote with me to-morrow night. I'll blow you off in good style."

While Wrinkles played an exuberant air on his guitar, little Pennoyer did part of a ballet. They cried ecstatically: "Will we? Well, I guess yes?"

When they were alone again, Grief said: "I'm not going, anyhow. I hate that fellow."

"Oh, fiddle," said Wrinkles. "You're an infernal crank. And besides, where's your dinner coming from to-morrow night if you don't go? Tell me that."

Little Pennoyer said: "Yes, that's so, Grief. Where's your dinner coming from if you don't go?"

Grief said: "Well, I hate him, anyhow."

* * * * * * *

As to Payment of the Rent.

Little Pennoyer's four dollars could not last for ever. When he received it he and Wrinkles and Great Grief went to a table d'hote. Afterwards little Pennoyer discovered that only two dollars and a half remained. A small magazine away down town had accepted one out of the six drawings that he had taken them, and later had given him four dollars for it. Penny was so disheartened when he saw that his money was not going to last for ever, that even with two dollars and a half in his pockets, he felt much worse than when he was penni- less, for at that time he anticipated twenty-four. Wrinkles lectured upon "Finance."

Great Grief said nothing, for it was established that when he received six dollar cheques from comic weeklies he dreamed of renting studios at seventy-five dollars per month, and was likely to go out and buy five dollars' worth of second-hand curtains and plaster casts.

When he had money Penny always hated the cluttered den in the old building. He desired to go out and breathe boastfully like a man. But he obeyed Wrinkles, the elder and the wise, and if you had visited that room about ten o'clock of a morning or about seven of an evening you would have thought that rye bread, frankfurters, and potato salad from Second Avenue were the only foods in the world.

Purple Sanderson lived there too, but then he really ate. He had learned parts of the gasfitter's trade before he came to be such a great artist, and when his opinions disagreed with that of every art manager in New York, he went to see a plumber, a friend of his, for whose opinion he had a great respect. In consequence, he frequented a very great restaurant on Twenty-third Street, and sometimes on Saturday nights he openly scorned his companions.

Purple was a good fellow, Grief said, but one of his singularly bad traits was that he always remembered everything. One night, not long after little Pennoyer's great discovery, Purple came in, and as he was neatly hanging up his coat, said: "Well, the rent will be due in four days."

"Will it?" demanded Penny, astounded. Penny was always astounded when the rent came due. It seemed to him the most extraordinary occurrence.

"Certainly it will," said Purple, with the irritated air of a superior financial man.

"My soul!" said Wrinkles.

Great Grief lay on the bed smoking a pipe and waiting for fame. "Oh, go home, Purple. You resent something. It wasn't me, it was the calendar."

"Try and be serious a moment, Grief."

"You're a fool, Purple."

Penny spoke from where he was at work. "Well, if those *Amazement Magazine* people pay me when they said they would I'll have money then."

"So you will, dear," said Grief, satirically. "You'll have money to burn. Did the *Amazement* people ever pay you when they said they would? You're wonderfully important all of a sudden, it seems to me. You talk like an artist."

Wrinkles, too, smiled at little Pennoyer. "The *Established Magazine* people wanted Penny to hire models and make a try for them too. It will only cost him a big blue chip. By the time he has invested all the money he hasn't got and the rent is two weeks' overdue, he will be able to tell the landlord to wait seven months until the Monday morning after the publication. Go ahead, Penny."

It was the habit to make game of little Pennoyer. He was always having gorgeous opportunities, with no opportunity to take advantage of his opportunities.

Penny smiled at them, his tiny, tiny smile of courage.

"You're a confident little cuss," observed Grief, irrelevantly.

"Well, the world has no objection to your being confident also, Grief," said Purple.

"Hasn't it?" said Grief. "Well, I want to know."

Wrinkles could not be light-spirited long. He was obliged to despair when occasion offered. At last he sank down in a chair and seized his guitar.

"Well, what's to be done?" he said. He began to play mournfully.

"Throw Purple out," mumbled Grief from the bed.

"Are you fairly certain that you will have money then, Penny?" asked Purple.

Little Pennoyer looked apprehensive. "Well, I don't know," he said.

And then began that memorable discussion, great in four minds. The tobacco was of the "Long John" brand. It smelled like burning mummies.

A Dinner on Sunday Evening.

Once Purple Sanderson went to his home in St. Lawrence county to enjoy some country air, and, incidentally, to explain his life failure to his people. Previously, Great Grief had given him odds that he would return sooner than he had planned, and everybody said that Grief had a good bet. It is not a glorious pastime, this explaining of life failures.

Later, Great Grief and Wrinkles went to Haverstraw to visit Grief's cousin and sketch. Little Pennoyer was disheartened, for it is bad to be imprisoned in brick and dust and cobbles when your ear can hear in the distance the harmony of the summer sunlight upon leaf and blade of green. Besides, he did not hear Wrinkles and Grief discoursing and quarrelling in the den, and Purple coming in at six o'clock with contempt.

On Friday afternoon he discovered that he only had fifty cents to last until Saturday morning, when he was to get his cheque from the *Gamin*. He was an artful little man by this time, however, and it is as true as the sky that when he walked toward the *Gamin* office on Saturday he had twenty cents remaining.

The cashier nodded his regrets, "Very sorry, Mr.—er—Pennoyer, but our pay-day, you know, is on Monday. Come around any time after ten."

"Oh, it don't matter," said Penny. As he walked along on his return he reflected deeply how he could invest his twenty cents in food to last until Monday morning any time after ten. He bought two coffee cakes in a third avenue bakery. They were very beautiful. Each had a hole in the centre, and a handsome scallop all around the edges.

Penny took great care of those cakes. At odd times he would rise from his work and go to see that no escape had been made. On Sunday he got up at noon and compressed breakfast and noon into one meal. Afterwards he had almost three-quarters of a cake still left to him. He congratulated himself that with strategy he could make it endure until Monday morning any time after ten.

At three in the afternoon there came a faint-hearted knock. "Come in," said Penny. The door opened and old Tim Connegan, who was trying to be a model, looked in apprehensively. "I beg pardon, sir," he said at once.

"Come in, Tim, you old thief," said Penny. Tim entered slowly and bashfully. "Sit down," said Penny. Tim sat down and began to rub his knees, for rheumatism had a mighty hold upon him.

Penny lit his pipe and crossed his legs. "Well, how goes it?"

Tim moved his square jaw upward and flashed Penny a little glance.

"Bad?" said Penny.

The old man raised his hand impressively. "I've been to every studio in the hull city, and I never see such absences in my life. What with the seashore and the mountains, and this and that resort, I think all the models will be starved by fall. I found one man in up on Fifty-seventh Street. He ses to me: 'Come around Tuesday—I may want yez and I may not.' That was last week. You know, I live down on the Bowery, Mr. Pennoyer, and when I got up there on Tuesday, he ses: 'Confound you, are you here again?' ses he. I went and sat down in the park, for I was too tired for the walk back. And there you are, Mr. Pennoyer. What with trampin' around to look for men that are thousand miles away, I'm near dead."

"It's hard," said Penny.

"It is, sir. I hope they'll come back soon. The summer is the death of us all, sir; it is. Sure, I never know where my next meal is coming until I get it. That's true."

"Had anything to-day?"

"Yes, sir, a little."

"How much?"

"Well, sir, a lady gave me a cup of coffee this morning. It was good, too, I'm telling you."

Penny went to his cupboard. When he returned, he said: "Here's some cake."

Tim thrust forward his hands, palms erect. "Oh, now, Mr. Pennoyer, I couldn't. You—"

"Go ahead. What's the odds?"

"Oh, now."

"Go ahead, you old bat."

Penny smoked.

When Tim was going out, he turned to grow eloquent again. "Well,

I can't tell you how much I'm obliged to you, Mr. Pennoyer. You—"

"Don't mention it, old man."

Penny smoked.

THE SILVER PAGEANT

"It's rotten," said Grief.

"Oh, it's fair, old man. Still, I would not call it a great contribution to American art," said Wrinkles.

"You've got a good thing, Gaunt, if you go at it right," said little Pennoyer.

These were all volunteer orations. The boys had come in one by one and spoken their opinions. Gaunt listened to them no more than if they had been so many match-peddlers. He never heard anything close at hand, and he never saw anything excepting that which transpired across a mystic wide sea. The shadow of his thoughts was in his eyes, a little grey mist, and, when what you said to him had passed out of your mind, he asked: "Wha—a—at?" It was understood that Gaunt was very good to tolerate the presence of the universe, which was noisy and interested in itself. All the younger men, moved by an instinct of faith, declared that he would one day be a great artist if he would only move faster than a pyramid. In the meantime he did not hear their voices. Occasionally when he saw a man take vivid pleasure in life, he faintly evinced an admiration. It seemed to strike him as a feat. As for him, he was watching that silver pageant across a sea.

When he came from Paris to New York somebody told him that he must make his living. He went to see some book publishers, and talked to them in his manner—as if he had just been stunned. At last one of them gave him drawings to do, and it did not surprise him. It was merely as if rain had come down.

Great Grief went to see him in his studio, and returned to the den to say: "Gaunt is working in his sleep. Somebody ought to set fire to him."

It was then that the others went over and smoked, and gave their opinions of a drawing. Wrinkles said: "Are you really looking at it, Gaunt? I don't think you've seen it yet, Gaunt?"

"What?"

"Why don't you look at it?"

When Wrinkles departed, the model, who was resting at that time, followed him into the hall and waved his arms in rage. "That feller's crazy. Yeh ought t' see—" and he recited lists of all the wrongs that can come to models.

It was a superstitious little band over in the den. They talked often of Gaunt. "He's got pictures in his eyes," said Wrinkles. They had expected genius to blindly stumble at the perface and ceremonies of the world, and each new flounder by Gaunt made a stir in the den. It awed them, and they waited.

At last one morning Gaunt burst into the room. They were all as dead men.

"I'm going to paint a picture." The mist in his eyes was pierced by a Coverian gleam. His gestures were wild and extravagant. Grief stretched out smoking on the bed, Wrinkles and little Pennoyer working at their drawing-boards tilted against the table—were suddenly frozen. If bronze statues had come and danced heavily before them, they could not have been thrilled further.

Gaunt tried to tell them of something, but it became knotted in his throat, and then suddenly he dashed out again.

Later they went earnestly over to Gaunt's studio. Perhaps he would tell them of what he saw across the sea.

He lay dead upon the floor. There was a little grey mist before his eyes.

When they finally arrived home that night they took a long time to undress for bed, and then came the moment when they waited for some one to put out the gas. Grief said at last, with the air of a man whose brain is desperately driven: "I wonder—I—what do you suppose he was going to paint?"

Wrinkles reached and turned out the gas, and from the sudden profound darkness, he said: "There is a mistake. He couldn't have had pictures in his eyes."

A STREET SCENE IN NEW YORK

The man and the boy conversed in Italian, mumbling the soft syllables and making little, quick egotistical gestures. Suddenly the man glared and wavered on his limbs for a moment as if some blinding light had flashed before his vision; then he swayed like a drunken man and fell. The boy grasped his arm convulsively, and made an attempt to support his companion so that the body slid to the side-walk with an easy motion like a corpse sinking into the sea. The boy screamed.

Instantly people from all directions turned their gaze upon that figure prone upon the side-walk. In a moment there was a dodging, peering, pushing crowd about the man. A volley of questions, replies, speculations flew to and fro among all the bobbing heads.

"What's th' matter? what's th' matter?"

"Oh, a jag, I guess!"

"Aw, he's got a fit!"

"What's th' matter? what's th' matter?"

Two streams of people coming from different directions met at this point to form a great crowd. Others came from across the street.

Down under their feet, almost lost under this mass of people, lay a man, hidden in the shadows caused by their forms, which, in fact, barely allowed a particle of light to pass between them. Those in the foremost rank bended down eagerly, anxious to see everything. Others behind them crowded savagely like starving men fighting for bread. Always, the question could be heard flying in the air. "What's th' matter." Some, near to the body, and perhaps feeling the danger of being forced over upon it, twisted their heads and protested violently to those unheeding ones who were scuffling in the rear: "Say, quit yer shovin', can't yeh? What do yeh want, anyhow? Quit!"

Somebody back in the throng suddenly said: "Say, young feller, cheese that pushin'! I ain't no peach!"

Another voice said: "Well, dat's all right—"

The boy who had been with the Italian was standing helplessly, a frightened look in his eyes, and holding the man's hand. Sometimes he looked about him dumbly, with indefinite hope, as if he expected sudden assistance to come from the clouds. The men about him frequently jostled him until he was obliged to put his hand upon the breast of the body to maintain his balance. Those nearest the man upon the sidewalk at first saw his body go through a singular contortion. It was as if an invisible hand had reached up from the earth and had seized him by the hair. He seemed dragged slowly, pitilessly backward, while his body stiffened convulsively, his hands clenched, and his arms swung rigidly upward. Through his pallid, half-closed lids one could see the steel-coloured, assassin-like gleam of his eye, that shone with a mystic light as a corpse might glare at those live ones who seemed about to trample it under foot. As for the men near, they hung back, appearing as if they expected it might spring erect and grab them. Their eyes, however, were held in a spell of fascination. They scarce seemed to breathe. They were contemplating a depth into which a human being had sunk, and the marvel of this mystery of life or death held them chained. Occasionally from the rear a man came thrusting his way impetuously, satisfied that there was a horror to be seen, and apparently insane to get a view of it. More self-contained men swore at these persons when they tread upon their toes.

The street cars jingled past this scene in endless parade. Occasionally, down where the elevated road crossed the street, one could hear sometimes a thunder, suddenly begun and suddenly ended. Over the heads of the crowd hung an immovable canvas sign: "Regular Dinner twenty cents."

The body on the pave seemed like a bit of debris sunk in this human ocean.

But after the first spasm of curiosity had passed away, there were those in the crowd who began to bethink themselves of some way to help. A voice called out: "Rub his wrists." The boy and a man on the other side of the body began to rub the wrists and slap the palms of the man. A tall German suddenly appeared, and resolutely began to push the crowd back. "Get back there—get back," he repeated continually while he pushed at them. He seemed to have authority; the crowd obeyed him. He and another man knelt down by the man in the darkness and loosened his shirt at the throat. Once they struck a match and held it close to the man's face. This livid visage suddenly appearing under their feet in the light of the match's yellow glare, made the crowd shudder. Half articulate exclamations could be heard. There were men who nearly created a riot in the madness of their desire to see the thing.

Meanwhile others had been questioning the boy. "What's his

name? Where does he live?"

Then a policeman appeared. The first part of this little drama had gone on without his assistance, but now he came, striding swiftly, his helmet towering over the crowd and shading that impenetrable police face. He charged the crowd as if he were a squadron of Irish Lancers. The people fairly withered before this onslaught. Occasionally he shouted: "Come, make way there. Come, now!" He was evidently a man whose life was half-pestered out of him by people who were sufficiently unreasonable and stupid as to insist on walking in the streets. He felt the rage toward them that a placid cow feels toward the flies that hover in clouds and disturb its repose. When he arrived at the centre of the crowd he first said, threateningly: "What's th' matter here?" And then when he saw that human bit of wreckage at the bottom of the sea of men, he said to it: "Come, git up out that! Git out a here!"

Whereupon hands were raised in the crowd and a volley of decorated information was blazed at the officer.

"Ah, he's got a fit, can't yeh see?"

"He's got a fit!"

"What th'ell yeh doin'? Leave 'im be!"

The policeman menaced with a glance the crowd from whose safe precincts the defiant voices had emerged.

A doctor had come. He and the policeman bended down at the man's side. Occasionally the officer reared up to create room. The crowd fell away before his admonitions, his threats, his sarcastic questions, and before the sweep of those two huge buckskin gloves.

At last the peering ones saw the man on the side-walk begin to breathe heavily, strainedly, as if he had just come to the surface from some deep water. He uttered a low cry in his foreign way. It was like a baby's squeal or the side wail of a little storm-tossed kitten. As this cry went forth to all those eager ears the jostling, crowding recommenced again furiously, until the doctor was obliged to yell warningly a dozen times. The policeman had gone to send the ambulance call.

Then a man struck another match, and in its meagre light the doctor felt the skull of the prostrate man carefully to discover if any wound had been caused by his fall to the stone side-walk. The crowd pressed and crushed again. It was as if they fully expected to see blood by the light of the match, and the desire made them appear almost insane. The policeman returned and fought with them. The doctor looked up occasionally to scold and demand room.

At last, out of the faint haze of light far up the street, there came the sound of a gong beating rapidly. A monstrous truck loaded to the sky with barrels scurried to one side with marvellous agility. And then the black waggon, with its gleam of gold lettering and bright brass gong, clattered into view, the horse galloping. A young man, as imperturbable almost as if he were at a picnic, sat upon the rear seat. When they picked up the limp body, from which came little moans and howls, the crowd almost turned into a mob. When the ambulance started on its banging and clanging return, they stood and gazed until it was quite out of sight. Some resumed their way with an air of relief. Others still continued to stare after the vanished ambulance and its burden as if they had been cheated, as if the curtain had been rung down on a tragedy that was but half completed; and this impenetrable blanket intervening between a sufferer and their curiosity seemed to make them feel an injustice.

MINETTA LANE, NEW YORK

Its Worst Days have Now Passed Away.
But its Inhabitants Still Include Many whose Deeds are Evil.
The Celebrated Resort of Mammy Ross.

Minetta Lane is a small and becobbled valley between hills and dingy brick. At night the street lamps, burning dimly, cause the shadows to be important, and in the gloom one sees groups of quietly conversant negroes, with occasionally the gleam of a passing growler. Everything is vaguely outlined and of uncertain identity, unless, indeed, it be the flashing buttons and shield of the policeman on his coast. The Sixth Avenue horse-cars jingle past one end of the lane, and a block eastward the little thoroughfare ends in the darkness of M'Dougall Street.

One wonders how such an insignificant alley could get such an assuredly large reputation, but, as a matter of fact, Minetta Lane and Minetta Street, which leads from it southward to Bleecker Street, were, until a few years ago, two of the most enthusiastically murderous thoroughfares in New York. Bleecker Street, M'Dougall Street, and nearly all the streets thereabouts were most unmistakably bad; the other streets went away and hid. To gain a reputation in Minetta Lane in those days a man was obliged to commit a number of furious crimes, and no celebrity was more important than the man who had a good honest killing to his credit. The inhabitants, for the most part, were negroes, and they represented the very worst element of their race. The razor habit clung to them with the tenacity of an epidemic, and every night the uneven cobbles felt blood. Minetta Lane was not a public thoroughfare at this period. It was a street set apart, a refuge for criminals. Thieves came here preferably with their gains, and almost any day peculiar sentences passed among the inhabitants. "Big Jim turned a thousand last night." "No-Toe's made another haul." And the worshipful citizens would make haste to be present at the consequent revel.

As has been said, Minetta Lane was then no thoroughfare. A peaceable citizen chose to make a circuit rather than venture through this place, that swarmed with the most dangerous people in the city. Indeed, the thieves of the district used to say: "Once get in the lane and you're all right." Even a policeman in chase of a criminal would probably shy away instead of pursuing him into the lane. The odds were too great against a lone officer.

Sailors, and any men who might appear to have money about them, were welcomed with all proper ceremony at the terrible dens of the lane. At departure they were fortunate if they still retained their teeth. It was the custom to leave very little else to them. There was every facility for the capture of coin, from trap-doors to plain ordinary knock-out drops.

And yet Minetta Lane is built on the grave of Minetta Brook, where, in olden times, lovers walked under the willows on the bank, and Minetta Lane, in later times, was the home of many of the best families of the town.

A negro named Bloodthirsty was perhaps the most luminous figure of Minetta Lane's aggregation of desperadoes. Bloodthirsty supposedly is alive now, but he has vanished from the lane. The police want him for murder. Bloodthirsty is a large negro, and very hideous. He has a rolling eye that shows white at the wrong time, and his neck, under the jaw, is dreadfully scarred and pitted.

Bloodthirsty was particularly eloquent when drunk, and in the wildness of a spree he would rave so graphically about gore that even the habitated wool of old timers would stand straight.

Bloodthirsty meant most of it, too. That is why his orations were impressive. His remarks were usually followed by the wide, lightning sweep of his razor. None cared to exchange epithets with Bloodthirsty. A man in a boiler iron suit would walk down to City Hall and look at the clock before he would ask the time of day from the single-minded and ingenuous Bloodthirsty.

After Bloodthirsty, in combative importance, came No-Toe Charley. Singularly enough, Charley was called No-Toe Charley because he did not have a toe on his feet. Charley was a small negro, and his manner of amusement befitting a smaller man. Charley was more wise, more sly, more round-about than the other man. The path of his crimes was like a corkscrew in architecture, and his method led him to make many tunnels. With all his cleverness, however, No-Toe was finally induced to pay a visit to the gentlemen in the grim, grey building up the river—Sing Sing.

Black-Cat was another famous bandit who made the land his home. Black-Cat is dead. Jube Tyler has been sent to prison, and after mentioning the recent disappearance of Old Man Spriggs it may be said that the lane is now destitute of the men who once crowned it with a glory of crime. It is hardly essential to mention Guinea Johnson.

Guinea is not a great figure. Guinea is just an ordinary little crook. Sometimes Guinea pays a visit to his friends, the other little crooks who make homes in the lane, but he himself does not live there, and with him out of it there is now no one whose industry's unlawfulness has yet earned him the dignity of a nickname. Indeed, it is difficult to find people now who remember the old gorgeous days, although it is but two years since the lane shone with sin like a new head-light. But after a search the reporter found three.

Mammy Ross is one of the last relics of the days of slaughter still living there. Her weird history also reaches back to the blossoming of the first members of the Whyo gang in the Old Sixth Ward, and her mind is stored with bloody memories. She at one time kept a sailors' boarding-house near the Tombs prison, and the accounts of all the festive crimes of that neighbourhood in ancient years roll easily from her tongue. They killed a sailor man every day, and pedestrians went about the streets wearing stoves for fear of the handy knives. At the present day the route to Mammy's home is up a flight of grimy stairs that are pasted on the outside of an old and tottering frame house. Then there is a hall blacker than a wolf's throat, and this hall leads to a little kitchen where Mammy usually sits groaning by the fire. She is, of course, very old, and she is also very fat. She seems always to be in great pain. She says she is suffering from "de very las' dregs of de yaller fever."

During the first part of a reporter's recent visit, old Mammy seemed most dolefully oppressed by her various diseases. Her great body shook and her teeth clicked spasmodically during her long and painful respirations. From time to time she reached her trembling hand and drew a shawl closer about her shoulders. She presented as true a picture of a person undergoing steady, unchangeable, chronic pain as a patent medicine firm could wish to discover for miraculous purposes. She breathed like a fish thrown out on the bank, and her old head continually quivered in the nervous tremors of the extremely aged and debilitated person. Meanwhile her daughter hung over the stove and placidly cooked sausages.

Appeals were made to the old woman's memory. Various personages who had been sublime figures of crime in the long-gone days were mentioned to her, and presently her eyes began to brighten. Her head no longer quivered. She seemed to lose for a period her sense of pain in the gentle excitement caused by the invocation of the spirits of her memory.

It appears that she had had a historic quarrel with Apple Mag. She first recited the prowess of Apple Mag; how this emphatic lady used to argue with paving stones, carving knives, and bricks. Then she told of the quarrel; what Mag said; what she said. It seems that they cited each other as spectacles of sin and corruption in more fully explanatory terms than are commonly known to be possible. But it was one of Mammy's most gorgeous recollections, and, as she told it, a smile widened over her face.

Finally she explained her celebrated retort to one of the most illustrious thugs that had blessed the city in bygone days. "Ah says to 'im, ah says: 'You—you'll die in yer boots like Gallopin' Thompson— dat's what you'll do. You des min' dat', honey. Ah got o'ny one chile, an' he ain't nuthin' but er cripple; but le'me tel' you, man, dat boy'll live t' pick de feathers f'm de goose dat'll eat de grass dat grows over your grave, man.' Dat's what I tol' 'm. But—law sake—how I know dat in less'n three day, dat man be lying in de gutter wif a knife stickin' out'n his back. Lawd, no, I sholy never s'pected noting like dat."

These reminiscences, at once maimed and reconstructed, have been treasured by old Mammy as carefully, as tenderly, as if they were the various little tokens of an early love. She applies the same black-handed sentiment to them, and, as she sits groaning by the fire, it is plainly to be seen that there is only one food for her ancient brain, and that is the recollection of the beautiful fights and murders of the past.

On the other side of the lane, but near Mammy's house, Pop Babcock keeps a restaurant. Pop says it is a restaurant, and so it must be one; but you could pass there ninety times each day and never know you were passing a restaurant. There is one obscure little window in the basement, and if you went close and peered in you might, after a time, be able to make out a small, dusty sign, lying amid jars on a dusty shelf. This sign reads: "Oysters in every style." If you are of a gambling turn of mind, you will probably stand out in the street and bet yourself black in the face that there isn't an oyster within a hundred yards. But Pop Babcock made that sign, and Pop Babcock could not tell an untruth. Pop is a model of all the virtues which an inventive fate has made for us. He says so.

As far as goes the management of Pop's restaurant, it differs from Sherry's. In the first place, the door is always kept locked. The wardmen of the Fifteenth precinct have a way of prowling through the restaurant almost every night, and Pop keeps the door locked in order to keep out the objectionable people that cause the wardmen's visits. He says so. The cooking stove is located in the main room of the restaurant, and it is placed in such a strategic manner that it occupies about all the space that is not already occupied by a table, a bench, and two chairs. The table will, on a pinch, furnish room for the plates of two people if they are willing to crowd. Pop says he is the best cook in the world.

When questioned concerning the present condition of the lane, Pop said: "Quiet! Quiet! Lo'd save us, maybe it ain't. Quiet! Quiet!" His emphasis was arranged crescendo, until the last word was really a vocal explosion. "Why, dish er' lane ain't nohow like what it uster be—no, indeed it ain't. No, sir. 'Deed it ain't. Why, I kin remember when dey was a-cuttin' an' a-slashin' long yere all night. 'Deed dey wos. My-my, dem times was different. Dat der Kent, he kep' de place at Green Gate cou't down yer ol' Mammy's—an' he was a hard baby—'deed he was—an' ol' Black-Cat an' ol' Bloodthirsty, dey was a-comin' round yere a-cuttin', an' a-slashin', an' a-cuttin', an' a-slashin'. Didn't dar' say boo to a goose in dose days, dat you didn't, less'n you lookin' fer a scrap. No, sir." Then he gave information concerning his own prowess at that time. Pop is about as tall as a picket of an undersized fence. "But dey didn't have nothin' ter say ter me. No, sir, 'deed dey didn't. I would lay down fer none of 'em. No, sir. Dey knew my gait, 'deed dey did. Man, man, many's de time I buck up agin 'em."

At this time Pop had three customers in his place, one asleep on the bench, one asleep on two chairs, and one asleep on the floor behind the stove.

But there is one who lends dignity of the real bevel-edged type to Minetta Lane, and that man is Hank Anderson. Hank, of course, does not live in the lane, but the shadows of his social perfections fall upon it as refreshingly as a morning dew.

Hank gave a dance twice in each week at a hall hard by in M'Dougall Street, and the dusky aristocracy of the neighbourhood know their guiding beacon. Moreover, Hank holds an annual ball in Forty-fourth Street. Also, he gives a picnic each year to the Montezuma Club, when he again appears as a guiding beacon. This picnic is usually held on a barge, and the excursion is a very joyous one. Some years ago it required the entire reserve squad of an up-town police precinct to properly control the enthusiasm of the gay picnickers, but that was an exceptional exuberance, and no measure of Hank's ability for management.

He is really a great manager. He was Boss Tweed's body-servant in the days when Tweed was a political prince, and any one who saw Bill Tweed through a spy-glass learned the science of leading, pulling, driving, and hauling men in a way to keep the men ignorant of it. Hank imbibed from this fount of knowledge, and he applied his information in Thompson Street. Thompson Street salaamed. Presently he bore a proud title: "The Mayor of Thompson Street." Dignities from the principal political organisations of the city adorned his brow, and he speedily became illustrious.

Hank knew the lane well in its direful days. As for the inhabitants, he kept clear of them, and yet in touch with them, according to a method that he might have learned in the Sixth ward. The Sixth ward was a good place in which to learn that trick. Anderson can tell many strange tales and good of the lane, and he tells them in the graphic way of his class. "Why, they could steal your shirt without moving a wrinkle on it."

The killing of Joe Carey was the last murder that happened in the Minettas. Carey had what might be called a mixed-ale difference with a man named Kenny. They went out to the middle of Minetta Street to affably fight it out and determine the justice of the question.

In the scrimmage Kenny drew a knife, thrust quickly, and Carey fell. Kenny had not gone a hundred feet before he ran into the arms of a policeman.

There is probably no street in New York where the police keep closer watch than they do in Minetta Lane. There was a time when the inhabitants had a profound and reasonable contempt for the public guardians, but they have it no longer apparently. Any citizen can walk through there at any time in perfect safety, unless, perhaps, he should happen to get too frivolous. To be strictly accurate, the change began under the reign of police Captain Chapman. Under Captain Groo, a commander of the Fifteenth precinct, the lane donned a complete new garb. Its denizens brag now of its peace, precisely as they once bragged of its war. It is no more a bloody lane. The song of the razor is seldom heard. There are still toughs and semi-toughs galore in it, but they can't get a chance with the copper looking the other way. Groo got the poor lane by the throat. If a man should insist upon becoming a victim of the badger game, he could probably succeed, upon search in Minetta Lane, as indeed, he could on any of the great avenues, but then Minetta Lane is not supposed to be a pearly street of Paradise.

In the meantime the Italians have begun to dispute the possession of the lane with the negroes. Green Gate Court is filled with them now, and a row of houses near the M'Dougall Street corner is occupied entirely by Italian families. None of them seem to be over fond of the old Mulberry Bend fashion of life, and there are no cutting affrays among them worth mentioning. It is the original negro element that makes the trouble when there is trouble.

But they are happy in this condition are these people. The most extraordinary quality of the negro is his enormous capacity for happiness under most adverse circumstances. Minetta Lane is a place of poverty and sin, but these influences cannot destroy the broad smile of the negro—a vain and simple child, but happy. They all smile here, the most evil as well as the poorest. Knowing the negro, one always expects laughter from him, be he ever so poor, but it was a new experience to see a broad grin on the face of the devil. Even old Pop Babcock had a laugh as fine and mellow as would be the sound of falling glass, broken saints from high windows, in the silence of some great cathedral's hollow.

THE ROOF GARDENS AND GARDENERS OF NEW YORK

A Phase of New York Life as Seen by a Close Observer.

When the hot weather comes the roof gardens burst into full bloom, and if an inhabitant of Chicago should take flight on his wings over this city, he would observe six or eight flashing spots in the darkness, spots as radiant as crowns. These are the roof gardens, and if a giant had flung a handful of monstrous golden coins upon the sombre-shadowed city he could not have benefited the metropolis more, although he would not have given the same opportunity to various commercial aspirants to charge a price and a half for everything. There are two classes of men—reporters and central office detectives—who do not mind these prices because they are very prodigal of their money.

Now is the time of the girl with the copper voice, the Irishman with circular whiskers, and the minstrel who had a reputation in 1833. To the street the noise of the band comes down on the wind in fitful gusts, and at the brilliantly illuminated rail there is suggestion of many straw hats.

One of the main features of the roof garden is the waiter, who stands directly in front of you whenever anything interesting transpires on the stage. This waiter is three hundred feet high and seventy-two feet wide. His finger can block your view of the golden-haired *soubrette*, and when he waves his arm the stage disappears as if by a miracle. What particularly fascinates you is his lack of self-appreciation. He doesn't know that his length over all is three hundred feet, and that his beam is seventy-two feet. He only knows that while the golden-haired *soubrette* is singing her first verse he is depositing beer on the table before some thirsty New Yorkers. He only knows that during the third verse the thirsty New Yorkers object to the roof-garden prices. He does not know that behind him are some fifty citizens who ordinarily would not give three whoops to see the golden-haired *soubrette*, but who, under these particular circumstances, are kept from swift assassination by sheer force of the human will. He gives an impressive exhibition of a man who is regardless of consequences, oblivious to everything save his task, which is to provide beer. Some day there may be a wholesale massacre of roof-garden waiters, but they will die with astonished faces and with questions on their lips. Skulls so steadfastly opaque defy axes, or any of the other methods which the populace occasionally use to cure colossal stupidity.

Between numbers on an ordinary roof-garden programme, the orchestra sometimes plays what the more enlightened and wary citizens of the town call a "beer overture." But, for reasons which no civil service commission could give, the waiter does not choose this time to serve the thirsty. No; he waits until the golden-haired *soubrette* appears, he waits until the haggard audience has goaded itself into some interest in the proceedings. Then he gets under way. Then he comes forth and blots out the stage. In case of war, all roof-garden waiters should be recruited in a special regiment and sent out in advance of everything. There is a peculiar quality of bullet-proofness about them which would turn a projectile pale.

If you have strategy enough in your soul you may gain furtive glimpses of the stage, despite the efforts of the waiters, and then, with something to engage the attention when the attention grows weary of the mystic wind, the flashing yellow lights, the music, and the undertone of the far street's roar, you should be happy.

Far up into the night there is a wildness, a temper to the air which suggests tossing tree boughs and the swift rustle of grass. The New Yorker, whose business will not allow him to go out to nature, perhaps, appreciates these little opportunities to go up to nature, although doubtless he thinks he goes to see the show.

One season two new roof gardens have opened. The one at the top of Grand Central Palace is large enough for a regimental drill room. The band is imprisoned still higher in a turreted affair, and a person who prefers gentle and unobtrusive amusement can gain deep pleasure and satisfaction from watching the leader of this band gesticulating upon the heavens. His figure is silhouetted beautifully against the sky, and every gesture in which he wrings noise from his band is interestingly accentuated.

The other new roof garden was Oscar Hammerstein's Olympia, which blazes on Broadway.

Oscar originally made a great reputation for getting out injunctions. All court judges in New York worked overtime when Oscar was in this business. He enjoined everybody in sight. He had a special machine made—"Drop a nickel in the judge and get an injunction." Then he sent a man to Washington for twenty-two thousand dollars' worth of nickels. In Harlem, where he then lived, it rained orders of the court every day at twelve o'clock. The street-cleaning commission was obliged to enlist a special force to deal with Oscar's injunctions. Citizens meeting on the street never said: "Good morning, how do you feel to-day?" They always said: "Good morning, have you been enjoined yet to-day?" When a man perhaps wished to enter a little game of draw, the universal form was changed when he sent a note to his wife: "Dear Louise, I have received an order of the court restraining me from coming home to dinner to-night. Yours, George."

But Oscar changed. He smashed his machine, girded himself, and resolved to provide the public with amusement. And now we see this great mind applying itself to a roof garden with the same unflagging industry and boundless energy which had previously expressed itself in injunctions. The Olympia, his new roof garden, is a feat. It has an exuberance which reminds one of the Union Depot train-shed of some western city. The steel arches of the roof make a wide and splendid sweep, and over in the corner there are real swans swimming in real water. The whole structure glares like a conflagration with the countless electric lights. Oscar has caused the execution of decorative paintings upon the walls. If he had caused the execution of the decorative painters he would have done better; but a man who has devoted the greater part of his life to the propagation of injunctions is not supposed to understand that wall decoration which appears to have been done with a nozzle is worse than none. But if carpers say that Oscar failed in his landscapes, none can say that he failed in his measurements of the popular mind. The people come in swarms to the Olympia. Two elevators are busy at conveying them to where the cool and steady night-wind insults the straw hat; and the scene here during the popular part of the evening is perhaps more gaudy and dazzling than any other in New York.

The bicycle has attained an economic position of vast importance. The roof garden ought to attain such a position, and it doubtless will soon—as we give it the opportunity it desires.

The Arab or the Moor probably invented the roof garden in some long-gone centuries, and they are at this day inveterate roof gardeners. The American, surprisingly belated—for him, has but recently seized upon the idea, and its development here has been only partial. The possibilities of the roof garden are still unknown.

Here is a vast city in which thousands of people in summer half stifle, cry out continually for air, fresher air. Just above their heads is what might be called a county of unoccupied land. It is not ridiculously small when compared with the area of New York county itself. But it is as lonely as a desert, this region of roofs. It is as untrodden as the corners of Arizona. Unless a man be a roof gardener, he knows practically nothing of this land.

Down in the slums necessity forces a solution of problems. It drives the people to the roofs. An evening upon a tenement roof with the great golden march of the stars across the sky, and Johnnie gone for a pail of beer, is not so bad if you have never seen the mountains nor heard, to your heart, the slow, sad song of the pines.

IN THE BROADWAY CARS

Panorama of a Day from the Down-town Rush of the Morning to the Uninterrupted Whirr of the Cable at Night—The Man, and the Woman, and the Conductor.

The cable cars come down Broadway as the waters come down at Lodore. Years ago Father Knickerbocker had convulsions when it was proposed to lay impious rails on his sacred thoroughfare. At the present day the cars, by force of column and numbers, almost dominate the great street, and the eye of even an old New Yorker is held by these long yellow monsters which prowl intently up and down, up and down, in a mystic search.

In the grey of the morning they come out of the up-town, bearing janitors, porters, all that class which carries the keys to set alive the great down-town. Later, they shower clerks. Later still, they shower more clerks. And the thermometer which is attached to a conductor's temper is steadily rising, rising, and the blissful time arrives when everybody hangs to a strap and stands on his neighbour's toes. Ten o'clock comes, and the Broadway cars, as well as elevated cars, horse cars, and ferryboats innumerable, heave sighs of relief. They have filled lower New York with a vast army of men who will chase to and fro and amuse themselves until almost nightfall.

The cable car's pulse drops to normal. But the conductor's pulse begins now to beat in split seconds. He has come to the crisis in his day's agony. He is now to be overwhelmed with feminine shoppers. They all are going to give him two-dollar bills to change. They all are going to threaten to report him. He passes his hand across his brow and curses his beard from black to grey and from grey to black.

Men and women have different ways of hailing a car. A man—if he is not an old choleric gentleman, who owns not this road but some other road—throws up a timid finger, and appears to believe that the King of Abyssinia is careering past on his war-chariot, and only his opinion of other people's Americanism keeps him from deep salaams. The gripman usually jerks his thumb over his shoulder and indicates the next car, which is three miles away. Then the man catches the last platform, goes into the car, climbs upon some one's toes, opens his morning paper, and is happy.

When a woman hails a car there is no question of its being the

King of Abyssinia's war-chariot. She has bought the car for three dollars and ninety-eight cents. The conductor owes his position to her, and the gripman's mother does her laundry. No captain in the Royal Horse Artillery ever stops his battery from going through a stone house in a way to equal her manner of bringing that car back on its haunches. Then she walks leisurely forward, and after scanning the step to see if there is any mud upon it, and opening her pocketbook to make sure of a two-dollar bill, she says: "Do you give transfers down Twenty-eighth Street?"

Some time the conductor breaks the bell strap when he pulls it under these conditions. Then, as the car goes on, he goes and bullies some person who had nothing to do with the affair.

The car sweeps on its diagonal path through the Tenderloin with its hotels, its theatres, its flower shops, its 10,000,000 actors who played with Booth and Barret. It passes Madison Square and enters the gorge made by the towering walls of great shops. It sweeps around the double curve at Union Square and Fourteenth Street, and a life insurance agent falls in a fit as the car dashes over the crossing, narrowly missing three old ladies, two old gentlemen, a newly-married couple, a sandwich man, a newsboy, and a dog. At Grace Church the conductor has an altercation with a brave and reckless passenger who beards him in his own car, and at Canal Street he takes dire vengeance by tumbling a drunken man on to the pavement. Meanwhile, the gripman has become involved with countless truck drivers, and inch by inch, foot by foot, he fights his way to City Hall Park. On past the Post Office the car goes, with the gripman getting advice, admonition, personal comment, an invitation to fight from the drivers, until Battery Park appears at the foot of the slope, and as the car goes sedately around the curve the burnished shield of the bay shines through the trees.

It is a great ride, full of exciting actions. Those inexperienced persons who have been merely chased by Indians know little of the dramatic quality which life may hold for them. These jungle of men and vehicles, these cañons of streets, these lofty mountains of iron and cut stone—a ride through them affords plenty of excitement. And no lone panther's howl is more serious in intention than the howl of the truck driver when the cable car bumps one of his rear wheels.

Owing to a strange humour of the gods that make our comfort, sailor hats with wide brims come into vogue whenever we are all engaged in hanging to cable-car straps. There is only one more serious combination known to science, but a trial of it is at this day impossible. If a troupe of Elizabethan courtiers in large ruffs should board a cable car, the complication would be a very awesome one, and the profanity would be in old English, but very inspiring. However, the combination of wide-brimmed hats and crowded cable cars is tremendous in its power to cause misery to the patient New York public.

Suppose you are in a cable car, clutching for life and family a creaking strap from overhead. At your shoulder is a little dude in a very wide-brimmed straw hat with a red band. If you were in your senses you would recognise this flaming band as an omen of blood. But you are not in your senses; you are in a Broadway cable car. You are not supposed to have any senses. From the forward end you hear the gripman uttering shrill whoops and running over citizens. Suddenly the car comes to a curve. Making a swift running start, it turns three hand-springs, throws a cart wheel for luck, bounds into the air, hurls six passengers over the nearest building, and comes down a-straddle of the track. That is the way in which we turn curves in New York.

Meanwhile, during the car's gamboling, the corrugated rim of the dude's hat has swept naturally across your neck, and has left nothing for your head to do but to quit your shoulders. As the car roars your head falls into the waiting arms of the proper authorities. The dude is dead; everything is dead. The interior of the car resembles the scene of the battle of Wounded Knee, but this gives you small satisfaction.

There was once a person possessing a fund of uncanny humour who greatly desired to import from past ages a corps of knights in full armour. He then purposed to pack the warriors into a cable car and send them around a curve. He thought that he could gain much pleasure by standing near and listening to the wild clash of steel upon steel—the tumult of mailed heads striking together, the bitter grind of armoured legs bending the wrong way. He thought that this would teach them that war is grim.

Towards evening, when the tides of travel set northward, it is curious to see how the gripman and conductor reverse their tempers. Their dispositions flop over like patent signals. During the down-trip they had in mind always the advantages of being at Battery Park. A perpetual picture of the blessings of Battery Park was before them, and every delay made them fume—made this picture all the more alluring. Now the delights of up-town appear to them. They have reversed the signs on the cars; they have reversed their aspirations. Battery Park has been gained and forgotten. There is a new goal. Here is a perpetual illustration which the philosophers of New York may use.

In the Tenderloin, the place of theatres, and of the restaurant where gayer New York does her dining, the cable cars in the evening carry a stratum of society which looks like a new one, but it is of the familiar strata in other clothes. It is just as good as a new stratum, however, for in evening dress the average man feels that he has gone up three pegs in the social scale, and there is considerable evening dress about a Broadway car in the evening. A car with its electric lamp resembles a brilliantly-lighted salon, and the atmosphere grows just a trifle strained. People sit more rigidly, and glance sidewise, perhaps, as if each was positive of possessing social value, but was doubtful of all others. The conductor says: "Ah, gwan. Git off th' earth." But this is to a man at Canal Street. That shows his versatility. He stands on the platform and beams in a modest and polite manner into the car. He notes a lifted finger and grabs swiftly for the bell strap. He reaches down to help a woman aboard. Perhaps his demeanour is a reflection of the manner of the people in the car. No one is in a mad New York hurry; no one is fretting and muttering; no one is perched upon his neighbour's toes. Moreover, the Tenderloin is a glory at night. Broadway of late years has fallen heir to countless signs illuminated with red, blue, green, and gold electric lamps, and the people certainly fly to these as the moths go to a candle. And perhaps the gods have allowed this opportunity to observe and study the best-dressed crowds in the world to operate upon the conductor until his mood is to treat us with care and mildness.

Late at night, after the diners and theatre-goers have been lost in Harlem, various inebriate persons may perchance emerge from the darker regions of Sixth Avenue and swing their arms solemnly at the gripman. If the Broadway cars run for the next 7000 years this will be the only time when one New Yorker will address another in public without an excuse sent direct from heaven. In these cars late at night it is not impossible that some fearless drunkard will attempt to inaugurate a general conversation. He is quite willing to devote his ability to the affair. He tells of the fun he thinks he has had; describes his feelings; recounts stories of his dim past. None reply, although all listen with every ear. The rake probably ends by borrowing a match, lighting a cigar, and entering into a wrangle with the conductor with an *abandon*, a ferocity, and a courage that do not come to us when we are sober.

In the meantime the figures on the street grow fewer and fewer. Strolling policemen test the locks of the great dark-fronted stores. Nighthawk cabs whirl by the cars on their mysterious errands. Finally the cars themselves depart in the way of the citizen, and for the few hours before dawn a new sound comes into the still thoroughfare— the cable whirring in its channel underground.

THE ASSASSIN IN MODERN BATTLES

The Torpedo Boat Destroyers that "Perform in the Darkness. An Act which Is more Peculiarly Murderous than most Things in War."

In the past century the gallant aristocracy of London liked to travel down the south bank of the Thames to Greenwich Hospital, where venerable pensioners of the crown were ready to hire telescopes at a penny each, and with these telescopes the lords and ladies were able to view at a better advantage the dried and enchained corpses of pirates hanging from the gibbets on the Isle of Dogs. In those times the dismal marsh was inhabited solely by the clanking figures whose feet moved in the wind like rather poorly-constructed weather cocks.

But even the Isle of Dogs could not escape the appetite of an expanding London. Thousands of souls now live on it, and it has changed its character from that of a place of execution, with mist, wet with fever, coiling forever from the mire and wandering among the black gibbets, to that of an ordinary, squalid, nauseating slum of London, whose streets bear a faint resemblance to that part of Avenue A which lies directly above Sixtieth Street in New York.

Down near the water front one finds a long brick building, three-storeyed and signless, which shuts off all view of the river. The windows, as well as the bricks, are very dirty, and you see no sign of life, unless some smudged workman dodges in through a little door. The place might be a factory for the making of lamps or stair rods, or any ordinary commercial thing. As a matter of fact, the building fronts the shipyard of Yarrow, the builder of torpedo boats, the maker of knives for the nations, the man who provides everybody with a certain kind of efficient weapon. One then remembers that if Russia fights England, Yarrow meets Yarrow; if Germany fights France, Yarrow meets Yarrow; if Chili fights Argentina, Yarrow meets Yarrow.

Besides the above-mentioned countries Yarrow has built torpedo boats for Italy, Austria, Holland, Japan, China, Ecuador, Brazil, Costa Rica, and Spain. There is a keeper of a great shop in London who is known as the Universal Provider. If a general conflagration of war should break out in the world, Yarrow would be known as one of the Universal Warriors, for it would practically be a battle between Yarrow, Armstrong, Krupp, and a few other firms. This is what makes interesting the dinginess of the cantonment on the Isle of Dogs.

The great Yarrow forte is to build speedy steamers of a tonnage of not more than 240 tons. This practically includes only yachts, launches, tugs, torpedo boat destroyers, torpedo boats, and of late shallow-draught gunboats for service on the Nile, Congo, and Niger. Some of the gunboats that shelled the dervishes from the banks of the Nile below Khartoum were built by Yarrow. Yarrow is always in action somewhere. Even if the firm's boats do not appear in every coming sea combat, the ideas of the firm will, for many nations, notably France and Germany, have bought specimens of the best models of Yarrow construction in order to reduplicate and reduplicate them in their own yards.

When the great fever to possess torpedo boats came upon the Powers of Europe, England was at first left far in the rear. Either Germany or France to-day has in her fleet more torpedo boats than has England. The British tar is a hard man to oust out of a habit. He had a habit of thinking that his battleships and cruisers were the final thing in naval construction. He scoffed at the advent of the torpedo boat. He did not scoff intelligently but because, mainly, he hated to be forced to change his ways.

You will usually find an Englishman balking and kicking at innovation up to the last moment. It takes him some years to get an idea into his head, and when finally it is inserted, he not only respects it, he reveres it. The Londoners have a fire brigade which would interest the ghost of a Babylonian, as an example of how much the method of extinguishing fires could degenerate in two thousand years, and in 1897, when a terrible fire devastated a part of the city, some voices were raised challenging the efficiency of the fire brigade. But that part of the London County Council which corresponds to fire commissioners in United States laid their hands upon their hearts and solemnly assured the public that they had investigated the matter, and had found the London fire brigade to be as good as any in the world. There were some isolated cases of dissent, but the great English public as a whole placidly accepted these assurances concerning the activity of the honoured corps.

For a long time England blundered in the same way over the matter of torpedo boats. They were authoritatively informed that there was nothing in all the talk about torpedo boats. Then came a great popular uproar, in which people tumbled over each other to get to the doors of the Admiralty and howl about torpedo boats. It was an awakening as unreasonable as had been the previous indifference and contempt. Then England began to build. She has never overtaken France or Germany in the number of torpedo boats, but she now heads the world with her collection of that marvel of marine architecture—the torpedo boat destroyer. She has about sixty-five of these vessels now in commission, and has about as many more in course of building.

People ordinarily have a false idea of the appearance of a destroyer. The common type is longer than an ordinary gunboat—a long, low, graceful thing, flying through the water at fabulous speed, with a great curve of water some yards back of the bow, and smoke flying horizontally from the three or four stacks.

Bushing this way and that way, circling, dodging, turning, they are like demons.

The best kind of modern destroyer has a length of 220 feet, with a beam of 26½ feet. The horse-power is about 6500, driving the boat at a speed of thirty-one knots or more. The engines are triple-expansion, with water tube boilers. They carry from 70 to 100 tons of coal, and at a speed of eight or nine knots can keep the sea for a week; so they are independent of coaling in a voyage of between 1300 and 1500 miles. They carry a crew of three or four officers, and about forty men.

They are armed usually with one twelve-pounder gun, and from three to five six-pounder guns, besides their equipment of torpedoes. Their hulls and top hamper are painted olive, buff, or preferably slate, in order to make them hard to find with the eye at sea.

Their principal functions, theoretically, are to discover and kill the enemy's torpedo boats, guard and scout for the main squadron, and perform messenger service. However, they are also torpedo boats of a most formidable kind, and in action will be found carrying out the torpedo boat idea in an expanded form. Four destroyers of this type building at the Yarrow yards were for Japan (1898).

The modern European ideal of a torpedo boat is a craft 152 feet long, with a beam of 15¼ feet. When the boat is fully loaded a speed of 24 knots is derived from her 2000 horse-power engines. The destroyers are twin screw, whereas the torpedo boats are commonly propelled by a single screw. The speed of twenty knots is for a run of three hours. These boats are not designed to keep at sea for any great length of time, and cannot raid toward a distant coast without the constant attendance of a cruiser to keep them in coal and provisions. Primarily they are for defence. Even with destroyers, England, in lately reinforcing her foreign stations, has seen fit to send cruisers in order to provide help for them in stormy weather.

Some years ago it was thought the proper thing to equip torpedo craft with rudders, which would enable them to turn in their own length when running at full speed. Yarrow found this to result in too much broken steering gear, and the firm's boats now have smaller rudders, which enable them to turn in a larger circle.

At one time a torpedo boat steaming at her best gait always carried a great bone in her teeth. During manœuvres the watch on the deck of a battleship often discovered the approach of the little enemy by the great white wave which the boat rolled at her bows during her headlong rush. This was mainly because the old-fashioned boats carried two torpedo tubes set in the bows, and the bows were consequently bluff.

The modern boat carries the great part of her armament amidships and astern on swivels, and her bow is like a dagger. With no more bow-waves, and with these phantom colours of buff, olive, bottle-green, or slate, the principal foe to a safe attack at night is bad firing in the stoke-room, which might cause flames to leap out of the stacks.

A captain of an English battleship recently remarked: "See those five destroyers lying there? Well, if they should attack me I would sink four of them, but the fifth one would sink me."

This was repeated to Yarrow's manager, who said: "He wouldn't sink four of them if the attack were at night and the boats were shrewdly and courageously handled." Anyhow, the captain's remark goes to show the wholesome respect which the great battleship has for these little fliers.

The Yarrow people say there is no sense in a torpedo flotilla attack on anything save vessels. A modern fortification is never built near enough to the water for a torpedo explosion to injure it, and, although some old stone flush-with-the-water castle might be badly crumpled, it would harm nobody in particular, even if the assault were wholly successful.

Of course, if a torpedo boat could get a chance at piers and dock gates they would make a disturbance, but the chance is extremely remote if the defenders have ordinary vigilance and some rapid fire guns. In harbour defence the searchlight would naturally play a most important part, whereas at sea experts are beginning to doubt its use as an auxiliary to the rapid fire guns against torpedo boats. About half the time it does little more than betray the position of the ship. On the other hand, a port cannot conceal its position anyhow, and searchlights would be invaluable for sweeping the narrow channels.

There could be only one direction from which the assault could come, and all the odds would be in favour of the guns on shore. A torpedo boat commander knows this perfectly. What he wants is a ship off at sea with a nervous crew staring into the encircling darkness from any point in which the terror might be coming.

Hi, then, for a grand, bold, silent rush and the assassin-like stab.

In stormy weather life on board a torpedo boat is not amusing. They tumble about like bucking bronchos, especially if they are going at anything like speed. Everything is battened down as if it were soldered, and the watch below feel that they are living in a football, which is being kicked every way at once.

And finally, while Yarrow and other great builders can make torpedo craft which are wonders of speed and manœuvring power, they cannot make that high spirit of daring and hardihood which is essential to a success.

That must exist in the mind of some young lieutenant who, knowing well that if he is detected, a shot or so from a rapid fire gun will cripple him if it does not sink him absolutely, nevertheless goes creeping off to sea to find a huge antagonist and perform stealthily in the darkness an act which is more peculiarly murderous than most things in war.

If a torpedo boat is caught within range in daylight, the fighting is all over before it begins. Any common little gunboat can dispose of it in a moment if the gunnery is not too Chinese.

IRISH NOTES

I. — AN OLD MAN GOES WOOING

The melancholy fisherman made his way through a street that was mainly as dark as a tunnel. Sometimes an open door threw a rectangle of light upon the pavement, and within the cottages were scenes of working women and men, who comfortably smoked and talked. From them came the sounds of laughter and the babble of children. Each time the old man passed through one of the radiant zones the light etched his face in profile with touches flaming and sombre until there was a resemblance to a stern and mournful Dante portrait.

Once a whistling lad came through the darkness. He peered intently for purposes of recognition. "Good avenin', Mickey," he cried cheerfully. The old man responded with a groan, which intimated that the lamentable reckless optimism of the youth had forced from him an expression of an emotion that he had been enduring in saintly patience and silence. He continued his pilgrimage toward the kitchen of the village inn.

The kitchen is a great and worthy place. The long range with its lurid heat continually emits the fragrance of broiling fish, roasting mutton, joints, and fowl. The high black ceiling is ornamented with hams and flitches of bacon. There is a long, dark bench against one wall, and it is fronted by a dark table, handy for glasses of stout. On an old mahogany dresser rows of plates face the distant range, and reflect the red shine of the peat. Smoke which has in it the odour of an American forest fire eddies through the air. The great stones of the floor are scarred by the black mud from the inn yard. And here the gossip of a country-side goes on amid the sizzle of broiling fish and the loud protesting splutter of joints taken from the oven.

When the old man reached the door of this paradise, he stopped for a moment with his finger on the latch. He sighed deeply; evidently he was undergoing some lachrymose reflection. For somewhere overhead in the inn he could hear the wild clamour of dining pig-buyers, men who were come for the pig fair to be held on the morrow. Evidently in the little parlour of the inn these men were dining amid an uproar of shouted jests and laughter. The revelry sounded like the fighting of two mobs amid a rain of missiles and crash of shop windows. The old man raised his hand as if, unseen there in the darkness, he was going to solemnly damn the dinner of the pig-buyers.

Within the kitchen Nora, tall, strong, intrepid, approached the fiery stove in the manner of a boxer. Her left arm was held high to guard her face, which was already crimson from the blaze. With a flourish of her apron she achieved a great brown humming joint from the oven, and, emerging a glowing and triumphant figure from the steam and smoke and rapid play of heat, she slid the pan upon the table, even as she saw the old man standing within the room and lugubriously cleaning the mud from his boots. "Tis you, Mickey?" she said.

He made no reply until he had found his way to the long bench. "It is," he said then. It was clear that in the girl's opinion he had gained some kind of strategic advantage. The sanctity of her kitchen was successfully violated, but the old man betrayed no elation. Lifting one knee and placing it over the other, he grunted in the blissful weariness of a venerable labourer returned to his own fireside. He coughed dismally. "Ah, 'tis no good a man gits from fishin' these days. I moind the toimes whin they would be hoppin' up clear o' the wather, there was that little room fur thim. I would be likin' a bottle o' stout."

"Niver fear you, Mickey," answered the girl. Swinging here and there in the glare of the fire, Nora, with her towering figure and bare brawny arms, was like a feminine blacksmith at a forge. The old man, pallid, emaciated, watched her from the shadows at the other side of the room. The lines from the sides of his nose to the corners of his mouth sank low to an expression of despair deeper than any moans. He should have been painted upon the door of a tomb with wringing willows arched above him and men in grey robes slowly booming the drums of death. Finally he spoke. "I would be likin' a bottle o' stout, Nora, me girrl," he said.

"Niver fear you, Mickey," again she replied with cheerful obstinacy. She was admiring her famous roast, which now sat in its platter on the rack over the range. There was a lull in her tumultuous duties. The old man coughed and moved his foot with a scraping sound on the stones. The noise of dining pig-buyers, now heard through doors and winding corridors of the inn, was a roll of far-away storm.

A woman in a dark dress entered the kitchen and keenly examined the roast and Nora's other feats. "Mickey here would be wantin' a bottle o' stout," said the girl to her mistress. The woman turned towards the spectral figure in the gloom, and regarded it quietly with a clear eye. "Have yez the money, Mickey?" repeated the woman of the house.

Profoundly embittered, he replied in short terms, "I have."

"There now," cried Nora, in astonishment and admiration. Poising a large iron spoon, she was motionless, staring with open mouth at the old man. He searched his pockets slowly during a complete silence in the kitchen. He brought forth two coppers and laid them sadly, reproachfully, and yet defiantly on the table.

"There now," cried Nora, stupefied.

They brought him a bottle of the black brew, and Nora poured it out for him with her own red hand, which looked to be as broad as his chest. A collar of brown foam curled at the top of the glass. With measured moments the old man filled a short pipe. There came a sudden howl from another part of the inn. One of the pig-buyers was at the head of the stairs bawling for the mistress. The two women hurriedly freighted themselves with the roast and the vegetables, and sprang with them to placate the pig-buyers. Alone, the old man studied the gleam of the fire on the floor. It faded and brightened in the way of lightning at the horizon's edge.

When Nora returned, the strapping grenadier of a girl was blushing and giggling. The pig-buyers had been humorous. "I moind the toime—" began the man sorrowfully. "I moind the toime whin yea was a wee bit of a girrl, Nora, an' wouldn't be havin' words wid min loike thim buyers."

"I moind the toime whin yea could attind to your own affairs, ye ould skileton," said the girl promptly. He made a gesture, which may have expressed his stirring grief at the levity of the new generation, and then lapsed into another stillness.

The girl, a giantess, carrying, lifting, pushing, an incarnation of dauntless labour, changing the look of the whole kitchen with a moment's manipulation of her great arms, did not heed the old man for a long time. When she finally glanced toward him, she saw that he was sunk forward with his grey face on his arms. A growl of heavy breathing ascended. He was asleep.

She marched to him and put both hands to his collar. Despite his feeble and dreamy protestations, she dragged him out from behind the table and across the floor. She opened the door and thrust him into the night.

II. — BALLYDEHOB

The illimitable inventive incapacity of the excursion companies has made many circular paths throughout Ireland, and on these well-pounded roads the guardians of the touring public may be seen drilling the little travellers in squads. To rise in rebellion, to face the superior clerk in his bureau, to endure his smile of pity and derision, and finally to wring freedom from him, is as difficult in some parts of Ireland as it is in all parts of Switzerland. To see the tourists chained in gangs and taken to see the Lakes of Killarney is a sad spectacle, because these people believe that they are learning Ireland, even as men believe that they are studying America when they contemplate the Niagara Falls.

But afterwards, if one escapes, one can go forth, unguided, untaught and alone, and look at Ireland. The joys of the pig-market, the delirium of a little tap-room filled with brogue, the fierce excitement of viewing the Royal Irish Constabulary fishing for trout, the whole quaint and primitive machinery of the peasant life—its melancholy, its sunshine, its humour—all this is then the property of the man who breaks like a Texan steer out of the pens and corrals of the tourist agencies. For what syndicate of maiden ladies—it is these who masquerade as tourist agencies—what syndicate of maiden ladies knows of the existence, for instance, of Ballydehob?

One has a sense of disclosure at writing the name of Ballydehob. It was really a valuable secret. There is in Ballydehob not one thing that is commonly pointed out to the stranger as a thing worthy of a half-tone reproduction in a book. There is no cascade, no peak, no lake, no guide with a fund of useless information, no gamins practised in the seduction of tourists. It is not an exhibit, an entry for a prize, like a heap of melons or cow. It is simply an Irish village wherein live some three hundred Irish and four constables.

If one or two prayer-towers spindled above Ballydehob it would be a perfect Turkish village. The red tiles and red bricks of England do not appear at all. The houses are low, with soiled white walls. The doors open abruptly upon dark old rooms. Here and there in the street is some crude cobbling done with round stones taken from the bed of a brook. At times there is a great deal of mud. Chickens depredate warily about the doorsteps, and intent pigs emerge for plunder from the alleys. It is unavoidable to admit that many people would consider

Ballydehob quite too grimy.

Nobody lives here that has money. The average English tradesman with his back-breaking respect for this class, his reflex contempt for that class, his reverence for the tin gods, could here be a commercial lord and bully the people in one or two ways, until they were thrown back upon the defence which is always near them, the ability to cut his skin into strips with a wit that would be a foreign tongue to him. For amid his wrongs and his rights and his failures—his colossal failures—the Irishman retains this delicate blade for his enemies, for his friends, for himself, the ancestral dagger of fast sharp speaking from fast sharp seeing—an inheritance which could move the world. And the Royal Irish Constabulary fished for trout in the adjacent streams.

Mrs. Kearney keeps the hotel. In Ireland male innkeepers die young. Apparently they succumb to conviviality when it is presented to them in the guise of a business duty. Naturally honest, temperate men, their consciences are lulled to false security by this idea of hard drinking being necessary to the successful keeping of a public-house. It is very terrible.

But they invariably leave behind them capable widows, women who do not recognise conviviality as a business obligation. And so all through Ireland one finds these brisk widows keeping hotels with a precision that is almost military.

In Kearney's there is always a wonderful collection of old women, bent figures shrouded in shawls who reach up scrawny fingers to take their little purchases from Mary Agnes, who presides sometimes at the bar, but more often at the shop that fronts it in the same room. In the gloom of a late afternoon these old women are as mystic as the swinging, chanting witches on a dark stage when the thunder-drum rolls and the lightning flashes by schedule. When a grey rain sweeps through the narrow street of Ballydehob, and makes heavy shadows in Kearney's tap-room, these old creatures, with their high mournful voices, and the mystery of their shawls, their moans and aged mutterings when they are obliged to take a step, raise the dead superstitions from the bottom of a man's mind.

"My boy," remarked my London friend cheerfully, "these might have furnished sons to be Aldermen or Congressmen in the great city of New York."

"Aldermen or Congressmen of the great city of New York always take care of their mothers," I answered meekly.

On a barrel, over in a corner, sat a yellow-bearded Irish farmer in tattered clothes who wished to exchange views on the Armenian massacres. He had much information and a number of theories in regard to them. He also advanced the opinion that the chief political aim of Russia at present is in the direction of China, and that it behoved other Powers to keep an eye on her. He thought the revolutionists in Cuba would never accept autonomy at the hands of Spain. His pipe glowed comfortably from his corner; waving the tuppenny glass of stout in the air, he discoursed on the business of the remote ends of the earth with the glibness of a fourth secretary of Legation. Here was a little farmer, digging betimes in a forlorn patch of wet ground, a man to whom a sudden two shillings would appear as a miracle, a ragged, unkempt peasant, whose mind roamed the world like the soul of a lost diplomat. This unschooled man believed that the earth was a sphere inhabited by men that are alike in the essentials, different in the manners, the little manners, which are accounted of such great importance by the emaciated. He was to a degree capable of knowing that he lived on a sphere and not on the apex of a triangle.

And yet, when the talk had turned another corner, he confidently assured the assembled company that a hair from a horse's tail when thrown in a brook would turn shortly to an eel.

III.—THE ROYAL IRISH CONSTABULARY

The newspapers called it a Veritable Arsenal. There was a description of how the sergeant of Constabulary had bent an ear to receive whispered information of the concealed arms, and had then marched his men swiftly and by night to surround a certain house. The search elicited a double-barrelled breech-loading shot-gun, some empty shells, powder, shot, and a loading machine. The point of it was that some of the Irish papers called it a Veritable Arsenal, and appeared to congratulate the Government upon having strangled another unhappy rebellion in its nest. They floundered and misnamed and mis-reasoned, and made a spectacle of the great modern craft of journalism, until the affair of this poor poacher was too absurd to be pitiable, and Englishmen over their coffee next morning must have almost believed that the prompt action of the Constabulary had quelled a rising. Thus it is that the Irish fight the Irish.

One cannot look Ireland straight in the face without seeing a great many constables. The country is dotted with little garrisons. It must have been said a thousand times that there is an absolute military occupation. The fact is too plain.

The constable himself becomes a figure interesting in its isolation. He has in most cases a social position which is somewhat analogous to that of a Turk in Thessaly. But then, in the same way, the Turk has the Turkish army. He can have battalions as companions and make the acquaintance of brigades. The constable has the Constabulary, it is true; but to be cooped with three or four others in a small white-washed iron-bound house on some bleak country side is not an exact parallel to the Thessalian situation. It looks to be a life that is infinitely lonely, ascetic, and barren. Two keepers of a lighthouse at a bitter end of land in a remote sea will, if they are properly let alone, make a murder in time. Five constables imprisoned 'mid a folk that will not turn a face toward them, five constables planted in a populated silence, may develop an acute and vivid economy, dwell in scowling dislike. A religious asylum in a snow-buried mountain pass will breed conspiring monks. A separated people will beget an egotism that is almost titanic. A world floating distinctly in space will call itself the only world. The progression is perfect.

But the constables take the second degree. They are next to the lighthouse keepers. The national custom of meeting stranger and friend alike on the road with a cheery greeting like "God save you" is too kindly and human a habit not to be missed. But all through the South of Ireland one sees the peasant turn his eyes pretentiously to the side of the road at the passing of the constable. It seemed to be generally understood that to note the presence of a constable was to make a conventional error. None looked, nodded, or gave sign. There was a line drawn so sternly that it reared like a fence. Of course, any police force in any part of the world can gather at its heels a riff-raff of people, fawning always on a hand licensed to strike that would be larger than the army of the Potomac, but of these one ordinarily sees little. The mass of the Irish strictly obey the stern tenet. One hears often of the ostracism or other punishment that befell some girl who was caught flirting with a constable.

Naturally the constable retreats to his pride. He is commonly a soldierly-looking chap, straight, lean, long-strided, well set-up. His little saucer of a forage cap sits obediently on his ear, as it does for the British soldier. He swings a little cane. He takes his medicine with a calm and hard face, and evidently stares full into every eye. But it is singular to find in the situation of the Royal Irish Constabulary the quality of pathos.

It is not known if these places in the South of Ireland are called disturbed districts. Over them hangs the peace of Surrey, but the word disturbance has an elastic arrangement by which it can be made to cover anything. All of the villages visited garrisoned from four to ten men. They lived comfortably in their white houses, strolled in pairs over the country roads, picked blackberries, and fished for trout. If at some time there came a crisis, one man was more than enough to surround it. The remaining nine add dignity to the scene. The crisis chiefly consisted of occasional drunken men who were unable to understand the local geography on Saturday nights.

The note continually struck was that each group of constables lived on a little social island, and there was no boat to take them off. There has been no such marooning since the days of the pirates. The sequestration must be complete when a man with a dinky little cap on his ear is not allowed to talk to the girls.

But they fish for trout. Isaac Walton is the father of the Royal Irish Constabulary. They could be seen on any fine day whipping the streams from source to mouth. There was one venerable sergeant who made a rod less than a yard long. With a line of about the same length attached to this rod, he hunted the gorse-hung banks of the little streams in the hills. An eight-inch ribbon of water lined with masses of heather and gorse will be accounted contemptible by a fisherman with an ordinary rod. But it was the pleasure of the sergeant to lay on his stomach at the side of such a stream and carefully, inch by inch, scout his hook through the pools. He probably caught more trout than any three men in county Cork. He fished more than any twelve men in the county Cork. Some people had never seen him in any other posture but that of crowding forward on his stomach to peer into a pool. They did not believe the rumour that he sometimes stood or walked like a human.

IV. — A FISHING VILLAGE

The brook curved down over the rocks, innocent and white, until it faced a little strand of smooth gravel and flat stones. It turned then to the left, and thereafter its guilty current was tinged with the pink of diluted blood. Boulders standing neck-deep in the water were rimmed with red; they wore bloody collars whose tops marked the supreme instant of some tragic movement of the stream. In the pale green shallows of the bay's edge, the outward flow from the criminal little brook was as eloquently marked as if a long crimson carpet had been laid upon the waters. The scene of the carnage was the strand of smooth gravel and flat stones, and the fruit of the carnage was cleaned mackerel.

Far to the south, where the slate of the sea and the grey of the sky wove together, could be seen Fastnet Rock, a mere button on the moving, shimmering cloth, while a liner, no larger than a needle, spun a thread of smoke aslant. The gulls swept screaming along the dull line of the other shore of roaring Water Bay, and near the mouth of the brook circled among the fishing boats that lay at anchor, their brown, leathery sails idle and straight. The wheeling, shrieking tumultuous birds stared with their hideous unblinking eyes at the Capers—men from Cape Clear—who prowled to and fro on the decks amid shouts and the creak of the tackle. Shoreward, a little shrivelled man, overcome by a profound melancholy, fished hopelessly from the end of the pier. Back of him, on a hillside, sat a white village, nestled among more trees than is common in this part of Southern Ireland.

A dinghy sculled by a youth in a blue jersey wobbled rapidly past the pier-head and stopped at the foot of the moss-green, dank, stone steps, where the waves were making slow but regular leaps to mount higher, and then falling back gurgling, choking, and waving the long, dark seaweeds. The melancholy fisherman walked over to the top of the steps. The young man was fastening the painter of his boat in an iron ring. In the dinghy were three round baskets heaped high with mackerel. They glittered like masses of new silver coin at times, and then other lights of faint carmine and peacock blue would chase across the sides of the fish in a radiance that was finer than silver.

The melancholy fisherman looked at this wealth. He shook his head mournfully. "Ah, now, Denny. This would not be a very good kill."

The young man snorted indignantly at his fellow-townsman. "This will be th' bist kill th' year, Mickey. Go along now."

The melancholy old man became immersed in deeper gloom. "Shure I have been in th' way of seein' miny a grand day whin th' fish was runnin' sthrong in these wathers, but there will be no more big kills here. No more. No more." At the last his voice was only a dismal croak.

"Come along outa that now, Mickey," cried the youth impatiently. "Come away wid you."

"All gone now. A-ll go-o-ne now!" The old man wagged his grey head, and, standing over the baskets of fishes, groaned as Mordecai groaned for his people.

"'Tis you would be cryin' out, Mickey, whativer," said the youth with scorn. He was giving his basket into the hands of five incompetent but jovial little boys to carry to a waiting donkey cart.

"An' why should I not?" said the old man sternly. "Me—in want—"

As the youth swung his boat swiftly out toward an anchored smack, he made answer in a softer tone. "Shure, if yez got for th' askin', 'tis you, Mickey, that would niver be in want." The melancholy old man returned to his line. And the only moral in this incident is that the young man is the type that America procures from Ireland, and the old man is one of the home types, bent, pallid, hungry, disheartened, with a vision that magnifies with a microscope glance any fly-wing of misfortune, and heroically and conscientiously invents disasters for the future. Usually the thing that remains to one of this type is a sympathy as quick and acute for others as is his pity for himself.

The donkey with his cart-load of gleaming fish, and escorted by the whooping and laughing boys, galloped along the quay and up a street of the village until he was turned off at the gravelly strand, at the point where the colour of the brook was changing. Here twenty people of both sexes and all ages were preparing the fish for market. The mackerel, beautiful as fire-etched salvers, first were passed to a long table, around which worked as many women as could have elbow room. Each one could clean a fish with two motions of the knife. Then the washers, men who stood over the troughs filled with running water from the brook, soused the fish until the outlet became a sinister element that in an instant changed the brook from a happy thing of gorse and heather of the hills to an evil stream, sullen and reddened. After being washed, the fish were carried to a group of girls with knives, who made the cuts that enabled each fish to flatten out in the manner known of the breakfast table. And after the girls came the men and boys, who rubbed each fish thoroughly with great handfuls of coarse salt, which was whiter than snow, and shone in the daylight from a multitude of gleaming points, diamond-like. Last came the packers, drilled in the art of getting neither too few nor too many mackerel into a barrel, sprinkling constantly prodigal layers of brilliant salt. There were many intermediate corps of boys and girls carrying fish from point to point, and sometimes building them in stacks convenient to the hands of the more important labourers.

A vast tree hung its branches over the place. The leaves made a shadow that was religious in its effect, as if the spot was a chapel consecrated to labour. There was a hush upon the devotees. The women at the large table worked intently, steadfastly, with bowed heads. Their old petticoats were tucked high, showing the coarse brogans which they wore—and the visible ankles were proportioned to the brogans as the diameter of a straw is to that of a half-crown. The national red under-petticoat was a fundamental part of the scene.

Just over the wall, in the sloping street, could be seen the bejerseyed Capers, brawny, and with shocks of yellow beard. They paced slowly to and fro amid the geese and children. They, too, spoke little, even to each other; they smoked short pipes in saturnine dignity and silence. It was the fish. They who go with nets upon the reeling sea grow still with the mystery and solemnity of the trade. It was Brittany; the first respectable catch of the year had changed this garrulous Irish hamlet into a hamlet of Brittany.

The Capers were waiting for high tide. It had seemed for a long time that, for the south of Ireland, the mackerel had fled in company with potato; but here, at any rate, was a temporary success, and the occasion was momentous. A strolling Caper took his pipe and pointed with the stem out upon the bay. There was little wind, but an ambitious skipper had raised his anchor, and the craft, her strained brown sails idly swinging, was drifting away on the first oily turn of the tide.

On the top of the pier the figure of the melancholy old man was portrayed upon the polished water. He was still dangling his line hopelessly. He gazed down into the misty water. Once he stirred and murmured: "Bad luck to thim." Otherwise he seemed to remain motionless for hours. One by one the fishing-boats floated away. The brook changed its colour, and in the dusk showed a tumble of pearly white among the rocks.

A cold night wind, sweeping transversely across the pier, awakened perhaps the rheumatism in the old man's bones. He arose and, mumbling and grumbling, began to wind his line. The waves were lashing the stones. He moved off towards the intense darkness of the village streets.

SULLIVAN COUNTY SKETCHES

FOUR MEN IN A CAVE

Likewise Four Queens, and a Sullivan County Hermit.

The moon rested for a moment on the top of a tall pine on a hill.

The little man was standing in front of the campfire making orations to his companions.

"We can tell a great tale when we get back to the city if we investigate this thing," said he, in conclusion.

They were won.

The little man was determined to explore a cave, because its black mouth had gaped at him. The four men took lighted pine-knot and clambered over boulders down a hill. In a thicket on the mountainside lay a little tilted hole. At its side they halted.

"Well?" said the little man.

They fought for last place and the little man was overwhelmed. He tried to struggle from under by crying that if the fat, pudgy man came after, he would be corked. But he finally administered a cursing over his shoulder and crawled into the hole. His companions gingerly followed.

A passage, the floor of damp clay and pebbles, the walls slimy, green-mossed, and dripping, sloped downward. In the cave atmosphere the torches became studies in red blaze and black smoke.

"Ho!" cried the little man, stifled and bedraggled, "let's go back." His companions were not brave. They were last. The next one to the little man pushed him on, so the little man said sulphurous words and cautiously continued his crawl.

Things that hung seemed to be on the wet, uneven ceiling, ready to drop upon the men's bare necks. Under their hands the clammy floor seemed alive and writhing. When the little man endeavoured to stand erect the ceiling forced him down. Knobs and points came out and punched him. His clothes were wet and mud-covered, and his eyes, nearly blinded by smoke, tried to pierce the darkness always before his torch.

"Oh, I say, you fellows, let's go back," cried he. At that moment he caught the gleam of trembling light in the blurred shadows before him.

"Ho!" he said, "here's another way out."

The passage turned abruptly. The little man put one hand around the corner, but it touched nothing. He investigated and discovered that the little corridor took a sudden dip down a hill. At the bottom shone a yellow light.

The little man wriggled painfully about, and descended feet in advance. The others followed his plan. All picked their way with anxious care. The traitorous rocks rolled from beneath the little man's feet and roared thunderously below him. Lesser stone, loosened by the men above him, hit him on the back. He gained seemingly firm foothold, and, turning half-way about, swore redly at his companions for dolts and careless fools. The pudgy man sat, puffing and perspiring, high in the rear of the procession. The fumes and smoke from four pine-knots were in his blood. Cinders and sparks lay thick in his eyes and hair. The pause of the little man angered him.

"Go on, you fool," he shouted. "Poor, painted man, you are afraid."

"Ho!" said the little man. "Come down here and go on yourself, imbecile!"

The pudgy man vibrated with passion. He leaned downward. "Idiot—!"

He was interrupted by one of his feet which flew out and crashed into the man in front of and below. It is not well to quarrel upon a slippery incline, when the unknown is below. The fat man, having lost the support of one pillar-like foot, lurched forward. His body smote the next man, who hurtled into the next man. Then they all fell upon the cursing little man.

They slid in a body down over the slippery, slimy floor of the passage. The stone avenue must have wibble-wobbled with the rush of this ball of tangled men and strangled cries. The torches went out with the combined assault upon the little man. The adventurers whirled to the unknown in darkness. The little man felt that he was pitching to death, but even in his convolutions he bit and scratched at his companions, for he was satisfied that it was their fault. The swirling mass went some twenty feet, and lit upon a level, dry place in a strong, yellow light of candles. It dissolved and became eyes.

The four men lay in a heap upon the floor of a grey chamber. A small fire smouldered in the corner, the smoke disappearing in a crack. In another corner was a bed of faded hemlock boughs and two blankets. Cooking utensils and clothes lay about, with boxes and a barrel.

Of these things the four men took small cognisance. The pudgy man did not curse the little man, nor did the little swear, in the abstract. Eight widened eyes were fixed upon the centre of the room of rocks.

A great, grey stone, cut squarely, like an altar, sat in the middle of the floor. Over it burned three candles, in swaying tin cups hung from the ceiling. Before it, with what seemed to be a small volume clasped in his yellow fingers, stood a man. He was an infinitely sallow person in the brown-checked shirt of the ploughs and cows. The rest of his apparel was boots. A long grey beard dangled from his chin. He fixed glinting, fiery eyes upon the heap of men, and remained motionless. Fascinated, their tongues cleaving, their blood cold, they arose to their feet. The gleaming glance of the recluse swept slowly over the group until it found the face of the little man. There it stayed and burned.

The little man shrivelled and crumpled as the dried leaf under the glass.

Finally, the recluse slowly, deeply spoke. It was a true voice from a cave, cold, solemn, and damp.

"It's your ante," he said.

"What?" said the little man.

The hermit tilted his beard and laughed a laugh that was either the chatter of a banshee in a storm or the rattle of pebbles in a tin box. His visitors' flesh seemed ready to drop from their bones.

They huddled together and cast fearful eyes over their shoulders. They whispered.

"A vampire!" said one.

"A ghoul!" said another.

"A Druid before the sacrifice," murmured another.

"The shade of an Aztec witch doctor," said the little man.

As they looked, the inscrutable face underwent a change. It became a livid background for his eyes, which blazed at the little man like impassioned carbuncles. His voice arose to a howl of ferocity. "It's your ante!" With a panther-like motion he drew a long, thin knife and advanced, stooping. Two cadaverous hounds came from nowhere, and, scowling and growling, made desperate feints at the little man's legs. His quaking companions pushed him forward.

Tremblingly he put his hand to his pocket.

"How much?" he said, with a shivering look at the knife that glittered.

The carbuncles faded.

"Three dollars," said the hermit, in sepulchral tones which rang against the walls and among the passages, awakening long-dead spirits with voices. The shaking little man took a roll of bills from a pocket and placed "three ones" upon the altar-like stone. The recluse looked at the little volume with reverence in his eyes. It was a pack of playing cards.

Under the three swinging candles, upon the altar-like stone, the grey beard and the agonised little man played at poker. The three other men crouched in a corner, and stared with eyes that gleamed with terror. Before them sat the cadaverous hounds licking their red lips. The candles burned low, and began to flicker. The fire in the corner expired.

Finally, the game came to a point where the little man laid down his hand and quavered: "I can't call you this time, sir. I'm dead broke."

"What?" shrieked the recluse. "Not call me! Villain! Dastard! Cur! I have four queens, miscreant." His voice grew so mighty that it could not fit his throat. He choked, wrestling with his lungs for a moment. Then the power of his body was concentrated in a word: "Go!"

He pointed a quivering, yellow finger at a wide crack in the rock. The little man threw himself at it with a howl. His erstwhile frozen companions felt their blood throb again. With great bounds they plunged after the little man. A minute of scrambling, falling, and pushing brought them to open air. They climbed the distance to their camp in furious springs.

The sky in the east was a lurid yellow. In the west the footprints of departing night lay on the pine trees. In front of their replenished camp fire sat John Willerkins, the guide.

"Hello!" he shouted at their approach. "Be you fellers ready to go deer huntin'?"

Without replying, they stopped and debated among themselves in whispers.

Finally, the pudgy man came forward.

"John," he inquired, "do you know anything peculiar about this cave below here?"

"Yes," said Willerkins at once; "Tom Gardner."

"What?" said the pudgy man.

"Tom Gardner."

"How's that?"

"Well, you see," said Willerkins slowly, as he took dignified pulls at his pipe, "Tom Gardner was once a fambly man, who lived in these here parts on a nice leetle farm. He uster go away to the city orften, and one time he got a-gamblin' in one of them there dens. He wentter the dickens right quick then. At last he kum home one time and tol' his folks he had up and sold the farm and all he had in the worl'. His leetle wife she died then. Tom he went crazy, and soon after—"

The narrative was interrupted by the little man, who became possessed of devils.

"I wouldn't give a cuss if he had left me 'nough money to get home on the doggoned, grey-haired red pirate," he shrilled, in a seething sentence. The pudgy man gazed at the little man calmly and sneeringly.

"Oh, well," he said, "we can tell a great tale when we get back to the city after having investigated this thing."

"Go to the devil," replied the little man.

THE MESMERIC MOUNTAIN

A Tale of Sullivan County.

On the brow of a pine-plumed hillock there sat a little man with his back against a tree. A venerable pipe hung from his mouth, and smoke-wreaths curled slowly skyward. He was muttering to himself with his eyes fixed on an irregular black opening in the green wall of forest at the foot of the hill. Two vague waggon ruts led into the shadows. The little man took his pipe in his hands and addressed the listening pines.

"I wonder what the devil it leads to," said he.

A grey, fat rabbit came lazily from a thicket and sat in the opening. Softly stroking his stomach with his paw, he looked at the little man in a thoughtful manner. The little man threw a stone, and the rabbit blinked and ran through an opening. Green, shadowy portals seemed to close behind him.

The little man started. "He's gone down that roadway," he said, with ecstatic mystery to the pines. He sat a long time and contemplated the door to the forest. Finally, he arose, and awakening his limbs, started away. But he stopped and looked back.

"I can't imagine what it leads to," muttered he. He trudged over the brown mats of pine needles, to where, in a fringe of laurel, a tent was pitched, and merry flames caroused about some logs. A pudgy man was fuming over a collection of tin dishes. He came forward and waved a plate furiously in the little man's face.

"I've washed the dishes for three days. What do you think I am—"

He ended a red oration with a roar: "Damned if I do it any more."

The little man gazed dim-eyed away. "I've been wonderin' what it leads to."

"What?"

"That road out yonder. I've been wonderin' what it leads to. Maybe, some discovery or something," said the little man.

The pudgy man laughed. "You're an idiot. It leads to ol' Jim Boyd's over on the Lumberland Pike."

"Ho!" said the little man, "I don't believe that."

The pudgy man swore. "Fool, what does it lead to, then?"

"I don't know just what, but I'm sure it leads to something great or something. It looks like it."

While the pudgy man was cursing, two more men came from

obscurity with fish dangling from birch twigs. The pudgy man made an obviously herculean struggle and a meal was prepared. As he was drinking his cup of coffee, he suddenly spilled it and swore. The little man was wandering off.

"He's gone to look at that hole," cried the pudgy man.

The little man went to the edge of the pine-plumed hillock, and, sitting down, began to make smoke and regard the door to the forest. There was stillness for an hour. Compact clouds hung unstirred in the sky. The pines stood motionless, and pondering.

Suddenly the little man slapped his knee and bit his tongue. He stood up and determinedly filled his pipe, rolling his eye over the bowl to the doorway. Keeping his eyes fixed he slid dangerously to the foot of the hillock and walked down the waggon ruts. A moment later he passed from the noise of the sunshine to the gloom of the woods.

The green portals closed, shutting out live things. The little man trudged on alone.

Tall tangled grass grew in the roadway, and the trees bended obstructing branches. The little man followed on over pine-clothed ridges and down through water-soaked swales. His shoes were cut by rocks of the mountains, and he sank ankle-deep in mud and moss of swamps. A curve just ahead lured him miles.

Finally, as he wended the side of a ridge, the road disappeared from beneath his feet. He battled with hordes of ignorant bushes on his way to knolls and solitary trees which invited him. Once he came to a tall, bearded pine. He climbed it, and perceived in the distance a peak. He uttered an ejaculation and fell out.

He scrambled to his feet, and said: "That's Jones's Mountain, I guess. It's about six miles from our camp as the crow flies."

He changed his course away from the mountain, and attacked the bushes again. He climbed over great logs, golden-brown in decay, and was opposed by thickets of dark-green laurel. A brook slid through the ooze of a swamp; cedars and hemlocks hung their sprays to the edges of pools.

The little man began to stagger in his walk. After a time he stopped and mopped his brow.

"My legs are about to shrivel up and drop off," he said.... "Still if I keep on in this direction, I am safe to strike the Lumberland Pike before sundown."

He dived at a clump of tag-alders, and emerging, confronted Jones's Mountain.

The wanderer sat down in a clear place and fixed his eyes on the summit. His mouth opened widely, and his body swayed at times. The little man and the peak stared in silence.

A lazy lake lay asleep near the foot of the mountain. In its bed of water-grass some frogs leered at the sky and crooned. The sun sank in red silence, and the shadows of the pines grew formidable. The expectant hush of evening, as if some thing were going to sing a hymn, fell upon the peak and the little man.

A leaping pickerel off on the water created a silver circle that was lost in black shadows. The little man shook himself and started to his feet, crying: "For the love of Mike, there's eyes in this mountain! I feel 'em! Eyes!"

He fell on his face.

When he looked again, he immediately sprang erect and ran.

"It's comin'!"

The mountain was approaching.

The little man scurried, sobbing through the thick growth. He felt his brain turning to water. He vanquished brambles with mighty bounds.

But after a time he came again to the foot of the mountain.

"God!" he howled, "it's been follerin' me." He grovelled.

Casting his eyes upward made circles swirl in his blood.

"I'm shackled I guess," he moaned. As he felt the heel of the mountain about crush his head, he sprang again to his feet. He grasped a handful of small stones and hurled them.

"Damn you," he shrieked loudly. The pebbles rang against the face of the mountain.

The little man then made an attack. He climbed with hands and feet wildly. Brambles forced him back and stones slid from beneath his feet. The peak swayed and tottered, and was ever about to smite with a granite arm. The summit was a blaze of red wrath.

But the little man at last reached the top. Immediately he swaggered with valour to the edge of the cliff. His hands were scornfully in his pockets.

He gazed at the western horizon, edged sharply against a yellow sky. "Ho!" he said. "There's Boyd's house and the Lumberland Pike."

The mountain under his feet was motionless.

MISCELLANEOUS

THE SQUIRE'S MADNESS

Linton was in his study remote from the interference of domestic sounds. He was writing verses. He was not a poet in the strict sense of the word, because he had eight hundred a year and a manor-house in Sussex. But he was devoted, at any rate, and no happiness was for him equal to the happiness of an imprisonment in this lonely study. His place had been a semi-fortified house in the good days when every gentleman was either abroad with a bared sword hunting his neighbours or behind oak-and-iron doors and three-feet walls while his neighbours hunted him. But in the life of Linton it may be said that the only part of the house which remained true to the idea of fortification was the study, which was free only to Linton's wife and certain terriers. The necessary appearance from time to time of a servant always grated upon Linton as much as if from time to time somebody had in the most well-bred way flung a brick through the little panes of his window.

This window looked forth upon a wide valley of hop-fields and sheep-pastures, dipping and rising this way and that way, but always a valley until it reached a high far away ridge upon which stood the upright figure of a windmill, usually making rapid gestures as if it were an excited sentry warning the old grey house of coming danger. A little to the right, on a knoll, red chimneys and parts of red-tiled roofs appeared among trees, and the venerable square tower of the village church rose above them.

For ten years Linton had left vacant Oldrestham Hall, and when at last it became known that he and his wife were to return from an incomprehensible wandering, the village, which for four centuries had turned a feudal eye toward the Hall, was wrung with a prospect of change, a proper change. The great family pew in Oldrestham church would be occupied each Sunday morning by a fat, happy-faced, utterly squire-looking man, who would be dutifully at his post when the parish was stirred by a subscription list. Then, for the first time in many years, the hunters would ride in the early morning merrily out through the park, and there would be also shooting parties, and in the summer groups of charming ladies would be seen walking the terrace, laughing on the lawns and in the rose gardens. The village expected to have the perfectly legal and fascinating privilege of discussing the performances of its own gentry.

The first intimation of calamity was in the news that Linton had rented all the shooting. This prepared the people for the blow, and it fell when they sighted the master of Oldrestham Hall. The older villagers remembered then that there had been nothing in the youthful Linton to promise a fat, happy-faced, dignified, hunting, shooting over-lord, but still they could not but resent the appearance of the new squire. There was no conceivable reason for his looking like a gaunt ascetic, who would surprise nobody if he borrowed a sixpence from the first yokel he met in the lanes.

Linton was in truth three inches more than six feet in height, but he had bowed himself to five feet eleven inches. His hair shocked out in front like hay, and under it were two spectacled eyes which never seemed to regard anything with particular attention. His face was pale and full of hollows, and the mouth apparently had no expression save a chronic pout of the under-lip. His hands were large and raw boned but uncannily white. His whole bent body was thin as that of a man from a long sick-bed, and all was finished by two feet which for size could not be matched in the county.

He was very awkward, but apparently it was not so much a physical characteristic as it was a mental inability to consider where he was going or what he was doing. For instance, when passing through a gate it was not uncommon for him to knock his side viciously against one of the posts. This was because he dreamed almost always, and if there had been forty gates in a row he would not then have noted them more than he did the one. As far as the villagers and farmers were concerned he never came out of this manner save in wide-apart cases, when he had forced upon him either some great exhibition of stupidity or some faint indication of double-dealing, and then this smouldering man flared out encrimsoning his immediate surrounding with a brief fire of ancestral anger. But the lapse back to indifference was more surprising. It was far quicker than the flare in the beginning. His feeling was suddenly ashes at the moment when one was certain it would lick the sky.

Some of the villagers asserted that he was mad. They argued it long in the manner of their kind, repeating, repeating, and repeating, and when an opinion confusingly rational appeared they merely shook their heads in pig-like obstinacy. Anyhow, it was historically clear that no such squire had before been in the line of Lintons of Oldrestham Hall, and the present incumbent was a shock.

The servants at the Hall—notably those who lived in the country-side—came in for a lot of questioning, and none were found too backward in explaining many things which they themselves did not understand. The household was most irregular. They all confessed that it was really so uncustomary that they did not know but what they would have to give notice. The master was probably the most extraordinary man in the whole world. The butler said that Linton would drink beer with his meals day in and day out like any carrier resting at a pot-house. It didn't matter even if the meal were dinner. Then suddenly he would change his tastes to the most valuable wines, and in ten days would make the wine-cellar look as if it had been wrecked at sea. What was to be done with a gentleman of that kind? The butler said for his part he wanted a master with habits, and he protested that Linton did not have a habit to his name, at least, none that could properly be called a habit.

Barring the cook, the entire establishment agreed categorically with the butler. The cook didn't agree because she was a very good cook indeed, which she thought entitled her to be extremely aloof from the other servants' hall opinions.

As for the squire's lady, they described her as being not much different from the master. At least she gave support to his most unusual manner of life, and evidently believed that whatever he chose to do was quite correct.

Linton had written—

> *"The garlands of her hair are snakes,*
> *Black and bitter are her hating eyes,*
> *A cry the windy death-hall makes,*
> *O, love, deliver us.*
> *The flung cup rolls to her sandal's tip,*
> *His arm—"*

Whereupon his thought fumed over the next two lines, coursing like greyhounds, after a fugitive vision of a writhening lover with the foam of poison on his lips dying at the feet of the woman. Linton arose, lit a cigarette, placed it on the window ledge, took another cigarette, looked blindly for the matches, thrust a spiral of paper into the flame of the log fire, lit the second cigarette, placed it toppling on a book and began a search among his pipes for one that would draw well. He gazed at his pictures, at the books on the shelves, out at the green spread of country-side, all without taking mental note. At the window ledge he came upon the first cigarette, and in a matter of fact way he returned it to his lips, having forgotten that he had forgotten it.

There was a sound of steps on the stone floor of the quaint little passage that led down to his study, and turning from the window he saw that his wife had entered the room and was looking at him strangely.

"Jack," she said in a low voice, "what is the matter?"

His eyes were burning out from under his shock of hair with a fierceness that belied his feeling of simple surprise. "Nothing is the matter," he answered. "Why do you ask?"

She seemed immensely concerned, but she was visibly endeavouring to hide her concern as well as to abate it.

"I—I thought you acted queerly."

He answered: "Why no. I'm not acting queerly. On the contrary," he added smiling, "I'm in one of my most rational moods."

Her look of alarm did not subside. She continued to regard him with the same stare. She was silent for a time and did not move. His own thoughts had quite returned to a contemplation of a poisoned lover, and he did not note the manner of his wife. Suddenly she came to him, and laying a hand on his arm said, "Jack, you are ill?"

"Why no, dear," he said with a first impatience, "I'm not ill at all. I never felt better in my life." And his mind beleaguered by this pointless talk strove to break through to its old contemplation of the poisoned lover. "Hear what I have written." Then he read—

> *"The garlands of her hair are snakes,*
> *Black and bitter are her hating eyes,*
> *A cry the windy death-hall makes,*
> *O, love, deliver us.*
> *The flung cup rolls to her sandal's tip,*
> *His arm—"*

Linton said: "I can't seem to get the lines to describe the man who is dying of the poison on the floor before her. Really I'm having a time with it. What a bore. Sometimes I can write like mad and other times I don't seem to have an intelligent idea in my head."

He felt his wife's hand tighten on his arm and he looked into her face. It was so alight with horror that it brought him sharply out of his dreams. "Jack," she repeated tremulously, "you are ill."

He opened his eyes in wonder. "Ill! ill? No; not in the least!"

"Yes, you are ill. I can see it in your eyes. You—act so strangely."

"Act strangely? Why, my dear, what have I done? I feel quite well. Indeed, I was never more fit in my life."

As he spoke he threw himself into a large wing chair and looked up at his wife, who stood gazing at him from the other side of the black oak table upon which Linton wrote his verses.

"Jack, dear," she almost whispered, "I have noticed it for days," and she leaned across the table to look more intently into his face. "Yes, your eyes grow more fixed every day—you—you—your head, does it ache, dear?"

Linton arose from his chair and came around the big table toward his wife. As he approached her, an expression akin to terror crossed her face and she drew back as in fear, holding out both hands to ward him off.

He had been smiling in the manner of a man reassuring a frightened child, but at her shrinking from his outstretched hand he stopped in amazement. "Why, Grace, what is it? tell me."

She was glaring at him, her eyes wide with misery. Linton moved his left hand across his face, unconsciously trying to brush from it that which alarmed her.

"Oh, Jack, you must see some one; I am wretched about you. You are ill!"

"Why, my dear wife," he said, "I am quite, quite well; I am anxious to finish these verses but words won't come somehow, the man dying—"

"Yes, that is it, you cannot remember, you see that you cannot remember. You must see a doctor. We will go up to town at once," she answered quickly.

"'Tis true," he thought, "that my memory is not as good as it used to be. I cannot remember dates, and words won't fit in somehow. Perhaps I don't take enough exercise, dear; is that what worries you?" he asked.

"Yes, yes, dear, you do not go out enough," said his wife. "You cling to this room as the ivy clings to the walls—but we must go to London, you *must* see some one; promise me that you will go, that you will go immediately."

Again Linton saw his wife look at him as one looks at a creature of pity. The faint lines from her nose to the corners of her mouth deepened as if she were in physical pain; her eyes, open to their fullest extent, had in them the expression of a mother watching her dying babe. What was this strange wall that had suddenly raised itself between them? Was he ill? No; he never was in better health in his life. He found himself vainly searching for aches in his bones. Again he brushed away this thing which seemed to be upon his face. There must be something on my face, he thought, else why does she look at me with such hopeless despair in her eyes; these kindly eyes that had hitherto been so responsive to each glance of his own. *Why* did she think that he was ill? She who knew well his every mood. *Was he mad?* Did this thing of the poisoned cup that rolled to her sandal's tip—and her eyes, her hating eyes, mean that his—no, it could not be. He fumbled among the papers on the table for a cigarette. He could not find one. He walked to the huge fireplace and peered nearsightedly at the ashes on the hearth.

"What, what do you want, Jack? Be careful! The fire!" cried his wife.

"Why, I want a cigarette," he said.

She started, as if he had spoken roughly to her. "I will get you some, wait, sit quietly, I will bring you some," she replied as she hastened through the small passage-way up the stone steps that led from his study.

Linton stood with his back still bent, in the posture of a man picking something from the ground. He did not turn from the fireplace until the echo of his wife's foot-fall on the stone floors had died away. Then he straightened himself and said, "Well, I'm damned!" And Linton was not a man who swore.

* * * * * * *

A month later the Squire and his wife were on their way to London to consult the great brain specialist, Doctor Redmond. Linton now believed that "something" was wrong with him. His wife's anxiety, which she could no longer conceal, forced him to this conclusion; "something" was wrong. Until these few last weeks Linton's wife had managed her household with the care and wisdom of a Chatelaine of mediæval times. Each day was planned for certain duties in house or village. She had theories as to the management and education of the village children, and this work occupied much of her time. She was the antithesis of her husband. He, a weaver of dream-stories, she of that type of woman who has ideas of the emancipation of women and who believe the problem could be solved by training the minds of the next generation of mothers. Linton was not interested in these questions, but he would smile indulgently at his wife as she talked of the equality of mind of the sexes and the public part in the world's history which would be played by the women of the future.

There was no talk of this kind now. The household management fell into the hands of servants. Night and day his wife watched Linton. He would awaken in the night to find her face close to his own, her eyes burning with feverish anxiety.

"What is it, Grace?" he would cry, "have I said anything? What is the reason you watch me in this fashion, dear?"

And she would sob, "Jack, you are ill, dear, you are ill; we must go to town, we must, indeed."

Then he would soothe her with fond words and promise that he would go to London.

This present journey was the outcome of those weeks of watching and fear in Linton's wife's mind.

* * * * * * *

Linton's wife was trembling violently as he helped her down from the cab in front of Doctor Redmond's door. They had made an appointment, so that they were sure of little delay before the portentous interview.

A small page in blue livery opened the door and ushered them into a waiting-room. Mrs. Linton dropped heavily into a chair, looking with a frightened air from side to side and biting her under lip nervously. She was moaning half under her breath, "Oh, Jack, you are ill, you are ill."

A short stout man with clean-shaven face and scanty black hair entered the room. His nose was huge and misshapen and his mouth was a straight firm line. Overhanging black brows tried in vain to shadow the piercing dark eyes, that darted questioning looks at every one, seeming to search for hidden thoughts as a flash-light from the conning tower of a ship searches for the enemy in time of war.

He advanced toward Mrs. Linton with outstretched hand. "Mrs. Linton?" he said. "Ah!"

She almost jumped from her chair as he came near her, crying, "Oh, doctor, my husband is ill, very ill, very ill!"

Again Doctor Redmond with his eyes fixed upon her face ejaculated, "Ah!" Turning to Linton he said, "Please wait here, Squire; I will first talk to your wife. Will you step into my study, madam?" he said to Mrs. Linton, bowing courteously.

Linton's wife ran into the room which the doctor pointed toward as his study.

Linton waited. He moved softly about the room looking at the photographs of Greek ruins which adorned the walls. He stopped finally before a large picture of the Gate of Hadrian. He travelled once more into his dream country. His fancy painted in the figures of men and women who had passed through that gate. He had forgotten his fear of the blotting out of his mind that could conjure these glowing colours. He had forgotten himself.

From this dream he was recalled to the present by a hand being placed gently upon his arm. He half turned and saw the doctor regarding him with sympathetic eyes.

"Come, my dear sir, come into my study," said the doctor. "I have asked your wife to await us here." Linton then turned fully toward the centre of the room and found that his wife was seated quietly by a table. Doctor Redmond bowed low to Mrs. Linton as he passed her, and Linton waved his hand, smiled, and said, "Only a moment, dear." She did not reply. The door closed behind them.

"Be seated, my dear sir," said the doctor, drawing forward a chair, "be seated. I want to say something to you, but you must drink this first." He handed Linton a small glass of brandy.

Linton sat down, took the glass mechanically, and gulped the brandy in one great swallow. The doctor stood by the mantel and said slowly, "I rejoice to say to you, sir, that I have never met a man more sound mentally than yourself"—

Linton half started from his chair.

"Stop!" said the doctor, "I have not yet finished—but it is my painful duty to tell you the truth—It is your Wife who is Mad! Mad as a Hatter!"

A DESERTION

The yellow gas-light that came with an effect of difficulty through the dust-stained windows on either side of the door, gave strange hues to the faces and forms of the three women who stood gabbling in the hall-way of the tenement. They made rapid gestures, and in the background their enormous shadows mingled in terrific conflict.

"Aye, she ain't so good as he thinks she is, I'll bet. He can watch over 'er an' take care of 'er all he pleases, but when she wants t' fool 'im, she'll fool 'im. An' how does he know she ain't foolin' 'im now?"

"Oh, he thinks he's keepin' 'er from goin' t' th' bad, he does. Oh, yes. He ses she's too purty t' let run round alone. Too purty! Huh! My Sadie—"

"Well, he keeps a clost watch on 'er, you bet. O'ny las' week, she met my boy Tim on th' stairs, an' Tim hadn't said two words to 'er b'fore th' ol' man begin to holler. 'Dorter, dorter, come here, come here!'"

At this moment a young girl entered from the street, and it was evident from the injured expression suddenly assumed by the three gossipers that she had been the object of their discussion. She passed them with a slight nod, and they swung about into a row to stare after her.

On her way up the long flights the girl unfastened her veil. One could then clearly see the beauty of her eyes, but there was in them a certain furtiveness that came near to marring the effects. It was a peculiar fixture of gaze, brought from the street, as of one who there saw a succession of passing dangers with menaces aligned at every corner.

On the top floor, she pushed open a door and then paused on the threshold, confronting an interior that appeared black and flat like a curtain. Perhaps some girlish idea of hobgoblins assailed her then, for she called in a little breathless voice, "Daddie!"

There was no reply. The fire in the cooking-stove in the room crackled at spasmodic intervals. One lid was misplaced, and the girl could now see that this fact created a little flushed crescent upon the ceiling. Also, a series of tiny windows in the stove caused patches of red upon the floor. Otherwise, the room was heavily draped with shadows.

The girl called again, "Daddie!"

Yet there was no reply.

"Oh, Daddie!"

Presently she laughed as one familiar with the humours of an old man. "Oh, I guess yer cussin' mad about yer supper, dad," she said, and she almost entered the room, but suddenly faltered, overcome by a feminine instinct to fly from this black interior, peopled with imagined dangers.

Again she called, "Daddie!" Her voice had an accent of appeal. It was as if she knew she was foolish but yet felt obliged to insist upon being reassured. "Oh, daddie!"

Of a sudden a cry of relief, a feminine announcement that the stars still hung, burst from her. For, according to some mystic process, the smouldering coals of the fire went aflame with sudden, fierce brilliance, splashing parts of the walls, the floor, the crude furniture, with a hue of blood-red. And in the light of this dramatic outburst of light, the girl saw her father seated at a table with his back turned toward her.

She entered the room, then, with an aggrieved air, her logic evidently concluding that somebody was to blame for her nervous fright. "Oh, yer on'y sulkin' 'bout yer supper. I thought mebbe ye'd gone somewheres."

Her father made no reply. She went over to a shelf in the corner, and, taking a little lamp, she lit it and put it where it would give her light as she took off her hat and jacket in front of the tiny mirror. Presently, she began to bustle among the cooking utensils that were crowded into the sink, and as she worked she rattled talk at her father, apparently disdaining his mood.

"I'd 'a come home earlier t'night, dad, o'ny that fly foreman, he kep' me in th' shop 'til half-past six. What a fool. He came t' me, yeh know, an' he ses, 'Nell, I wanta give yeh some brotherly advice.' Oh, I know him an' his brotherly advice. 'I wanta give yeh some brotherly advice. Yer too purty, Nell,' he ses, 't' be workin' in this shop an' paradin' through the streets alone, without somebody t' give yeh good brotherly advice, an' I wanta warn yeh, Nell. I'm a bad man, but I ain't as bad as some, an' I wanta warn yeh.' 'Oh, g'long 'bout yer business,' I ses. I know 'im. He's like all of 'em, o'ny he's a little slyer. I know 'im. 'You g'long 'bout yer business,' I ses. Well, he ses after a while that he guessed some evenin' he'd come up an' see me. 'Oh, yeh will,' I ses, 'yeh will? Well, you jest let my ol' man ketch yeh comin' foolin' 'round our place. Yeh'll wish yeh went t' some other girl t' give brotherly advice.' 'What th' 'ell do I care fer yer father?' he ses. 'What's he t' me?' 'If he throws yeh down stairs, yeh'll care for 'im,' I ses. 'Well,' he ses, 'I'll come when 'e ain't in, b' Gawd, I'll come when 'e ain't in.' 'Oh, he's allus in when it means takin' care 'a me,' I ses. 'Don't yeh fergit it either. When it comes t' takin' care 'a his dorter, he's right on deck every single possible time.'"

After a time, she turned and addressed cheery words to the old man. "Hurry up th' fire, daddie! We'll have supper pretty soon."

But still her father was silent, and his form in its sullen posture was motionless.

At this, the girl seemed to see the need of the inauguration of a feminine war against a man out of temper. She approached him breathing soft, coaxing syllables.

"Daddie! Oh, Daddie! O—o—oh, Daddie!"

It was apparent from a subtle quality of valour in her tones that this manner of onslaught upon his moods had usually been successful, but to-night it had no quick effect. The words, coming from her lips, were like the refrain of an old ballad, but the man remained stolid.

"Daddie! My Daddie! Oh, Daddie are yeh mad at me, really—truly mad at me!"

She touched him lightly upon the arm. Should he have turned then he would have seen the fresh, laughing face, with dew-sparkling eyes, close to his own.

"Oh, Daddie! My Daddie! Pretty Daddie!"

She stole her arm about his neck, and then slowly bended her face toward his. It was the action of a queen who knows that she reigns notwithstanding irritations, trials, tempests.

But suddenly, from this position, she leaped backward with the mad energy of a frightened colt. Her face was in this instant turned to a grey, featureless thing of horror. A yell, wild and hoarse as a brute-cry, burst from her. "Daddie!" She flung herself to a place near the door, where she remained, crouching, her eyes staring at the motion-less figure, spattered by the quivering flashes from the fire. Her arms extended, and her frantic fingers at once besought and repelled. There was in them an expression of eagerness to caress and an expression of the most intense loathing. And the girl's hair that had been a splen-dour, was in these moments changed to a disordered mass that hung and swayed in witchlike fashion.

Again, a terrible cry burst from her. It was more than the shriek of agony—it was directed, personal, addressed to him in the chair, the first word of a tragic conversation with the dead.

It seemed that when she had put her arm about its neck, she had jostled the corpse in such a way, that now she and it were face to face. The attitude expressed an intention of arising from the table. The eyes, fixed upon hers, were filled with an unspeakable hatred.

* * * * * * *

The cries of the girl aroused thunders in the tenement. There was a loud slamming of doors, and presently there was a roar of feet upon the boards of the stairway. Voices rang out sharply.

"What is it?"

"What's th' matter?"

"He's killin' her!"

"Slug 'im with anythin' yeh kin lay hold of, Jack."

But over all this came the shrill shrewish tones of a woman. "Ah, th' damned ol' fool, he's drivin' 'er inteh th' street—that's what he's doin.' He's drivin' 'er inteh th' street."

HOW THE DONKEY
LIFTED THE HILLS

Many people suppose that the donkey is lazy. This is a great mistake. It is his pride.

Years ago, there was nobody quite so fine as the donkey. He was a great swell in those times. No one could express an opinion of anything without the donkey showing where he was in it. No one could mention the name of an important personage without the donkey declaring how well he knew him.

The donkey was, above all things, a proud and aristocratic beast.

One day a party of animals were discussing one thing and another, until finally the conversation drifted around to mythology.

"I have always admired that giant, Atlas," observed the ox in the course of the conversation. "It was amazing how he could carry things."

"Oh, yes, Atlas," said the donkey, "I knew him very well. I once met a man and we got talking of Atlas. I expressed my admiration for the giant and my desire to meet him some day, if possible. Whereupon the man said there was nothing quite so easy. He was sure that his dear friend, Atlas, would be happy to meet so charming a donkey. Was I at leisure next Monday? Well, then, could I dine with him upon that date? So, you see, it was all arranged. I found Atlas to be a very pleasant fellow."

"It has always been a wonder to me how he could have carried the earth on his back," said the horse.

"Oh, my dear sir, nothing is more simple," cried the donkey. "One has only to make up one's mind to it, and then—do it. That is all. I am quite sure that if I wished I could carry a range of mountains upon my back."

All the others said, "Oh, my!"

"Yes, I could," asserted the donkey, stoutly. "It is merely a question of making up one's mind. I will bet."

"I will wager also," said the horse. "I will wager my ears that you can't carry a range of mountains upon your back."

"Done," cried the donkey.

Forthwith the party of animals set out for the mountains. Suddenly, however, the donkey paused and said, "Oh, but look here. Who will place this range of mountains upon my back? Surely I can not be expected to do the loading also."

Here was a great question. The party consulted. At length the ox said, "We will have to ask some men to shovel the mountain upon the donkey's back."

Most of the others clapped their hoofs or their paws and cried, "Ah, that is the thing."

The horse, however, shook his head doubtfully. "I don't know about these men. They are very sly. They will introduce some deviltry into the affair."

"Why, how silly," said the donkey. "Apparently you do not understand men. They are the most gentle, guileless creatures."

"Well," retorted the horse, "I will doubtless be able to escape since I am not to be encumbered with any mountains. Proceed."

The donkey smiled in derision at these observations by the horse.

Presently they came upon some men who were labouring away like mad, digging ditches, felling trees, gathering fruits, carrying water, building huts.

"Look at these men, would you," said the horse. "Can you trust them after this exhibition of their depravity? See how each one selfishly—"

The donkey interrupted with a loud laugh.

"What nonsense!"

And then he cried out to the men, "Ho, my friends, will you please come and shovel a range of mountains upon my back?"

"What?"

"Will you please come and shovel a range of mountains upon my back?"

The men were silent for a time. Then they went apart and debated. They gesticulated a great deal.

Some apparently said one thing and some another. At last they paused and one of their number came forward.

"Why do you wish a range of mountains shovelled upon your back?"

"It is a wager," cried the donkey.

The men consulted again. And as the discussion became older, their heads went closer and closer together, until they merely whispered, and did not gesticulate at all. Ultimately they cried, "Yes, certainly we will shovel a range of mountains upon your back for you."

"Ah, thanks," said the donkey.

"Here is surely some deviltry," said the horse behind his hoof to the ox.

The entire party proceeded then to the mountains. The donkey drew a long breath and braced his legs.

"Are you ready?" asked the men.

"All ready," cried the donkey.

The men began to shovel.

The dirt and stones flew over the donkey's back in showers. It was not long before his legs were hidden. Presently only his neck and head remained in view. Then at last this wise donkey vanished. There had been made no great effect upon the range of mountains. They still towered toward the sky.

The watching crowd saw a heap of dirt and stones make a little movement and then was heard a muffled cry. "Enough! Enough! It was not two ranges of mountains! It is not fair! It is not fair!"

But the men only laughed as they shovelled on.

"Enough! Enough! Oh, woe is me—thirty snow-capped peaks upon my little back. Ah, these false, false men! Oh, virtuous, wise, and holy men, desist."

The men again laughed. They were as busy as fiends with their shovels.

"Ah, brutal, cowardly, accursed men; ah, good, gentle, and holy men, please remove some of those damnable peaks. I will adore your beautiful shovels forever. I will be slave to the beckoning of your little fingers. I will no longer be my own donkey—I will be your donkey."

The men burst into a triumphant shout and ceased shovelling.

"Swear it, mountain-carrier."

"I swear! I swear! I swear!"

The other animals scampered away then, for these men in their plots and plans were very terrible. "Poor old foolish fellow," cried the horse; "he may keep his ears. He will need them to hear and count the blows that are now to fall upon him."

The men unearthed the donkey. They beat him with their shovels. "Ho, come on, slave." Encrusted with earth, yellow-eyed from fright, the donkey limped toward his prison. His ears hung down like leaves of the plantain during the great rain.

So, now, when you see a donkey with a church, a palace, and three villages upon his back, and he goes with infinite slowness, moving but one leg at a time, do not think him lazy. It is his pride.

A MAN BY THE NAME OF MUD

Deep in a leather chair, the Kid sat looking out at where the rain slanted before the dull brown houses and hammered swiftly upon an occasional lonely cab. The happy crackle from the great and glittering fireplace behind him had evidently no meaning of content for him. He appeared morose and unapproachable, and when a man appears morose and unapproachable it is a fine chance for his intimate friends. Three or four of them discovered his mood, and so hastened to be obnoxious.

"What's wrong, Kid? Lost your thirst?"

"He can never be happy again. He has lost his thirst."

"That's right, Kid. When you quarrel with a man who can whip you, resort to sarcastic reflection and distance."

They cackled away persistently, but the Kid was mute and continued to stare gloomily at the street.

Once a man who had been writing letters looked up and said, "I saw your friend at the Comique the other night." He waited a moment and then added, "In back."

The Kid wheeled about in his chair at this information, and all the others saw then that it was important. One man said with deep intelligence, "Ho, ho, a woman, hey? A woman's come between the two Kids. A woman. Great, eh?" The Kid launched a glare of scorn across the room, and then turned again to a contemplation of the rain. His friends continued to do all in their power to worry him, but they fell ultimately before his impregnable silence.

As it happened, he had not been brooding upon his friend's mysterious absence at all. He had been concerned with himself. Once in a while he seemed to perceive certain futilities and lapsed them immediately into a state of voiceless dejection. These moods were not frequent.

An unexplained thing in his mind, however, was greatly enlightened by the words of the gossip. He turned then from his harrowing scrutiny of the amount of pleasure he achieved from living, and settled into a comfortable reflection upon the state of his comrade, the other Kid.

Perhaps it could be indicated in this fashion: "Went to Comique, I suppose. Saw girl. Secondary part, probably. Thought her rather natural. Went to Comique again. Went again. One time happened to meet omnipotent and good-natured friend. Broached subject to him with great caution. Friend said—'Why, certainly, my boy, come round to-night, and I'll take you in back. Remember, it's against all rules, but I think that in your case, etc.' Kid went. Chorus girls winked same old wink. 'Here's another dude on the prowl.' Kid aware of this, swearing under his breath and looking very stiff. Meets girl. Knew beforehand that the footlights might have sold him, but finds her very charming. Does not say single thing to her which she naturally expected to hear. Makes no reference to her beauty nor her voice—if she has any. Perhaps takes it for granted that she knows. Girl don't exactly love this attitude, but then feels admiration, because after all she can't tell whether he thinks her nice or whether he don't. New scheme this. Worked by occasional guys in Rome and Egypt, but still, new scheme. Kid goes away. Girl thinks. Later, nails omnipotent and good-natured friend. 'Who was that you brought back?' 'Oh, him? Why, he—' Describes the Kid's wealth, feats, and virtues—virtues of disposition. Girl propounds clever question—'Why did he wish to meet me?' Omnipotent person says, 'Damned if I know.'"

Later, Kid asks girl to supper. Not wildly anxious, but very evident that he asks her because he likes her. Girl accepts; goes to supper. Kid very good comrade and kind. Girl begins to think that here at last is a man who understands her. Details ambitions—long, wonderful ambitions. Explains her points of superiority over the other girls of stage. Says their lives disgust her. She wants to work and study and make something of herself. Kid smokes vast number of cigarettes. Displays and feels deep sympathy. Recalls, but faintly, that he has heard it on previous occasions. They have an awfully good time. Part at last in front of apartment house. "Good-night, old chap." "Good-night." Squeeze hands hard. Kid has no information at all about kissing her good-night, but don't even try. Noble youth. Wise youth. Kid goes home and smokes. Feels strong desire to kill people who say intolerable things of the girl in rows. "Narrow, mean, stupid, ignorant, damnable people." Contemplates the broad, fine liberality of his experienced mind.

Kid and girl become very chumy. Kid like a brother. Listens to her troubles. Takes her out to supper regularly and regularly. Chorus girls now tacitly recognise him as the main guy. Sometimes, may be, girl's mother sick. Can't go to supper. Kid always very noble. Understands perfectly the probabilities of there being others. Lays for 'em, but makes no discoveries. Begins to wonder whether he is a winner or whether she is a girl of marvellous cleverness. Can't tell. Maintains himself with dignity, however. Only occasionally inveighs against the men who prey upon the girls of the stage. Still noble.

Time goes on. Kid grows less noble. Perhaps decides not to be noble at all, or as little as he can. Still inveighs against the men who prey upon the girls of the stage. Thinks the girl stunning. Wants to be dead sure there are no others. Once suspects it, and immediately makes the colossal mistake of his life. Takes the girl to task. Girl won't stand it for a minute. Harangues him. Kid surrenders and pleads with her—pleads with her. Kid's name is mud.

A POKER GAME

Usually a poker game is a picture of peace. There is no drama so low-voiced and serene and monotonous. If an amateur loser does not softly curse, there is no orchestral support. Here is one of the most exciting and absorbing occupations known to intelligent American manhood; here a year's reflection is compressed into a moment of thought; here the nerves may stand on end and scream to themselves, but a tranquillity as from heaven is only interrupted by the click of chips. The higher the stakes the more quiet the scene; this is a law that applies everywhere save on the stage.

And yet sometimes in a poker game things happen. Everybody remembers the celebrated corner on bay rum that was triumphantly consummated by Robert F. Cinch, of Chicago, assisted by the United States Courts and whatever other federal power he needed. Robert F. Cinch enjoyed his victory four months. Then he died, and young Bobbie Cinch came to New York in order to more clearly demonstrate that there was a good deal of fun in twenty-two million dollars.

Old Henry Spuytendyvil owns all the real estate in New York save that previously appropriated by the hospitals and Central Park. He had been a friend of Bob's father. When Bob appeared in New York, Spuytendyvil entertained him correctly. It came to pass that they just naturally played poker.

One night they were having a small game in an up-town hotel. There were five of them, including two lawyers and a politician. The stakes depended on the ability of the individual fortune.

Bobbie Cinch had won rather heavily. He was as generous as sunshine, and when luck chases a generous man it chases him hard, even though he cannot bet with all the skill of his opponents.

Old Spuytendyvil had lost a considerable amount. One of the lawyers from time to time smiled quietly, because he knew Spuytendyvil well, and he knew that anything with the name of loss attached to it sliced the old man's heart into sections.

At midnight Archie Bracketts, the actor, came into the room. "How you holding 'em, Bob?" said he.

"Pretty well," said Bob.

"Having any luck, Mr. Spuytendyvil?"

"Blooming bad," grunted the old man.

Bracketts laughed and put his foot on the round of Spuytendyvil's chair. "There," said he, "I'll queer your luck for you." Spuytendyvil sat at the end of the table. "Bobbie," said the actor, presently, as young Cinch won another pot, "I guess I better knock your luck." So he took his foot from the old man's chair and placed it on Bob's chair. The lad grinned good-naturedly and said he didn't care.

Bracketts was in a position to scan both of the hands. It was Bob's ante, and old Spuytendyvil threw in a red chip. Everybody passed out up to Bobbie. He filled in the pot and drew a card.

Spuytendyvil drew a card. Bracketts, looking over his shoulder, saw him holding the ten, nine, eight, and seven of diamonds. Theatrically speaking, straight flushes are as frequent as berries on a juniper tree, but as a matter of truth the reason that straight flushes are so admired is because they are not as common as berries on a juniper tree. Bracketts stared; drew a cigar slowly from his pocket, and placing it between his teeth forgot its existence.

Bobbie was the only other stayer. Bracketts flashed an eye for the lad's hand and saw the nine, eight, six, and five of hearts. Now, there are but six hundred and forty-five emotions possible to the human mind, and Bracketts immediately had them all. Under the impression that he had finished his cigar, he took it from his mouth and tossed it toward the grate without turning his eyes to follow its flight.

There happened to be a complete silence around the green-clothed table. Spuytendyvil was studying his hand with a kind of contemptuous smile, but in his eyes there perhaps was to be seen a cold, stern light expressing something sinister and relentless.

Young Bob sat as he had sat. As the pause grew longer, he looked up once inquiringly at Spuytendyvil.

The old man reached for a white chip. "Well, mine are worth about that much," said he, tossing it into the pot. Thereupon he leaned back comfortably in his chair and renewed his stare at the five straight diamond. Young Bob extended his hand leisurely toward his stack. It occurred to Bracketts that he was smoking, but he found no cigar in his mouth.

The lad fingered his chips and looked pensively at his hand. The silence of those moments oppressed Bracketts like the smoke from a conflagration.

Bobbie Cinch continued for some moments to coolly observe his cards. At last he breathed a little sigh and said, "Well, Mr. Spuytendyvil, I can't play a sure thing against you." He threw in a white chip. "I'll just call you. I've got a straight flush." He faced down his cards.

Old Spuytendyvil's fear, horror, and rage could only be equalled in volume to a small explosion of gasolene. He dashed his cards upon the table. "There!" he shouted, glaring frightfully at Bobbie. "I've got a straight flush, too! And mine is Jack high!"

Bobbie was at first paralysed with amazement, but in a moment he recovered, and apparently observing something amusing in the situation he grinned.

Archie Bracketts, having burst his bond of silence, yelled for joy and relief. He smote Bobbie on the shoulder. "Bob, my boy," he cried exuberantly, "you're no gambler, but you're a mighty good fellow, and if you hadn't been you would be losing a good many dollars this minute."

Old Spuytendyvil glowered at Bracketts. "Stop making such an infernal din, will you, Archie," he said morosely. His throat seemed filled with pounded glass. "Pass the whisky."

THE SNAKE

Where the path wended across the ridge, the bushes of huckle-
berry and sweet fern swarmed at it in two curling waves until it was
a mere winding line traced through a tangle. There was no interference by clouds, and as the rays of the sun fell full upon the ridge, they
called into voice innumerable insects which chanted the heat of the
summer day in steady, throbbing, unending chorus.

A man and a dog came from the laurel thickets of the valley where
the white brook brawled with the rocks. They followed the deep
line of the path across the ridge. The dog—a large lemon and white
setter—walked, tranquilly meditative, at his master's heels.

Suddenly from some unknown and yet near place in advance there
came a dry, shrill whistling rattle that smote motion instantly from
the limbs of the man and the dog. Like the fingers of a sudden death,
this sound seemed to touch the man at the nape of the neck, at the
top of the spine, and change him, as swift as thought, to a statue of
listening horror, surprise, rage. The dog, too—the same icy hand was
laid upon him, and he stood crouched and quivering, his jaw dropping, the froth of terror upon his lips, the light of hatred in his eyes.

Slowly the man moved his hands toward the bushes, but his glance
did not turn from the place made sinister by the warning rattle. His
fingers, unguided, sought for a stick of weight and strength. Presently
they closed about one that seemed adequate, and holding this weapon
poised before him, the man moved slowly forward, glaring. The dog
with his nervous nostrils fairly fluttering moved warily, one foot at a
time, after his master.

But when the man came upon the snake, his body underwent a
shock as if from a revelation, as if after all he had been ambushed.
With a blanched face, he sprang forward, and his breath came in
strained gasps, his chest heaving as if he were in the performance of
an extraordinary muscular trial. His arm with the stick made a spasmodic, defensive gesture.

The snake had apparently been crossing the path in some mystic
travel when to his sense there came the knowledge of the coming of
his foes. The dull vibration perhaps informed him, and he flung his
body to face the danger. He had no knowledge of paths; he had no
wit to tell him to slink noiselessly into the bushes. He knew that his
implacable enemies were approaching; no doubt they were seeking

him, hunting him. And so he cried his cry, an incredibly swift jangle of tiny bells, as burdened with pathos as the hammering upon quaint cymbals by the Chinese at war—for, indeed, it was usually his death-music.

"Beware! Beware! Beware!"

The man and the snake confronted each other. In the man's eyes were hatred and fear. In the snake's eyes were hatred and fear. These enemies manœuvred, each preparing to kill. It was to be a battle without mercy. Neither knew of mercy for such a situation. In the man was all the wild strength of the terror of his ancestors, of his race, of his kind. A deadly repulsion had been handed from man to man through long dim centuries. This was another detail of a war that had begun evidently when first there were men and snakes. Individuals who do not participate in this strife incur the investigations of scientists. Once there was a man and a snake who were friends, and at the end, the man lay dead with the marks of the snake's caress just over his East Indian heart. In the formation of devices, hideous and horrible, Nature reached her supreme point in the making of the snake, so that priests who really paint hell well fill it with snakes instead of fire. These curving forms, these scintillant colourings create at once, upon sight, more relentless animosities than do shake barbaric tribes. To be born a snake is to be thrust into a place a-swarm with formidable foes. To gain an appreciation of it, view hell as pictured by priests who are really skilful.

As for this snake in the pathway, there was a double curve some inches back of its head, which, merely by the potency of its lines, made the man feel with tenfold eloquence the touch of the death-fingers at the nape of his neck. The reptile's head was waving slowly from side to side and its hot eyes flashed like little murder-lights. Always in the air was the dry, shrill whistling of the rattles.

"Beware! Beware! Beware!"

The man made a preliminary feint with his stick. Instantly the snake's heavy head and neck were bended back on the double curve and instantly the snake's body shot forward in a low, straight, hard spring. The man jumped with a convulsive chatter and swung his stick. The blind, sweeping blow fell upon the snake's head and hurled him so that steel-coloured plates were for a moment uppermost. But he rallied swiftly, agilely, and again the head and neck bended back to the double curve, and the steaming, wide-open mouth made its desperate effort to reach its enemy. This attack, it could be seen, was despairing, but it was nevertheless impetuous, gallant, ferocious, of the same quality as the charge of the lone chief when the walls of white faces close upon him in the mountains. The stick swung unerringly again, and the snake, mutilated, torn, whirled himself into the last coil.

And now the man went sheer raving mad from the emotions of his forefathers and from his own. He came to close quarters. He gripped the stick with his two hands and made it speed like a flail. The snake, tumbling in the anguish of final despair, fought, bit, flung itself upon this stick which was taking his life.

At the end, the man clutched his stick and stood watching in silence. The dog came slowly and with infinite caution stretched his nose forward, sniffing. The hair upon his neck and back moved and ruffled as if a sharp wind was blowing. The last muscular quivers of the snake were causing the rattles to still sound their treble cry, the shrill, ringing war chant and hymn of the grave of the thing that faces foes at once countless, implacable, and superior.

"Well, Rover," said the man, turning to the dog with a grin of victory, "we'll carry Mr. Snake home to show the girls."

His hands still trembled from the strain of the encounter, but he pried with his stick under the body of the snake and hoisted the limp thing upon it. He resumed his march along the path, and the dog walked, tranquilly meditative, at his master's heels.

A SELF-MADE MAN

An Example of Success that Any One can Follow.

Tom had a hole in his shoe. It was very round and very uncomfortable, particularly when he went on wet pavements. Rainy days made him feel that he was walking on frozen dollars, although he had only to think for a moment to discover he was not.

He used up almost two packs of playing cards by means of putting four cards at a time inside his shoe as a sort of temporary sole, which usually lasted about half a day. Once he put in four aces for luck. He went down town that morning and got refused work. He thought it wasn't a very extraordinary performance for a young man of ability, and he was not sorry that night to find his packs were entirely out of aces.

One day Tom was strolling down Broadway. He was in pursuit of work, although his pace was slow. He had found that he must take the matter coolly. So he puffed tenderly at a cigarette and walked as if he owned stock. He imitated success so successfully, that if it wasn't for the constant reminder (king, queen, deuce, and tray) in his shoe, he would have gone into a store and bought something.

He had borrowed five cents that morning off his landlady, for his mouth craved tobacco. Although he owed her much for board, she had unlimited confidence in him, because his stock of self-assurance was very large indeed. And as it increased in a proper ratio with the amount of his bills, his relations with her seemed on a firm basis. So he strolled along and smoked with his confidence in fortune in nowise impaired by his financial condition.

Of a sudden he perceived on old man seated upon a railing and smoking a clay pipe.

He stopped to look, because he wasn't in a hurry, and because it was an unusual thing on Broadway to see old men seated upon railings and smoking clay pipes.

And to his surprise the old man regarded him very intently in return. He stared, with a wistful expression, into Tom's face, and he clasped his hands in trembling excitement.

Tom was filled with astonishment at the old man's strange demeanour. He stood puffing at his cigarette, and tried to understand matters. Failing, he threw his cigarette away, took a fresh one from his pocket, and approached the old man.

"Got a match?" he inquired, pleasantly.

The old man, much agitated, nearly fell from the railing as he leaned dangerously forward.

"Sonny, can you read?" he demanded in a quavering voice.

"Certainly, I can," said Tom, encouragingly. He waived the affair of the match.

The old man fumbled in his pocket. "You look honest, sonny. I've been looking for an honest feller fur a'most a week. I've set on this railing fur six days," he cried, plaintively.

He drew forth a letter and handed it to Tom. "Read it fur me, sonny, read it," he said, coaxingly.

Tom took the letter and leaned back against the railings. As he opened it and prepared to read, the old man wriggled like a child at a forbidden feast.

Thundering trucks made frequent interruptions, and seven men in a hurry jogged Tom's elbow, but he succeeded in reading what follows:—

Office of Ketchum R. Jones, Attorney-at-Law,
Tin Can, Nevada, May 19, 18—.

Rufus Wilkins, Esq.

Dear Sir,—I have as yet received no acknowledgment of the draft from the sale of the north section lots, which I forwarded to you on 25th June. I would request an immediate reply concerning it.

Since my last I have sold the three corner lots at five thousand each. The city grew so rapidly in that direction that they were surrounded by brick stores almost before you would know it. I have also sold for four thousand dollars the ten acres of out-laying sage bush, which you once foolishly tried to give away. Mr. Simpson, of Boston, bought the tract. He is very shrewd, no doubt, but he hasn't been in the west long. Still, I think if he holds it for about a thousand years, he may come out all right.

I worked him with the projected-horse-car-line gag.

Inform me of the address of your New York attorneys, and I will send on the papers. Pray do not neglect to write me concerning the draft sent on 25th June.

In conclusion, I might say that if you have any eastern friends who are after good western investments inform them of the glorious future of Tin Can. We now have three rail-roads, a bank, an electric light plant, a projected horse-car line, and an art society. Also, a saw manufactory, a patent car-wheel mill, and a Methodist Church. Tin Can is marching forward to take her proud stand as the metropolis of the west. The rose-hued future holds no glories to which Tin Can does not—

Tom stopped abruptly. "I guess the important part of the letter came first," he said.

"Yes," cried the old man, "I've heard enough. It is just as I thought. George has robbed his dad."

The old man's frail body quivered with grief. Two tears trickled slowly down the furrows of his face.

"Come, come, now," said Tom, patting him tenderly on the back. "Brace up, old feller. What you want to do is to get a lawyer and go put the screws on George."

"Is it really?" asked the old man, eagerly.

"Certainly, it is," said Tom.

"All right," cried the old man, with enthusiasm. "Tell me where to get one." He slid down from the railing and prepared to start off.

Tom reflected. "Well," he said, finally, "I might do for one myself."

"What," shouted the old man in a voice of admiration, "are you a lawyer as well as a reader?"

"Well," said Tom again, "I might appear to advantage as one. All you need is a big front," he added, slowly. He was a profane young man.

The old man seized him by the arm. "Come on, then," he cried, "and we'll go put the screws on George."

Tom permitted himself to be dragged by the weak arms of his companion around a corner and along a side street. As they proceeded, he was internally bracing himself for a struggle, and putting large bales of self-assurance around where they would be likely to obstruct the advance of discovery and defeat.

By the time they reached a brown-stone house, hidden away in a street of shops and warehouses, his mental balance was so admi-rable that he seemed to be in possession of enough information and brains to ruin half of the city, and he was no more concerned about the king, queen, deuce, and tray than if they had been discards that didn't fit his draw. He infused so much confidence and courage into his companion, that the old man went along the street, breathing war, like a decrepit hound on the scent of new blood.

He ambled up the steps of the brown-stone house as if he were charging earthworks. He unlocked the door and they passed along a dark hallway. In a rear room they found a man seated at table engaged with a very late breakfast. He had a diamond in his shirt front and a bit of egg on his cuff.

"George," said the old man in a fierce voice that came from his aged throat with a sound like the crackle of burning twigs, "here's my lawyer, Mr. er—ah—Smith, and we want to know what you did with the draft that was sent on 25th June."

The old man delivered the words as if each one was a musket shot. George's coffee spilled softly upon the tablecover, and his fingers worked convulsively upon a slice of bread. He turned a white, astonished face toward the old man and the intrepid Thomas.

The latter, straight and tall, with a highly legal air, stood at the old man's side. His glowing eyes were fixed upon the face of the man at the table. They seemed like two little detective cameras taking pictures of the other man's thoughts.

"Father, what d—do you mean," faltered George, totally unable to withstand the two cameras and the highly legal air.

"What do I mean?" said the old man with a feeble roar as from an ancient lion. "I mean that draft—that's what I mean. Give it up or we'll—we'll"—he paused to gain courage by a glance at the formidable figure at his side—"we'll put the screws on you."

"Well, I was—I was only borrowin' it for 'bout a month," said George.

"Ah," said Tom.

George started, glared at Tom, and then began to shiver like an animal with a broken back. There were a few moments of silence. The old man was fumbling about in his mind for more imprecations. George was wilting and turning limp before the glittering orbs of the valiant attorney. The latter, content with the exalted advantage he had gained by the use of the expression "Ah," spoke no more, but continued to stare.

"Well," said George, finally, in a weak voice, "I s'pose I can give you a cheque for it, 'though I was only borrowin' it for 'bout a month. I don't think you have treated me fairly, father, with your lawyers and your threats, and all that. But I'll give you the cheque."

The old man turned to his attorney. "Well?" he asked.

Tom looked at the son and held an impressive debate with himself. "I think we may accept the cheque," he said coldly after a time.

George arose and tottered across the room. He drew a cheque that made the attorney's heart come privately into his mouth. As he and his client passed triumphantly out, he turned a last highly legal glare upon George that reduced that individual to a mere paste.

On the side-walk the old man went into a spasm of delight and called his attorney all the admiring and endearing names there were to be had.

"Lord, how you settled him," he cried ecstatically.

They walked slowly back toward Broadway. "The scoundrel," murmured the old man. "I'll never see 'im again. I'll desert 'im. I'll find a nice quiet boarding-place and—"

"That's all right," said Tom. "I know one. I'll take you right up," which he did.

He came near being happy ever after. The old man lived at advanced rates in the front room at Tom's boarding-house. And the latter basked in the proprietress' smiles, which had a commercial value, and were a great improvement on many we see.

The old man, with his quantities of sage bush, thought Thomas owned all the virtues mentioned in high-class literature, and his opinion, too, was of commercial value. Also, he knew a man who knew another man who received an impetus which made him engage Thomas on terms that were highly satisfactory. Then it was that the latter learned he had not succeeded sooner because he did not know a man who knew another man.

So it came to pass that Tom grew to be Thomas G. Somebody. He achieved that position in life from which he could hold out for good wines when he went to poor restaurants. His name became entangled with the name of Wilkins in the ownership of vast and valuable tracts of sage bush in Tin Can, Nevada.

At the present day he is so great that he lunches frugally at high prices. His fame has spread through the land as a man who carved his way to fortune with no help but his undaunted pluck, his tireless energy, and his sterling integrity.

Newspapers apply to him now, and he writes long signed articles to struggling young men, in which he gives the best possible advice as to how to become wealthy. In these articles, he, in a burst of glorification, cites the king, queen, deuce, and tray, the four aces, and all that. He alludes tenderly to the nickel he borrowed and spent for cigarettes as the foundation of his fortune.

"To succeed in life," he writes, "the youth of America have only to see an old man seated upon a railing and smoking a clay pipe. Then go up and ask him for a match."

A TALE OF MERE CHANCE

Being an Account of the Pursuit of the Tiles, the Statement of the Clock, and the Grip of a Coat of Orange Spots, together with some Criticism of a Detective said to be Carved from an Old Table-leg.

Yes, my friend, I killed the man, but I would not have been detected in it were it not for some very extraordinary circumstances. I had long considered this deed, but I am a delicate and sensitive person, you understand, and I hesitated over it as the diver hesitates on the brink of a dark and icy mountain pool. A thought of the shock of the contact holds one back.

As I was passing his house one morning, I said to myself, "Well, at any rate, if she loves him, it will not be for long." And after that decision I was not myself, but a sort of a machine.

I rang the bell and the servants admitted me to the drawing-room. I waited there while the old tall clock placidly ticked its speech of time. The rigid and austere chairs remained in possession of their singular imperturbability, although, of course, they were aware of my purpose, but the little white tiles of the floor whispered one to another and looked at me. Presently he entered the room, and I, drawing my revolver, shot him. He screamed—you know that scream—mostly amazement—and as he fell forward his blood was upon the little white tiles. They huddled and covered their eyes from this rain. It seemed to me that the old clock stopped ticking as a man may gasp in the middle of a sentence, and a chair threw itself in my way as I sprang toward the door.

A moment later, I was walking down the street, tranquil, you understand, and I said to myself, "It is done. Long years from this day I will say to her that it was I who killed him. After time has eaten the conscience of the thing, she will admire my courage."

I was elated that the affair had gone off so smoothly, and I felt like returning home and taking a long, full sleep, like a tired working man. When people passed me, I contemplated their stupidity with a sense of satisfaction.

But those accursed little white tiles.

I heard a shrill crying and chattering behind me, and, looking back, I saw them, blood-stained and impassioned, raising their little hands and screaming "Murder! It was he!" I have said that they had little hands. I am not sure of it, but they had some means of indicating me as unerringly as pointing fingers. As for their movement, they swept along as easily as dry, light leaves are carried by the wind. Always they were shrilly piping their song of my guilt.

My friend, may it never be your fortune to be pursued by a crowd of little blood-stained tiles. I used a thousand means to be free from the clash-clash of these tiny feet. I ran through the world at my best speed, but it was no better than that of an ox, while they, my pursuers, were always fresh, eager, relentless.

I am an ingenious person, and I used every trick that a desperate, fertile man can invent. Hundreds of times I had almost evaded them when some smouldering, neglected spark would blaze up and discover me.

I felt that the eye of conviction would have no terrors for me, but the eyes of suspicion which I saw in city after city, on road after road, drove me to the verge of going forward and saying, "Yes, I have murdered."

People would see the following, clamorous troops of blood-stained tiles, and give me piercing glances, so that these swords played continually at my heart. But we are a decorous race, thank God. It is very vulgar to apprehend murderers on the public streets. We have learned correct manners from the English. Besides, who can be sure of the meaning of clamouring tiles? It might be merely a trick in politics.

Detectives? What are detectives? Oh, yes, I have read of them and their deeds, when I come to think of it. The prehistoric races must have been remarkable. I have never been able to understand how the detective navigated in stone boats. Still, specimens of their pottery excavated in Taumalipas show a remarkable knowledge of mechanics. I remember the little hydraulic—what's that? Well, what you say may be true, my friend, but I think you dream.

The little stained tiles. My friend, I stopped in an inn at the ends of the earth, and in the morning they were there flying like little birds and pecking at my window.

I should have escaped. Heavens, I should have escaped. What was more simple? I murdered and then walked into the world, which is wide and intricate.

Do you know that my own clock assisted in the hunting of me? They asked what time I left my home that morning, and it replied at once, "Half-after eight." The watch of a man I had chanced to pass near the house of the crime told the people "Seven minutes after nine." And, of course, the tall, old clock in the drawing-room went about day after day repeating, "Eighteen minutes after nine."

Do you say that the man who caught me was very clever? My friend, I have lived long, and he was the most incredible blockhead of my experience. An enslaved, dust-eating Mexican vaquero wouldn't hitch his pony to such a man. Do you think he deserves credit for my capture? If he had been as pervading as the atmosphere, he would never have caught me. If he was a detective, as you say, I could carve a better one from an old table-leg. But the tiles. That is another matter. At night I think they flew in long high flock, like pigeons. In the day, little mad things, they murmured on my trail like frothy-mouthed weasels.

I see that you note these great, round, vividly orange spots on my coat. Of course, even if the detective were really carved from an old table-leg, he could hardly fail to apprehend a man thus badged. As sores come upon one in the plague so came these spots upon my coat. When I discovered them, I made effort to free myself of this coat. I tore, tugged, wrenched at it, but around my shoulders it was like a grip of a dead man's arms. Do you know that I have plunged into a thousand lakes? I have smeared this coat with a thousand paints. But day and night the spots burn like lights. I might walk from this jail to-day if I could rid myself of this coat, but it clings—clings—clings.

At any rate, the person you call a detective was not so clever to discover a man in a coat of spotted orange, followed by shrieking, blood-stained tiles. Yes, that noise from the corridor is most peculiar. But they are always there, muttering and watching, clashing and jostling. It sounds as if the dishes of Hades were being washed. Yet I have become used to it. Once, indeed, in the night, I cried out to them, "In God's name, go away, little blood-stained tiles." But they doggedly answered, "It is the law."

AT CLANCY'S WAKE

Scene—*Room in the house of the lamented Clancy. The curtains are pulled down. A perfume of old roses and whisky hangs in the air. A weeping woman in black it seated at a table in the centre. A group of wide-eyed children are sobbing in a corner. Down the side of the room is a row of mourning friends of the family. Through an open door can be seen, half hidden in shadows, the silver and black of a coffin.*

Widow—Oh, wirra, wirra, wirra!

Children—B-b boo-hoo-hoo!

Friends (*conversing in low tones*)—Yis, Moike Clancy was a foine mahn, sure! None betther! No, I don't t'ink so. Did he? Sure, all th' elictions! He was th' bist in the warrud! He licked 'im widin an inch of his loife, aisy, an' th' other wan a big, shtrappin' buck of a mahn, an' him jes' free of th' pneumonia! Yis, he did! They carried th' warrud by six hunder! Yis, he was a foine mahn. None betther. Gawd sav' 'im!

(*Enter* Mr. Slick, *of the "Daily Blanket," shown in by a maidservant, whose hair has become disarranged through much tear-shedding. He is attired in a suit of grey check, and wears a red rose in his buttonhole.*)

Mr. Slick—Good afternoon, Mrs. Clancy. This is a sad misfortune for you, isn't it?

Widow—Oh, indade, indade, young mahn, me poor heart is bruk.

Mr. Slick—Very sad, Mrs. Clancy. A great misfortune, I'm sure. Now, Mrs. Clancy, I've called to—

Widow—Little did I t'ink, young mahn, win they brought poor Moike in that it was th' lasht!

Mr. Slick (*with conviction*)—True! True! Very true, indeed. It was a great grief to you, Mrs. Clancy. I've called this morning, Mrs. Clancy, to see if I could get from you a short obituary notice for the *Blanket* if you could—

Widow—An' his hid was done up in a rag, an' he was cursin' frightful. A damned Oytalian lit fall th' hod as Moike was walkin' pasht as dacint as you plaze. Win they carried 'im in, him all bloody, an' ravin' tur'ble 'bout Oytalians, me heart was near bruk, but I niver tawt—I niver tawt—I—I niver—(*Breaks forth into a long, forlorn cry. The children join in, and the chorus echoes wailfully through the rooms.*)

Mr. Slick (*as the yell, in a measure, ceases*)—Yes, indeed, a sad, sad affair. A terrible misfortune. Now, Mrs. Clancy—

Widow (*turning suddenly*)—Mary Ann. Where's thot lazy divil of a Mary Ann? (*As the servant appears.*) Mary Ann, bring th' bottle! Give th' gintlemin a dhrink!... Here's to Hiven savin' yez, young mahn. (*Drinks.*)

Mr. Slick (*drinks*)—A noble whisky, Mrs. Clancy. Many thanks. Now, Mrs. Clancy—

Widow—Take anodder wan! Take anodder wan! (*Fills his glass.*)

Mr. Slick (*impatiently*)—Yes, certainly, Mrs. Clancy, certainly. (*He drinks.*) Now, could you tell me, Mrs. Clancy, where your late husband was—

Widow—Who—Moike? Oh, young mahn, yez can just say thot he was the foinest mahn livin' an' breathin', an' niver a wan in th' warrud was betther. Oh, but he had th' tindther heart for 'is fambly, he did. Don't I remimber win he clipped little Patsey wid th' bottle, an' didn't he buy th' big rockin'-horse th' minit he got sober? Sure he did. Pass th' bottle, Mary Ann! (*Pours a beer-glass about half-full for her guest.*)

Mr. Slick (*taking a seat*)—True, Mr. Clancy was a fine man, Mrs. Clancy—a *very* fine man. Now, I—

Widow (*plaintively*)—An' don't yez loike th' rum? Dhrink th' rum, mahn! It was me own Moike's fav'rite bran'. Well I remimber win he fotched it home, an' half th' demijohn gone a'ready, an' him a-cursin' up th' stairs as dhrunk as Gawd plazed. It was a—Dhrink th' rum, young mahn, dhrink th' rum! If he cud see yez now, Moike Clancy wud git up from 'is—

Mr. Slick (*desperately*)—Very well, very well, Mrs. Clancy. Here's your good health. Now, can you tell me, Mrs. Clancy, when was Mr. Clancy born?

Widow—Win was he borrun. Sure, divil a bit do I care win he was borrun. He was th' good mahn to me an' his childher; an' Gawd knows I don't care win he was borrun. Mary Ann, pass th' bottle! Wud yez kape th' gintlemin starvin' for a dhrink here in Moike Clancy's own house? Gawd save yez.

(*When the bottle appears she pours a huge quantity out for her guest.*)

Mr. Slick—Well, then, Mrs. Clancy, *where* was he born?

Widow (*staring*)—In Oirland, mahn, in Oirland! Where did yez t'ink? (*Then, in sudden, wheedling tones.*) An' ain't yez goin' to dhrink th' rum? Are yez goin' to shirk th' good whisky what was th' pride of Moike's life, an' him gettin' full on it an' breakin' th' furnitir t'ree nights a week hard-runnin'? Shame an yez, an' Gawd save yer soul. Dhrink it oop now, there's a dear, dhrink it oop now, an' say: "Moike Clancy, be all th' powers in th' shky, Hiven sind yez rist!"

Mr. Slick—(*to himself*)—Holy smoke! (*He drinks, then regards the glass for a long time.*) ... Well, now, Mrs. Clancy, give me your attention for a moment, please. When did—

Widow—An' oh, but he was a power in th' warrud! Divil a mahn cud vote right widout Moike Clancy at 'is elbow. An' in th' calkus, sure didn't Mulrooney git th' nominashun jes' by raison of Moike's atthackin' th' opposashun wid th' shtove-poker. Mulrooney got it as aisy as dhirt, wid Moike rowlin' under th' tayble wid th' other candeedate. He was a good sit'zen, was Moike—divil a wan betther.

Mr. Slick *spends some minutes in collecting his faculties.*

Mr. Slick (*after he decides that he has them collected*)—Yes, yes, Mrs. Clancy, your husband's h-highly successful pol-pol-political career was w-well known to the public; but what I want to know is— what I want to know—(*Pauses to consider.*)

Widow (*finally*)—Pass th' glasses, Mary Ann, yez lazy divil; give th' gintlemin a dhrink! Here (*tendering him a glass*), take anodder wan to Moike Clancy, an' Gawd save yez for yer koindness to a poor widee woman!

Mr. Slick (*after solemnly regarding the glass*)—Certainly, I—I'll take a drink. Certainly, M—Mish Clanshy. Yes, certainly, Mish Clanshy. Now, Mish Clanshy, w-w-wash was Mr. Clanshy's n-name before he married you, Mish Clanshy?

Widow (*astonished*)—Why, divil a bit else but Clancy.

Mr. Slick (*after reflection*)—Well, but I mean—I mean, Mish Clanshy, I mean—what was date of birth? Did marry you 'fore then, or d-did marry you when 'e was born in N' York, Mish Clanshy?

Widow—Phwat th' divil—

Mr. Slick (*with dignity*)—Ansher my queshuns, pleash, Mish Clanshy. Did 'e bring chil'en withum f'm Irelan', or was you, after married in N' York, mother those chil'en 'e brought f'm Irelan'?

Widow—Be th' powers above, I—

Mr. Slick (*with gentle patience*)—I don't shink y' unnerstan' m' queshuns, Mish Clanshy. What I wanna fin' out is, what was 'e born in N' York for when he, before zat, came f'm Irelan'? Dash what puzzels me. I-I'm completely puzzled. An' alsho, I wanna fin' out—I wanna fin' out, if poshble—zat is, if it's poshble shing, I wanna fin' out—I wanna fin' out—if poshble—I wanna-shay, who the blazesh is dead here, anyhow?

AN EPISODE OF WAR

The lieutenant's rubber blanket lay on the ground, and upon it he had poured the company's supply of coffee. Corporals and other representatives of the grimy and hot-throated men who lined the breastwork had come for each squad's portion.

The lieutenant was frowning and serious at this task of division. His lips pursed as he drew with his sword various crevices in the heap until brown squares of coffee, astoundingly equal in size, appeared on the blanket. He was on the verge of a great triumph in mathematics, and the corporals were thronging forward, each to reap a little square, when suddenly the lieutenant cried out and looked quickly at a man near him as if he suspected it was a case of personal assault. The others cried out also when they saw blood upon the lieutenant's sleeve.

He has winced like a man stung, swayed dangerously, and then straightened. The sound of his hoarse breathing was plainly audible. He looked sadly, mystically, over the breastwork at the green face of a wood, where now were many little puffs of white smoke. During this moment the men about him gazed statue-like and silent, astonished and awed by this catastrophe which happened when catastrophes were not expected—when they had leisure to observe it.

As the lieutenant stared at the wood, they too swung their heads, so that for another instant all hands, still silent, contemplated the distant forest as if their minds were fixed upon the mystery of a bullet's journey.

The officer had, of course, been compelled to take his sword into his left hand. He did not hold it by the hilt. He gripped it at the middle of the blade, awkwardly. Turning his eyes from the hostile wood, he looked at the sword as he held it there, and seemed puzzled as to what to do with it, where to put it. In short, this weapon had of a sudden become a strange thing to him. He looked at it in a kind of stupefaction, as if he had been endowed with a trident, a sceptre, or a spade.

Finally he tried to sheath it. To sheath a sword held by the left hand, at the middle of the blade, in a scabbard hung at the left hip, is a feat worthy of a sawdust ring. This wounded officer engaged in a desperate struggle with the sword and the wobbling scabbard, and during the time of it he breathed like a wrestler.

But at this instant the men, the spectators, awoke from their stone-like poses and crowded forward sympathetically. The orderly-sergeant took the sword and tenderly placed it in the scabbard. At the time, he leaned nervously backward, and did not allow even his finger to brush the body of the lieutenant. A wound gives strange dignity to him who bears it. Well men shy from this new and terrible majesty. It is as if the wounded man's hand is upon the curtain which hangs before the revelations of all existence—the meaning of ants, potentates, wars, cities, sunshine, snow, a feather dropped from a bird's wing; and the power of it sheds radiance upon a bloody form, and makes the other men understand sometimes that they are little. His comrades look at him with large eyes thoughtfully. Moreover, they fear vaguely that the weight of a finger upon him might send him headlong, precipitate the tragedy, hurl him at once into the dim, grey unknown. And so the orderly-sergeant, while sheathing the sword, leaned nervously backward.

There were others who proffered assistance. One timidly presented his shoulder and asked the lieutenant if he cared to lean upon it, but the latter waved him away mournfully. He wore the look of one who knows he is the victim of a terrible disease and understands his helplessness. He again stared over the breastwork at the forest, and then turning went slowly rearward. He held his right wrist tenderly in his left hand as if the wounded arm was made of very brittle glass.

And the men in silence stared at the wood, then at the departing lieutenant—then at the wood, then at the lieutenant.

As the wounded officer passed from the line of battle, he was enabled to see many things which as a participant in the fight were unknown to him. He saw a general on a black horse gazing over the lines of blue infantry at the green woods which veiled his problems. An aide galloped furiously, dragged his horse suddenly to a halt, saluted, and presented a paper. It was, for a wonder, precisely like an historical painting.

To the rear of the general and his staff a group, composed of a bugler, two or three orderlies, and the bearer of the corps standard, all upon maniacal horses, were working like slaves to hold their ground, preserve their respectful interval, while the shells boomed in the air about them, and caused their chargers to make furious quivering leaps.

A battery, a tumultuous and shining mass, was swirling toward the right. The wild thud of hoofs, the cries of the riders shouting blame and praise, menace and encouragement, and, last, the roar of the wheels, the slant of the glistening guns, brought the lieutenant to an intent pause. The battery swept in curves that stirred the heart; it made halts as dramatic as the crash of a wave on the rocks, and when it fled onward, this aggregation of wheels, levers, motors, had a beautiful unity, as if it were a missile. The sound of it was a war-chorus that reached into the depths of man's emotion.

The lieutenant, still holding his arm as if it were of glass, stood watching this battery until all detail of it was lost, save the figures of the riders, which rose and fell and waved lashes over the black mass.

Later, he turned his eyes toward the battle where the shooting sometimes crackled like bush-fires, sometimes sputtered with exasperating irregularity, and sometimes reverberated like the thunder. He saw the smoke rolling upward and saw crowds of men who ran and cheered, or stood and blazed away at the inscrutable distance.

He came upon some stragglers, and they told him how to find the field hospital. They described its exact location. In fact, these men, no longer having part in the battle, knew more of it than others. They told the performance of every corps, every division, the opinion of every general. The lieutenant, carrying his wounded arm rearward, looked upon them with wonder.

At the roadside a brigade was making coffee and buzzing with talk like a girls' boarding-school. Several officers came out to him and inquired concerning things of which he knew nothing. One, seeing his arm, began to scold. "Why, man, that's no way to do. You want to fix that thing." He appropriated the lieutenant and the lieutenant's wound. He cut the sleeve and laid bare the arm, every nerve of which softly fluttered under his touch. He bound his handkerchief over the wound, scolding away in the meantime. His tone allowed one to think that he was in the habit of being wounded every day. The lieutenant hung his head, feeling, in this presence, that he did not know how to be correctly wounded.

The low white tents of the hospital were grouped around an old school-house. There was here a singular commotion. In the foreground two ambulances interlocked wheels in the deep mud. The drivers were tossing the blame of it back and forth, gesticulating and berating, while from the ambulances, both crammed with wounded, there came an occasional groan. An interminable crowd of bandaged men were coming and going. Great numbers sat under the trees nursing heads or arms or legs. There was a dispute of some kind raging on the steps of the school-house. Sitting with his back against a tree a man with a face as grey as a new army blanket was serenely smoking a corn-cob pipe. The lieutenant wished to rush forward and inform him that he was dying.

A busy surgeon was passing near the lieutenant. "Good-morning," he said, with a friendly smile. Then he caught sight of the lieutenant's arm and his face at once changed. "Well, let's have a look at it." He seemed possessed suddenly of a great contempt for the lieutenant. This wound evidently placed the latter on a very low social plane. The doctor cried out impatiently, "What mutton-head had tied it up that way anyhow?" The lieutenant answered, "Oh, a man."

When the wound was disclosed the doctor fingered it disdainfully. "Humph," he said. "You come along with me and I'll 'tend to you." His voice contained the same scorn as if he were saying, "You will have to go to jail."

The lieutenant had been very meek, but now his face flushed, and he looked into the doctor's eyes. "I guess I won't have it amputated," he said.

"Nonsense, man! Nonsense! Nonsense!" cried the doctor. "Come along, now. I won't amputate it. Come along. Don't be a baby."

"Let go of me," said the lieutenant, holding back wrathfully, his glance fixed upon the door of the old school-house, as sinister to him as the portals of death.

And this is the story of how the lieutenant lost his arm. When he reached home, his sisters, his mother, his wife, sobbed for a long time at the sight of the flat sleeve. "Oh, well," he said, standing shamefaced amid these tears, "I don't suppose it matters so much as all that."

THE VOICE OF THE MOUNTAIN

The old man Popocatepetl was seated on a high rock with his white mantle about his shoulders. He looked at the sky, he looked at the sea, he looked at the land—nowhere could he see any food. And he was very hungry, too.

Who can understand the agony of a creature whose stomach is as large as a thousand churches, when this same stomach is as empty as a broken water jar?

He looked longingly at some island in the sea. "Ah, those flat cakes! If I had them." He stared at storm-clouds in the sky. "Ah, what a drink is there." But the King of Everything, you know, had forbidden the old man Popocatepetl to move at all, because he feared that every footprint would make a great hole in the land. So the old fellow was obliged to sit still and wait for his food to come within reach. Any one who has tried this plan knows what intervals lie between meals.

Once his friend, the little eagle, flew near, and Popocatepetl called to him. "Ho, tiny bird, come and consider with me as to how I shall be fed."

The little eagle came and spread his legs apart and considered manfully, but he could do nothing with the situation. "You see," he said, "this is no ordinary hunger which one goat will suffice—"

Popocatepetl groaned an assent.

"—but it is an enormous affair," continued the little eagle, "which requires something like a dozen stars. I don't see what can be done unless we get that little creature of the earth—that little animal with two arms, two legs, one head, and a very brave air, to invent something. He is said to be very wise."

"Who claims it for him?" asked Popocatepetl.

"He claims it for himself," responded the eagle.

"Well, summon him. Let us see. He is doubtless a kind little animal, and when he sees my distress he will invent something."

"Good!" The eagle flew until he discovered one of these small creatures. "Oh, tiny animal, the great chief Popocatepetl summons you!"

"Does he, indeed!"

"Popocatepetl, the great chief," said the eagle again, thinking that the little animal had not heard rightly.

"Well, and why does he summon me?"

"Because he is in distress, and he needs your assistance."

The little animal reflected for a time, and then said, "I will go."

When Popocatepetl perceived the little animal and the eagle he stretched forth his great, solemn arms. "Oh, blessed little animal with two arms, two legs, a head, and a very brave air, help me in my agony. Behold I, Popocatepetl, who saw the King of Everything fashioning the stars, I, who knew the sun in his childhood, I, Popocatepetl, appeal to you, little animal. I am hungry."

After a while the little animal asked: "How much will you pay?"

"Pay?" said Popocatepetl.

"Pay?" said the eagle.

"Assuredly," quoth the little animal, "pay!"

"But," demanded Popocatepetl, "were you never hungry? I tell you I am hungry, and is your first word then 'pay'?"

The little animal turned coldly away. "Oh, Popocatepetl, how much wisdom has flown past you since you saw the King of Everything fashioning the stars and since you knew the sun in his childhood? I said pay, and, moreover, your distress measures my price. It is our law. Yet it is true that we did not see the King of Everything fashioning the stars. Nor did we know the sun in his childhood."

Then did Popocatepetl roar and shake in his rage. "Oh, louse—louse—louse! Let us bargain then! How much for your blood?" Over the little animal hung death.

But he instantly bowed himself and prayed: "Popocatepetl, the great, you who saw the King of Everything fashioning the stars, and who knew the sun in his childhood, forgive this poor little animal. Your sacred hunger shall be my care. I am your servant."

"It is well," said Popocatepetl at once, for his spirit was ever kindly. "And now, what will you do?"

The little animal put his hand upon his chin and reflected. "Well, it seems you are hungry, and the King of Everything has forbidden you to go for food in fear that your monstrous feet will riddle the earth with holes. What you need is a pair of wings."

"A pair of wings!" cried Popocatepetl delightedly.

"A pair of wings!" screamed the eagle in joy.

"How very simple, after all."

"And yet how wise!"

"But," said Popocatepetl, after the first outburst, "who can make me these wings?"

The little animal replied: "I and my kind are great, because at times we can make one mind control a hundred thousand bodies. This is the secret of our performance. It will be nothing for us to make wings for even you, great Popocatepetl. I and my kind will come"—continued the crafty, little animal—"we will come and dwell on this beautiful plain that stretches from the sea to the sea, and we will make wings for you."

Popocatepetl wished to embrace the little animal. "Oh, glorious! Oh, best of little brutes! Run! run! run! Summon your kind, dwell in the plain and make me wings. Ah, when once Popocatepetl can soar on his wings from star to star, then, indeed—"

* * * * * * *

Poor old stupid Popocatepetl! The little animal summoned his kind, they dwelt on the plains, they made this and they made that, but they made no wings for Popocatepetl.

And sometimes when the thunderous voice of the old peak rolls and rolls, if you know that tongue, you can hear him say: "Oh, traitor! Traitor! Traitor! Where are my wings? My wings, traitor! I am hungry! Where are my wings?"

But the little animal merely places his finger beside his nose and winks.

"Your wings, indeed, fool! Sit still and howl for them! Old idiot!"

WHY DID THE YOUNG CLERK SWEAR? OR, THE UNSATISFACTORY FRENCH

All was silent in the little gent's furnishing store. A lonely clerk with a blonde moustache and a red necktie raised a languid hand to his brow and brushed back a dangling lock. He yawned and gazed gloomily at the blurred panes of the windows.

Without, the wind and rain came swirling round the brick buildings and went sweeping over the streets. A horse-car rumbled stolidly by. In the mud on the pavements, a few pedestrians struggled with excited umbrellas.

"The deuce!" remarked the clerk. "I'd give ten dollars if somebody would come in and buy something, if 'twere only cotton socks."

He waited amid the shadows of the grey afternoon. No customers came. He heaved a long sigh and sat down on a high stool. From beneath a stack of unlaundried shirts he drew a French novel with a picture on the cover. He yawned again, glanced lazily toward the street, and settled himself as comfortable as the gods would let him upon the high stool.

He opened the book and began to read. Soon it could have been noticed that his blonde moustache took on a curl of enthusiasm, and the refractory locks on his brow showed symptoms of soft agitation.

"Silvere did not see the young girl for some days," read the clerk. "He was miserable. He seemed always to inhale that subtle perfume from her hair. At night he saw her eyes in the stars.

"His dreams were troubled. He watched the house. Heloise did not appear. One day he met Vibert. Vibert wore a black frock-coat. There were wine-stains on the right breast. His collar was soiled. He had not shaved.

"Silvere burst into tears. 'I love her! I love her! I shall die!' Vibert laughed scornfully. His necktie was second-hand. Idiotic, this boy in love. Fool! Simpleton! But at last he pitied him. She goes to the music-teacher's every morning. Silly Silvere embraced him.

"The next day Silvere waited at the street corner. A vendor was selling chestnuts. Two gamins were fighting in an alley. A woman was scrubbing some steps. This great Paris throbbed with life.

"Heloise came. She did not perceive Silvere. She passed with a happy smile on her face. She looked fresh, fair, innocent. Silvere felt himself swooning. 'Ah, my God!'

"She crossed the street. The young man received a shock that sent the warm blood to his brain. It had been raining. There was mud. With one slender hand Heloise lifted her skirts. Silvere leaning forward, saw her—"

A young man in a wet mackintosh came into the little gent's furnishing store.

"Ah, beg pardon," said he to the clerk, "but do you have an agency for a steam laundry here? I have been patronising a Chinaman down th' avenue for some time, but he—what? No? You have none here? Well, why don't you start one, anyhow? It'd be a good thing in this neighbourhood. I live just round the corner, and it'd be a great thing for me. I know lots of people who would—what? Oh, you don't? Oh!"

As the young man in the wet mackintosh retreated, the clerk with a blonde moustache made a hungry grab at the novel. He continued to read: "Handkerchief fall in a puddle. Silvere sprang forward. He picked up the handkerchief. Their eyes met. As he returned the handkerchief, their hands touched. The young girl smiled. Silvere was in ecstacies. 'Ah, my God!'

"A baker opposite was quarrelling over two sous with an old woman.

"A grey-haired veteran with a medal upon his breast and a butcher's boy were watching a dog-fight. The smell of dead animals came from adjacent slaughter-houses. The letters on the sign over the tinsmith's shop on the corner shone redly like great clots of blood. It was hell on roller skates."

Here the clerk skipped some seventeen chapters descriptive of a number of intricate money transactions, the moles on the neck of a Parisian dressmaker, the process of making brandy, the milk-leg of Silvere's aunt, life in the coal-pits, and scenes in the Chamber of Deputies. In these chapters the reputation of the architect of Charlemagne's palace was vindicated, and it was explained why Heloise's grandmother didn't keep her stockings pulled up.

Then he proceeded: "Heloise went to the country. The next day Silvere followed. They met in the fields. The young girl had donned the garb of the peasants. She blushed. She looked fresh, fair, innocent. Silvere felt faint with rapture. 'Ah, my God!'

"She had been running. Out of breath, she sank down in the hay. She held out her hand. 'I am so glad to see you.' Silvere was enchanted at this vision. He bended toward her. Suddenly he burst into tears. 'I love you! I love you! I love you!' he stammered.

"A row of red and white shirts hung on a line some distance away. The third shirt from the left had a button off the neck. A cat on the rear steps of a cottage near the shirt was drinking milk from a platter. The north-east portion of the platter had a crack in it.

"'Heloise!' Silvere was murmuring hoarsely. He leaned toward her until his warm breath moved the curls on her neck. 'Heloise!' murmured Jean."

"Young man," said an elderly gentleman with a dripping umbrella to the clerk with a blonde moustache, "have you any night-shirts open front and back? Eh? Night-shirts open front and back, I said. D'you hear, eh? *Night-shirts open front and back.* Well, then, why didn't you say so? It would pay you to be a trifle more polite, young man. When you get as old as I am, you will find out that it pays to—what? I didn't see you adding any column of figures. In that case I am sorry. You have no night-shirts open front and back, eh? Well, good-day."

As the elderly gentleman vanished, the clerk with a blonde moustache grasped the novel like some famished animal. He read on: "A peasant stood before the two children. He wrung his hands. 'Have you seen a stray cow?' 'No,' cried the children in the same breath. The peasant wept. He wrung his hands. It was a supreme moment.

"'She loves me!' cried Silvere to himself, as he changed his clothes for dinner.

"It was evening. The children sat by the fire-place. Heloise wore a gown of clinging white. She looked fresh, fair, innocent. Silvere was in raptures. 'Ah, my God!'

"Old Jean, the peasant, saw nothing. He was mending harness. The fire crackled in the fire-place. The children loved each other. Through the open door to the kitchen came the sound of old Marie shrilly cursing the geese who wished to enter. In front of the window two pigs were quarrelling over a vegetable. Cattle were lowing in a distant field. A hay-waggon creaked slowly past. Thirty-two chickens were asleep in the branches of a tree. This subtle atmosphere had a mighty effect upon Heloise. It was beating down her self-control. She felt herself going. She was choking.

"The young girl made an effort. She stood up. 'Good-night, I must go.' Silvere took her hand. 'Heloise,' he murmured. Outside the two pigs were fighting.

"A warm blush overspread the young girl's face. She turned wet eyes toward her lover. She looked fresh, fair, innocent. Silvere was maddened. 'Ah, my God!'

"Suddenly the young girl began to tremble. She tried vainly to withdraw her hand. But her knee—"

"I wish to get my husband some shirts," said a shopping-woman with six bundles. The clerk with a blonde moustache made a private gesture of despair, and rapidly spread a score of different-patterned shirts upon the counter. "He's very particular about his shirts," said the shopping-woman. "Oh, I don't think any of these will do. Don't you keep the Invincible brand? He only wears that kind. He says they fit him better. And he's very particular about his shirts. What? You don't keep them? No? Well, how much do you think they would come at?" "Haven't the slightest idea." "Well, I suppose I must go somewhere else, then. Um, good-day."

The clerk with the blonde moustache was about to make further private gestures of despair, when the shopping-woman with six bundles turned and went out. His fingers instantly closed nervously over the book. He drew it from its hiding-place, and opened it at the place where he had ceased. His hungry eyes seemed to eat the words upon the page. He continued: "—struck cruelly against a chair. It seemed to awaken her. She started. She burst from the young man's arms. Outside the two pigs were grunting amiably.

"Silvere took his candle. He went toward his room. He was in despair. 'Ah, my God!'

"He met the young girl on the stairs. He took her hand. Tears were raining down his face. 'Heloise!' he murmured.

"The young girl shivered. As Silvere put his arms about her, she faintly resisted. This embrace seemed to sap her life. She wished to die. Her thoughts flew back to the old well and the broken hayrakes at Plassans.

"The young girl looked fresh, fair, innocent 'Heloise!' murmured Silvere. The children exchanged a long, clinging kiss. It seemed to unite their souls.

"The young girl was swooning. Her head sank on the young man's shoulder. There was nothing in space except these warm kisses on her neck. Silvere enfolded her. 'Ah, my God!'"

"Say, young fellow," said a youth with a tilted cigar to the clerk with a blonde moustache, "where th'll is Billie Carcart's joint round here? Know?"

"Next corner," said the clerk fiercely.

"Oh, th'll," said the youth, "yehs needn't git gay. See! When a feller asts a civil question yehs needn't git gay. See! Th'll!"

The youth stood and looked aggressive for a moment. Then he went away.

The clerk seemed almost to leap upon the book. His feverish fingers twirled the pages. When he found his place he glued his eyes to it. He read:

"Then a great flash of lightning illumined the hall-way. It threw livid hues over a row of flowerpots in the window-seat. Thunder shook the house to its foundation. From the kitchen arose the voice of old Marie in prayer.

"Heloise screamed. She wrenched herself from the young man's arms. She sprang inside her room. She locked the door. She flung herself face downward on the bed. She burst into tears. She looked fresh, fair, innocent.

"The rain pattering upon the thatched roof sounded in the stillness like the footsteps of spirits. In the sky toward Paris there shone a crimson light.

"The chickens had all fallen from the tree. They stood, sadly, in a puddle. The two pigs were asleep under the porch.

"Upstairs, in the hall-way, Silvers was furious."

The clerk with a blonde moustache gave here a wild scream of disappointment. He madly hurled the novel with the picture on the cover from him. He stood up and said: "Damn!"

THE VICTORY OF THE MOON

The Strong Man of the Hills lost his wife. Immediately he went abroad, calling aloud. The people all crouched afar in the dark of their huts, and cried to him when he was yet a long distance away: "No, no, great chief, we have not even seen the imprint of your wife's sandal in the sand. If we had seen it, you would have found us bowed down in worship before the marks of her ten glorious brown toes, for we are but poor devils of Indians, and the grandeur of the sun rays on her hair would have turned our eyes to dust."

"Her toes are not brown. They are pink," said the Strong Man from the Hills. "Therefore do I believe that you speak the truth when you say you have not seen her, good little men of the valley. In this matter of her great loveliness, however, you speak a little too strongly. As she is no longer among my possessions, I have no mind to hear her praised. Whereabouts is the best man of you?"

None of them had stomach for this honour at the time. They surmised that the Strong Man of the Hills had some plan for combat, and they knew that the best of them would have in this encounter only the strength of the meat in the grip of the fire. "Great King," they said, in one voice, "there is no best man here."

"How is this?" roared the Strong Man. "There must be one who excels. It is a law. Let him step forward then."

But they solemnly shook their heads. "There is no best man here."

The Strong Man turned upon them so furiously that many fell to the ground. "There must be one. Let him step forward." Shivering, they huddled together and tried, in their fear, to thrust each other toward the Strong Man.

At this time a young philosopher approached the throng slowly. The philosophers of that age were all young men in the full heat of life. The old greybeards were, for the most part, very stupid, and were so accounted.

"Strong Man from the Hills," said the young philosopher, "go to yonder brook and bathe. Then come and eat of this fruit. Then gaze for a time at the blue sky and the green earth. Afterward I have something to say to you."

"You are not so wise that I am obliged to bathe before listening to you?" demanded the Strong Man, insolently.

"No," said the young philosopher. All the people thought this reply very strange.

"Why, then, must I bathe and eat of fruit and gaze at the earth and the sky?"

"Because they are pleasant things to do."

"Have I, do you think, any thirst at this time for pleasant things?"

"Bathe, eat, gaze," said the young philosopher with a gesture.

The Strong Man did, indeed, whirl his bronzed and terrible limbs in the silver water. Then he lay in the shadow of a tree and ate the cool fruit and gazed at the sky and the earth. "This is a fine comfort," he said. After a time he suddenly struck his forehead with his finger. "By the way, did I tell you that my wife had fled from me?"

"I know it," said the young philosopher.

Later the Strong Man slept peacefully. The young philosopher smiled.

But in the night the little men of the valley came clamouring: "Oh, Strong Man of the Hills, the moon derides you!"

The philosopher went to them in the darkness. "Be still, little people. It is nothing. The derision of the moon is nothing."

But the little men of the valley would not cease their uproar. "Oh, Strong Man! Strong Man, awake! Awake! The moon derides you!"

Then the Strong Man aroused and shook his locks away from his eyes. "What is it, good little men of the valley?"

"Oh, Strong Man, the moon derides you! Oh, Strong Man!"

The Strong Man looked, and there, indeed, was the moon laughing down at him. He sprang to his feet and roared. "Ah, old, fat, lump of moon, you laugh! Have you seen my wife?"

The moon said no word, but merely smiled in a way that was like a flash of silver bars.

"Well, then, moon, take this home to her," thundered the Strong Man, and he hurled his spear.

The moon clapped both hands to its eye, and cried: "Oh! Oh!"

The little people of the valley cried: "Oh, this is terrible, Strong Man! He has smitten our sacred moon in the eye!"

The young philosopher cried nothing at all.

The Strong Man threw his coat of crimson feathers upon the ground. He took his knife and felt its edge. "Look you, philosopher," he said. "I have lost my wife, and the bath, the meal of fruit in the shade, the sight of sky and earth are still good to me, but when this false moon derides me, there must be a killing."

"I understand you," said the young philosopher.

The Strong Man ran off into the night. The little men of the valley clapped their hands in ecstacy and terror. "Ah! ah! what a battle will there be!"

The Strong Man went into his own hills and gathered there many great rocks and trunks of trees. It was strange to see him erect upon a peak of the mountains and hurling these things at the moon. He kept the air full of them.

"Fat moon, come closer," he shouted. "Come closer, and let it be my knife against your knife. Oh, to think that we are obliged to tolerate such an old, fat, stupid, lazy, good-for-nothing moon. You are ugly as death, while I—Oh, moon, you stole my beloved, and it was nothing, but when you stole my beloved and laughed at me, it became another matter. And yet you are so ugly, so fat, so stupid, so lazy, so good-for-nothing. Ah, I shall go mad! Come closer, moon, and let me examine your round, grey skull with this club."

And he always kept the air full of great missiles.

The moon merely laughed, and said: "Why should I come closer?"

Wildly did the Strong Man pile rock upon rock. He built him a tower that was the father of all towers. It made the mountains to appear to be babes. Upon the summit of it he swung his great club and flourished his knife.

The little men in the valley far below beheld a great storm, and at the end of it they said: "Look, the moon is dead." The cry went to and fro on the earth: "The moon is dead!"

The Strong Man went to the home of the moon. She, the sought one, lay upon a cloud, and her little foot dangled over the side of it. The Strong Man took this little foot in his two hands and kissed it. "Ah, beloved!" he moaned, "I would rather this little foot was upon my dead neck than that moon should ever have the privilege of seeing it."

She leaned over the edge of the cloud and gazed at him. "How dusty you are. Why do you puff so? Veritably, you are an ordinary person. Why did I ever find you interesting?"

The Strong Man flung his knife into the air and turned back toward the earth. "If the young philosopher had been at my elbow," he reflected, bitterly, "I would doubtless have gone at the matter in another way. What does my strength avail me in this contest?"

The battered moon, limping homeward, replied to the Strong Man from the Hills: "Aye, surely. My weakness is in this thing as strong as your strength. I am victor with ugliness, my age, my stoutness, my laziness, my good-for-nothingness. Woman is woman. Men are equal in everything save good fortune. I envy you not."